Beyond Expectations

A Contemporary Interracial Romance

Decisions and Destiny
Book 1

Natasha Allen

To the girls who love reading,
yet always felt
unseen
unheard
and unrepresented

This one's for you.

"Love is blind despite the world's attempt to give it eyes."

— Matshona Dhliwayo

Chapter 1

Serena

"What's the German word for order or order number?" my dad bellowed, covering his phone's speaker.

"Umm, I think it's *Bestellnummer*," I replied, as I eyed the oil cap under the hood of the car.

He should already know this by now as he'd been ordering car parts from across the world, especially Germany, for over twenty years.

I was just about to return to the oil change I was doing, when his frustrated groan echoed across the garage.

"Why do I always get cut off after being passed back and forth from one place to the next?"

"I don't know why you don't just do the orders online. I've shown you countless times how much easier it is."

"I did try, but they could not process the order and said I needed to call the customer service line."

"Why don't you try the chat button on their website?"

His lack of response made me look up, and I couldn't stop

the smile spreading across my face as I watched him glare at me with slow-blinking eyes.

"I'm not chatting to a robot."

I didn't know why he felt the need to use air quotes. I knew arguing with him about technology was an utterly wasted effort. The slight wrinkles around his eyes crinkled as he scratched the white stubble along his jaw, which stood out in such contrast against his sepia skin.

"I'm going to try to call again from the phone in the office. I've got no more bookings for the rest of the day, but shout me if you need anything."

"Yes, I know."

Turning the radio back up, I returned under the hood of the '74 Datoun.

It wasn't often I got the chance to work on cars anymore with the hours I worked and living in Manhattan, but Dad always let me tinker with something every time I came to visit.

The distinct sound of constant rattling accompanied the rumble of an engine. It wasn't just the continual rattling but the godawful rotten egg smell that accompanied the car that pulled through the open doors of the garage.

Still grimacing at the smell that now permeated my nostrils, I attempted to breathe slowly through my mouth as I watched the driver's door open.

Looking up, I expected to see one of our regulars. However, to my surprise, one of the hottest guys I had ever seen stood before me.

He was tall, about six feet three inches, with broad swimmer's shoulders that encased a Ralph Lauren blue checked shirt, his sleeves rolled up, exposing muscular forearms with a luxury gold watch on his right wrist. Dark jeans hugged his thighs, and he wore a pair of brown leather loafers.

My eyes cruised back over his body and found his face. He

had stubble that did nothing to hide his strong jaw. His eyes were a shade of blue I would only see in the oceans of the Caribbean, and he had dark blonde bed hair that couldn't look any sexier if he tried.

Eyeing the keys in his hand, I gazed at the lovely car he was leaning against. I wiped away the beads of sweat I could feel forming on my temple.

"Can I help you?" I asked.

"I need someone to look at my car," he answered sternly.

His impatient tone didn't shock me, but the cold smirk and the singular raised brow on his face contradicted it.

I bet this guy had never had to work hard for anything in this life. I was sure the Abercrombie model-looking, blue-blooded guy got everything and every woman he'd ever wanted. I'd had my fair share of these types of guys at Columbia.

Rich, spoilt, and would go on to inherit their fortune without a care in the world. Although they thoroughly annoyed me with their snide, underhanded, sexist, and racist comments and jabs, they gave me more glory and satisfaction by coming to the top of my class.

So why was this guy making my nipples hard?

I took the keys from him, making sure not to get the oil that was still on my hands on his. I opened the door and popped the bonnet open to look.

"Do you know what you're doing?" he asked me.

Ugh. Typical man. Does he think women knew nothing about cars?

"Yes. It looks like your head gasket has gone."

The smirk on his face had now transformed into a look of shock.

Ha, that shut him up.

"This is my father's shop. He's on a call right now but

should be done in a minute and can then book you in for the repairs."

"Thank you."

I looked back at him as I wiped the grease off my hands and saw his outstretched hand.

"Um..."

My eyes bounced from the stark contrast between my hand and his. Mine, which still had traces of grease smears on them, looked small and dirty next to his, which were large, smooth, and perfectly manicured. As I tentatively shook his hand, I almost gasped as it felt like a zap of electricity sparked through me. And as I pulled my hand away, I could still feel ghost-like tingles skating across my fingertips.

Needing to break through some of this tension, I returned to his car, marveling at its exquisite craftsmanship.

"I haven't seen this color before. Did you get it customized?"

There was a beat of silence, and all I could hear was the rapid beating of my heart before he spoke.

"No."

The grave timber of his voice, despite him speaking at a low volume, further piqued my interest.

"I saw it at an auction and knew I had to have it. Besides, with something as classic and beautiful as this, I'd never risk damaging it for simple aesthetic purposes."

I knew he was talking about the car, but those words tapped right into my thoughts, and I couldn't help the slight gasp that left my lips.

Not allowing my mind to stray down that dark path of my past, I focused my attention back on the present and the man standing beside me. There was something enigmatic about him. His aloofness teetered on cold and insular, while his eyes had a magnetism that made it hard for you to look away.

"So, what brings you here? Besides the obvious car trouble?" I queried.

"What makes you think I'm not from here?"

His quick response felt like we were starting a game of sorts, yet I couldn't put my finger on what.

"Hmm. Just the car?"

Laughter bubbled out of me at the cockiness of the guy, yet the rigidness in his posture and the fact he still held himself physically back made me want to continue this little charade.

"Yes, it is a thing of beauty. And you still haven't answered my question."

"I was visiting family and decided to take her for a drive instead of flying back."

Lifting his hand to his mouth, I watched as he ran his thumb across his lower lip, and it was then that I noticed the walnut-brown leather driving glove he still wore on his left hand.

He clenched his fist, causing the leather to creak, and the sound sent a shiver down my spine. Biting my lip to stop the moan from escaping, my mind wondered how that leather would feel brushing against my skin. Quickly glancing back up at him, I saw his pupils were blown wide, and his nostrils flared as though he could smell the arousal that was pouring out of me.

What on earth was going on?

We'd hardly said two words to one another, and my body's reaction to a man whose name I didn't even know was electric. I watched as his eyes roamed down my body, the feeling so intense that I could feel it as though it were his physical touch. Once his eyes finally returned to mine. Neither one of us wanted to break whatever spell we were under.

"Can I get your name?"

I was just about to answer when the sound of the office

door opening interrupted me. I watched as Dad made his way over to the guy who was still watching me with a look that did nothing, for how turned on his body was making me feel.

"Good afternoon. Sorry to keep you waiting. What can I help you with?"

The stranger continued to look at me for a second before turning to Dad. I watched his expression change as the ice cold mask slipped back across his face.

I listened as Dad introduced himself and checked over the guy's Mercedes-Benz 300 SL Gull-Wing. After looking at the engine for a minute, he said he believed the head gasket had gone.

I knew it.

Looking up at the stranger's face, I saw him smirk in a way that sent blood straight to my clit.

Oh. My. God.

Serena, sort yourself out.

Mentally, I shouted at myself, and without wanting to give this guy the satisfaction of knowing how much he turned me on, I gave him the smugest look that said, *see, I know what I'm talking about.*

Perspiration still clung to my skin, and a consistent buzzing continuously ran through my veins as I returned to the office, stopping only to grab my keys and bag that I'd chucked on the armchair in the corner of the office.

Not a single part of me could understand why I had such a visceral reaction to him. Especially considering how cold and aloof he was, yet a fire burned in his eyes that drew me in like a moth to a flame.

Shaking myself out of this trance-like state, I decided to go out the back way to avoid another encounter. I'd parked my car in the back lot, which meant driving past the front doors to get onto the main street.

Despite my love of classic cars, I was never more grateful for my Audi A7 and its dark-tinted windows as I slowly passed the front, where I could still see my dad talking to the enigmatic stranger.

I wasn't precisely spying, more like my eyes were reeled in on the way his thighs filled his dark jeans, and don't even get me started on his ass that looked like it'd been carved out of marble. I thought I'd gotten away with my ogling when I sensed him looking straight at me. And despite the tint of the windows, those aqua eyes pierced straight into mine.

I watched as Dad followed the guy's line of vision and reached his hand out to wave me off. Lowering my window, I took a deep, steadying breath, smiled, and shouted to Dad.

"I'll get a start on dinner. Let me know when you're on your way."

Just before pulling away, I glanced back over to the mystery man and felt the heat of his gaze right through to my bones.

The corner of my mouth lifted slightly, and I raised my eyebrow, getting one last little game of cat and mouse, before putting my foot on the pedal and peeling out of there.

As I glanced in my rearview mirror, I could see that he had turned, watching me leave, and despite the distance, I could have sworn I saw a smile on his face.

Chapter 2

Serena

The sweet and spicy smell of dinner made my mouth water, and at the same time, I heard my brother Roman's stomach growl.

Lifting my bottle of Corona, I waited for Dad to take a seat.

"Cheers, and thanks for dinner. It smells divine."

I toasted, clinking my bottle with Dad and Roman's before diving straight in.

I was too busy devouring my food and not paying attention to the two of them, as they argued about some play or something that had happened in the football game over the weekend. Football was something the two of them could go on for hours about, especially given that the Green Bay Packers had signed Roman, but en route to training camp, he was hit head-on by a drunk driver who was never apprehended. Luckily, he survived the crash, but his shoulder was damaged severely, ending his football career instantly.

I was just about to tuck into my third smoked pulled pork sub when I heard my name mentioned, followed by Roman's laugh.

"What's so funny?" I muttered, knowing my dad always thought it funny that I loved demolishing my food.

"Ignore your brother. I was telling him about the guy that turned up at the garage yesterday and how impressed he was with your knowledge of cars."

"He was probably worried you would mess up his car even more than it already was. Well, at least until you batted your lashes at him," Roman quipped.

"Shut up. What are you, fifteen?" I retorted.

"Well, considering I'm ten months older, you kinda insult yourself too with that comment," Roman teased and continued laughing, which made me want to go off on him further.

But before I could say anything, Dad gave me the look I knew all too well.

Serena, ignore him.

I don't know why I let my brother rile me up like that, especially considering I was a successful lawyer who came top of my class at Columbia and was running my own firm at thirty-three. I didn't even react to that extreme when I was in court.

Deciding it wasn't an argument worth continuing, I picked up my plate and loaded it into the dishwasher.

"Dad, do you need me to help clean up? I think I'm gonna have an early night," I offered.

Glancing over my shoulder, I caught the glare my dad shot Roman before looking over at me.

"No, sweetie, it's fine."

I walked back to the table and gave him a kiss on the head.

"Good night, Dad."

"Good night, Serena."

Not wanting to be too petty, I looked over at Roman, whose eyes still shone with amusement.

"Night, Ro," I quipped.

"Night, S."

I shook my head at the grin plastered on his face and made my way upstairs.

After washing my face and doing my nighttime routine, I fell asleep almost the second my head hit the cool silk pillowcase.

~

My back arched up against the cold bonnet of the car, and my skin tingled as if it had electricity running through it. Every fiber and nerve came alive as he continued his delicious torture of licking, teasing, and biting each nipple.

His other hand traveled down my body, leaving a blazing fire across every inch he touched. Strong, yet supple hands kneaded my hips with such intensity and dedication.

It felt as if my body were like opium to him, and he couldn't get enough. Finally, he reached his hand between my legs and found me already dripping wet.

I could feel him smile against my neck as he kissed his way up to my mouth. He slid two fingers in and used the pad of his thumb to rub my over-sensitive clit.

My pussy screamed for more—and as if he could read my mind, he stood up and pulled his white and blue striped shirt off to reveal big, broad, solid shoulders and chiseled abdominal muscles.

He started popping the buttons off his jeans until I could see his erect cock straining to stay within his Calvin Klein briefs. He leaned back, sliding me down the bonnet to anchor me into position, lubricating himself by rubbing against my now-drenched pussy.

The moans escaping my lips almost didn't sound human. I had never been so turned on by a man in my life.

His first hard thrust almost made me come. He stretched

and filled me nearly to the point of pain. Not only did he have considerable length, but also eye-watering girth. How did a man like this even exist?

I was going to come as I'd never come before... and then, the loud shriek of my phone alarm ruined everything.

And then, I woke up.

Panting and sore with want.

My nipples peaked hard and rubbed against my cotton camisole. My whole body was flush with perspiration. My whole face burned with both embarrassment and excitement.

It wasn't as if it was the first time I'd had a sex dream. But I'd never had one that felt real and made me feel so alive.

An ice-cold shower was just what I needed to get my head out of my dream and back on the list of things I needed to do.

Standing in my dad's kitchen, watching him and Roman prepare dinner, I grabbed a piece of cucumber from the salad bowl when the doorbell rang.

"Do something useful and get that, will you?" my brother said, while swatting my hand away.

Opening the door, I was almost tackled to the ground by my two nieces.

"Auntie Rena."

"Aahh, Auntie Rena, Mommy said I couldn't have dessert if I didn't stop singing in the car."

Bending down and laughing, I scooped my six-year-old twin nieces, Eden and Amelia, into a bear hug.

"Now, girls, you know I would never let your mommy withhold dessert when I visit."

My mocking scowl at my sister had the girls in a fit of giggles before they rushed past me into the kitchen. I loved my nieces, and I knew it was common for people to say the kids in their family were the best, but I knew my nieces were the most gorgeous children I had ever seen. I always tried to push for my sister to sign them up with a modeling agency, but she always shut me down.

"Trust me. You would too if you'd been made to listen to *Let It Go* for the ten thousandth time."

"Come on, Olivia, think of all the Disney tunes we used to belt out in the car when we were younger."

My sister squeezed me before holding me at arm's length.

"Damn, why do you always look so effortlessly put together? I swear my wardrobe is always in a simple rotation of scrubs, tracksuits, mom jeans, and a sweater."

Growing up, I'd always been a bit of a tomboy. Since college, and now living in New York and having all the different established and up-and-coming designers, it allowed me to evolve and embrace my love of fashion. I knew I was very fortunate, both financially and being unattached without children, that I could indulge more than Olivia. I had always suppressed the pang of judgment from her. Especially given that when we were younger, she and I were never as close as Roman and me. My dad used to say it was simply because she was older, but I just thought she was a bitch. We had gotten closer the older we'd gotten, and she could understand I was not simply her annoying little sister. And I learned to appreciate everything she had done to help my dad raise us.

"Oh, stop it. You look great, and God knows how you do it running after those two and working a full-time job. How's work going, anyway?"

My sister was a dental hygienist who was either busy at the practice or running around after the girls.

"It's fine, crazy busy at the moment, but we've got two new

trainees that will hopefully become full-time staff, so that should help things settle down in the next few weeks."

Following behind Olivia was her husband, Calvin.

"Serena, always a pleasure to see you."

"Aww, thanks. How are you doing? What's the name of the movie you're working on again?"

Calvin was an indie film producer and split his time between here and LA. He was such a sweet and funny guy, but he also had backbone, which one required if he was going to be going up against my sister in any shape or form.

"Don't get him started on that. I've made him take the weekend off, and that means no work talk."

I watched as Calvin mouthed, *I'll tell you about it later,* and I rolled my lips in to suppress my laugh.

Minutes later, the doorbell rang again. It was my uncle Martin, his wife Angela, and my cousin Anthony. We could finally sit down and eat.

Spending quality time together as a family had always brought me immense happiness.

After dinner, I was listening to Dad talk about visiting the other branches of his garage, as he'd succeeded in expanding my grandpa's auto shop into a chain of luxury and vintage car repair garages. Along with my uncle's help, he had a Portland, Austin, and Atlanta branch.

Leaning against the countertop, I took in this moment of happiness and relaxation when I noticed Roman sitting at the table alone and looking down. Walking over, I put my arm around my brother.

"Hey, what's gotten you so down?"

"Nothing. I'm just tired," he grumbled.

"Liar, Roman. I know you, and I know when you're lying to me."

"It's nothing. I was just wondering whether it's a clever idea for me to go to Ruby's party, that's all."

His face was etched with longing and regret as he spoke.

Ruby had been my best friend since high school, and she also used to date Roman. In high school, they were the 'it' couple, but after his accident, he spiraled into a deep depression and broke up with Ruby. Then he moved back and decided to help Dad run the shop.

"You guys haven't been together in years. And it's not as if you've spent time in each other's company. Come on, she's my best friend and your friend, too."

I kept my tone light and cheerful, not wanting to pressure him. I'd always suspected that he regretted breaking up with her.

His slight wince at the word friend felt like confirmation of my suspicions.

"Well, if you want to go, you know it'll be a good night."

I smiled.

I was never really a party girl, even in my college years. Still, after moving to Manhattan and running my business, I always appreciated the rare nights out I allowed myself, and most of those consisted of Ruby and me getting all glammed up and hitting various bars and clubs.

"I know it will be a good night. But I don't know if I want to go, plus I'd have to stay at yours... and I might cramp your style."

I knew what he was doing, trying to find any excuse to not go, and it wasn't because he'd be staying at mine.

"Roman, you know you're always welcome at mine. You're my brother, and I love you. But if you don't want to go, that's fine. I'll tell Rubs you're busy, and then you can send her a card, and she'll be happy."

With a sigh of relief, he nodded.

"I'll send her a bunch of calla lilies."

I gave him a warm smile for remembering her favorite flowers and mentally rolled my eyes at why men always seemed to struggle with being honest and honest with themselves.

By the time everyone had left, it was seven. The air had slightly cooled, and I walked over to my car with my weekend bag in hand, giving my dad and Roman one last wave goodbye. Even though I got to see my family once a month, saying goodbye was always tricky, and the drive back always felt bittersweet.

Chapter 3

Rhett

It had been four days since I saw that fiery beauty in the garage.

Four days of her being the desire of my dreams.

Four days of not being able to focus.

I couldn't stop thinking about her. I couldn't function properly. Every time my cell rang, for a split second, I plugged the hope that it was her calling to say my car was ready and that she was waiting with it at the garage for me, naked in the backseat.

Yes, like that was going to happen.

The past two days at work had dragged on. Walking down the street, I kept thinking I'd see her, only to turn and see nobody there. I needed to get a grip.

Looking at the time on my computer, I had three minutes until my next meeting. If it was just any meeting, I'd get Charlotte, my PA, to reschedule, but it was with my father, the other heads of departments, and my damn brother. Putting on my jacket, I started going to the boardroom. As I was walking, I thought I saw her in the corner of my eye.

God, I needed to sort my shit out. I was starting to halluci-nate the damn woman.

Entering the room, I greeted my father, our lawyer, Dominic, and two other heads seated on either side of me. I was the last to enter, and my father's PA handed the other gentlemen and I a folder outlining the points covered in this meeting.

Pouring myself a glass of water, I glanced over the notes, and a wave of irritation came over me as I remembered the reason for this meeting. My father wanted to expand the company's portfolio deeper into Queens and Brooklyn. We'd already agreed and come to terms with twenty-five out of the thirty-five blocks we needed, but our legal department couldn't get the fucking deal sorted. So now they were bringing in specialists to help.

I was just about to signal to Charlotte when the specialist lawyers walked in, and I stopped breathing. Walking towards my father is *the* woman from the garage.

Part of me was convinced all of this was a dream or just another one of the morbid hallucinations I'd been having of her. But it wasn't. She was there.

Every fiber in my body was paying attention to her every move. My eyes cataloged every curve and dip, but her smol-dering eyes drew me in. All her focus was on my father. She showed confidence, grace, elegance, and professionalism—all the attributes my father and other men there acknowledged and appreciated.

Although I could understand all these characteristics, I couldn't get over how stunning this woman was. As my eyes continued to examine her from head to toe greedily, I became instantly hard.

Fuck.

"Good morning. Will you be taking down the minutes?" Julian asked with a smarmy grin on his face.

I noticed a smile on a few other men's faces, which did nothing for my rising anger. With a look of determination and the slightest hint of frustration, I watched as she straightened her back and opened her folder.

"No. I've been hired to help you close on the remaining ten blocks you're struggling to negotiate on."

Putting the folder down, she raised her hand to shake with my father's outstretched one.

"Serena Parker, of Parker and Associates."

The specialist firm we needed was hers.

What were the odds?

Ha.

That grin was wiped straight off my brother's face. Then, her attention fell upon me. I'd just managed to discreetly adjust my hard-on into the waistband of my slacks when she walked over and offered me her hand.

She introduced herself. "Serena Parker."

"Rhett Chambers," I responded.

A shot of electricity shot through my body as our hands connected. The shock in her eyes as she registered it was me showed a slight sense of vulnerability, but it was only briefly visible before she schooled her face.

Her eyes felt like they could pierce through my soul, making me slightly uneasy. Her gaze darted to my mouth, and in what felt like slow motion, she ran her tongue across her glossy and juicy lips, making me instantly aware of what was going through her mind.

This would be the most challenging meeting I'd ever sat through.

How did the delectable Serena Parker go from mechanic to lawyer?

I was torn about which role I was more turned on by. At the garage, she wore daisy dukes and black leather biker boots. Her very impressive rack had strained against a white tank top, and a red and black flannel shirt was wrapped around her hips. Her golden caramel skin glistened under the fluorescent lights. She had beautiful, curly, jet-black hair that cascaded down to her breasts.

Today, she epitomized a sexy businesswoman wearing a cream-colored pencil dress, dove gray heels, and a large matching bag.

Her dress fell to just below the knee, and it clung to every sexy curve of her hourglass figure. Her straightened hair in a high and provocative ponytail made me wonder what it would be like to wrap my hand around it, gently pulling her head back and allowing me to bite the shell of her ear. As my other hand glided up her smooth thighs, my fingers pushing past her panties, then sliding into her wet pussy.

Damn it, Rhett, snap out of it.

I needed to focus on the business at hand.

"As you can see, the last ten blocks will cost you around five million each in purchases and payouts. I know you plan on turning them into restaurants, hotels, shopping outlets, spas, and luxury condominiums. But fundamentally, this seems to be a negating issue with those withholding."

Listening to her was like being wrapped in velvet, and I couldn't miss the chance to get her to engage with me.

"Can you explain how so?"

Her eyes briefly flared at my question before handing out a stack of what looked like reports.

She continued to guide the conversation mainly towards my father, but also the rest of the board. I could tell she was trying to avoid turning in my direction as much as possible.

Once again, this made me want to push for another reaction. Not wanting to let her see her effect on me, I relaxed back into my chair, skimming through the issues listed from the withholding parties.

"We had already run a preliminary evaluation, including speaking to members of the co-ops and individual residents. Half of these concerns weren't reported to our reps at the beginning of these negotiations."

I wasn't trying to belittle her or underestimate her clear capabilities. I hated being ignored. But most of all, I wanted to get her attention. And the way she had continued to avoid my gaze and gave off an air of indifference pierced me irrationally.

Her eyes shot over to mine, and her fiery gaze was the exact reaction I had hoped for. Give me fire over disinterested and unconcerned.

Maintaining eye contact, I watched as she opened her mouth. I was sure she was ready with a rapid response, but my brother Julian's scoff cut her off as an interruption.

I saw him sneering, smirking, and grimacing at her. As I looked around and saw some of the other heads of departments, I noticed a few of them behaving similarly, dismissing her in the same manner. Simon from our accounts and finance division piped up and, showing no respect for this woman's capabilities, asked a question.

"Why don't we just increase our offer by one percent? Surely, these people should just be happy being offered more money than they would ever see in a lifetime. Tell them to stop being so pigheaded and agree to the damn deal."

"It's not about the money," Serena countered.

Julian chuckled. "What do you mean, it's not about the money? Everything in this world evolves around money."

I never thought I'd be as embarrassed about being Julian's brother as I was now. A part of me did understand where he was coming from, but he came across as the ignorant, lazy prick that I knew he was.

"When was the last time you visited the sites you're trying to acquire as opposed to your architects, site managers and representatives?" Serena asked.

She hadn't just directed that question to Julian, but to everyone, including me. I scanned the boardroom and looked at the puzzled and bored faces around the table. Yet no one answered.

"Are you telling me that neither you nor anyone else sat at this meeting has ever gone out and personally inspected these blocks? The importance they have in those communities?"

She looked astonished and utterly bewildered, and I had to admit, she had a point.

"And why would I do anything as mundane and insignificant as that when we have a team of people who have presented us with all the necessary information?" Julian pressed.

Serena shook her head.

"Quite simply because you couldn't even begin to understand the type of people that live there. The things they count as important, the things they value and cherish. They don't want luxury condominiums they can't afford, gyms most can't get memberships to, casinos, spas, and restaurants they'll never be able to afford to visit. You won't be able to make a deal unless you know how to talk to them, understand them, and value what they say."

Julian leaned forward.

"And, of course, you would. Such feminine empathy and delicate sensibilities have no place in business. That kind of mentality is better left at home."

I was about to lunge for him when my father shouted, "Julian, you best apologize to Ms. Parker at once."

"Ms. Parker, I wholeheartedly hope you accept my apology."

Every single word Julian uttered dripped with sarcasm. She looked at him and nodded. Then, she explained what she could do to help us have the best chance of getting these contracts.

I had never wanted to beat up anyone as painfully and savagely as I wished to punch Julian right there, right then. I was utterly shocked at how everyone else seemed to carry on as though nothing had happened while I was shaking with anger and embarrassment.

The meeting concluded, and I uncurled my fists, which had been white-knuckle-clenched for the past five minutes.

I had hoped to have a quick word with Serena, but I was still too angry to catch her before she and her team left. Making my way back to my office, Charlotte glanced over at me.

My face must say it all, as she left me alone and continued typing on her computer. Sitting back at my desk and looking out the window, I did everything possible to rein in my anger. But nothing worked. The more I tried to find my equilibrium, the angrier I got.

What has gotten into Julian?

I knew how much of a jerk he could be at the best of times, but his behavior towards the delicious Ms Parker even went beyond his sense of decency.

What the fuck was his problem?

Picking up the phone, I called Charlotte in.

"Will you call my father and Julian into my office ASAP?"

She peered down at me, and I at once regretted my tone. Taking a gentler approach, I asked, "Can we also go through my appointments for this week so I can carve out my free time in my schedule? I have something important I need to deal with."

I couldn't go much longer without seeing Serena, but I

didn't need Charlotte to know she was the reason for my frustration.

"Of course, Mr. Chambers."

She took out her PDA and began going through the week's calendar.

"Thursday, you have the breakfast meeting with the mayor about the Inner-City Children's Home Charity Gala you have coming up, followed by your mother's birthday dinner. On Friday, you have a meeting at one o'clock with Wallace Maynard, followed by a presentation from the PR department. And, finally, on Saturday, you and Julian meet with Ted Summers at The Mount."

I'd completely forgotten I had to go with my damn brother to meet with the infamous Ted Summers. He was New York's biggest and best events planner and the head of PR. They organized the meeting as they knew it would give us the best exposure to have Mr. Summers host our next event.

The downside was that he wanted to meet with either me or my father, and as I was younger and more likely, into that sort of place myself. My father delegated the task to me. And if that wasn't bad enough, I had to have Julian go with me as Father wanted him more integrated into the company.

"Thanks, Charlotte. If you could call my father and Julian in."

The knock at my door brought me back to the task ahead. Charlotte let my father and Julian into my office, and each sat before me. Simply seeing Julian again brought all my anger back.

"What can we help you with?"

Father's somber tone had always mellowed me, especially when I looked into his eyes and could tell he had noticed my anger toward my brother.

"Well, first, I need to address Julian's total lack of respect and decorum, which he showed in the meeting. The way he spoke to Ms. Parker was rude and obnoxious."

"I've already had words with Julian, and I have made it clear that his behavior today is never to be repeated," my father insisted.

Looking over at Julian, I saw him roll his eyes, reach into his jacket pocket, and retrieve his phone.

"Secondly, it would be best to rearrange my meeting with the mayor and that you, Father, should go instead. It'll have more impact, plus the guy makes me angry."

I knew I was expected to aid my father in building and expanding our family's business. It was something that had been ingrained in me since infancy. Not that I'd ever had any other choice or even been asked if it was what I genuinely wanted to do. My father must have seen something in my expression that showed how frustrated I was.

"I guess you're right. I'll have my PA rearrange it," Father agreed.

Walking over to my drink cabinet, he made himself a whiskey. He offered me one, but I declined.

"I'll take one," Julian remarked, but to my relief, my father shook his head. "I don't think so, especially as you have a meeting in thirty minutes."

The look on my brother's face couldn't have been more tedious and reluctant if he had tried, which made my following suggestion for my father even sweeter.

"I also think it would be great for Julian to accompany you to the meeting with the mayor, as I believe it would be a wonderful opportunity for him to see you weave your magic firsthand."

My father looked at me and grinned. We looked over at Julian, who was not impressed, and grunted in response.

"Carter is on his way over. I was going to order lunch to be delivered. Do you want to join us?"

The last thing I wanted to do was spend more time around Julian, but I could see the plea in my father's eyes, so with great reluctance, I agreed.

"Tell him to head straight to my office. I need to work through lunch."

An hour later, I re-emerged from my bathroom, having brushed my teeth as Julian, my father, and Carter, my father's best friend, lawyer, and also my godfather, were still sitting and eating around the coffee table.

"Max sent me a copy of this quarter's projections, and I have to say they are very impressive."

I'd always respected and cared for my godfather, so I obviously appreciated the praise. Still, my eyes instantly went to my father, just as they always did, seeking his approval, and the proud smile he gave me eased the knot that had been building in my stomach.

Everyone seemed to ignore Julian's huff as he got up to use the bathroom.

"I'm thrilled with the reports I have read, and Rhett seems to be handling everything in his stride. When I took over from my father, I felt like a deer in headlights. I was overwhelmed, and we had less than half our current assets. That's why it's always been so important for me to show you everything from the ground up. When the time comes for you to take over, I won't have any worries about you handling things. Every obstacle that has come your way, you have taken in your stride. So I know you'll be able to manage it just like I managed it. It's in our blood."

Once again, I endured the heavy burden that was on my shoulders.

"I mean it, Rhett. Just continue to do what you're doing.

You have been coming to meetings and watching me handle business longer than some staff members have been employed. I promise you, if you continue the way you are and the way we always have been, I know you will help Chambers Industries continue to prosper and grow even more in the years to come."

His words had a heavy finality that sent an uneasy feeling through me.

I focused my attention back on the emails and reports I was working on, barely listening to the three of them as they talked in the background, but I could feel eyes on me.

As I looked up, I saw my father staring at me, and it was a look of love and respect but also worry. And that was something I had never seen from him before. But just as quickly, his eyes focused back on Carter, and my brother and I focused once again on work.

Once my father, Carter, and Julian left my office, I decided to make it my sole mission to find a way to repair the damage my ass of a brother had caused with Serena and do everything in my power to prove that not all of us Chambers were made that way.

Plus, I wanted to see her again.

Chapter 4

Serena

"Hey, Ruby, I'm not sure whether these gold heels go with the dress," I shouted out to my best friend, who was putting the last touches to her makeup at my vanity.

Standing in my closet, staring at my reflection in the mirror, I studied my hair, which had been blow-dried into long, loose waves rolling down my bare shoulders.

I wore a white halter-neck dress with a plunging neckline and a low scooping back. Ruby walked in, wearing her gorgeous scarlet Herve Ledger bandage dress that complemented the olive undertones of her complexion. Her espresso brunette hair was blown out in big bouncy curls, and the light smokey eyes of her makeup made her look like Mila Kunis's long-lost twin.

My bestie looked stunning, and I'd been looking forward to celebrating her birthday that night.

"Serena, those Zanotti shoes look drop-dead gorgeous. Of course, they go with that dress. How about one more shot before we head out?"

Ruby was already making her way to my kitchen before I

could reply. Grabbing my clutch, I made my way out to her. After handing me a glass, we raised them in a toast.

"Rubs, you have been my best friend since kindergarten. We have been through love, losing loved ones, joy, heartbreak, success, and everything. You are one of the kindest, fiercest, and most loving people I know, and I can't wait for all the fun and memories we still have. Wishing you a super happy birthday."

She clinked my glass, and the fiery taste of Patrone burned smoothly down my throat.

"Thanks, babes, but no more emotional speeches. I must look hot tonight, not a weepy mess, especially as I turn thirty-three."

I gave her arm a reassuring squeeze, and then we grabbed our stuff and went out the door.

Ruby chose one of the newest clubs in the city to celebrate her birthday, which had already been tipped as becoming the hottest new place in town. And the smile she had on her face when they showed us to the top table in the VIP section that I'd booked as a surprise for her... well, it was worth the extra cost.

Deciding to give my feet a five-minute rest as we'd been dancing our butts off since we arrived, I took a seat, grabbed my phone, and quickly checked my emails and messages. The last one is from Roman apologizing again for not coming and asking if Ruby was having a good night. I fast-typed my reply as I saw her coming over.

> Hey, Ro. We're having a great night. It's a shame you couldn't make it. I'll pass on the message to Ruby. Speak soon, love you xx

I hastily put my phone back in my clutch as I knew Ruby wouldn't be happy with me checking in on work on a night out.

"Serena, Serena, come here quick!" she said with a slight slur.

She would have to slow down if she wanted to last the night. Making my way over to the edge of the dance floor where she stood, I could see her doing all her trademark *how to get a guy's attention* moves. Standing with her spine straight, boobs up and out, hand on the hip, her eyes hooded, which just intensified her smoky eye, and finished off with the infamous Ruby Tanner pout.

"So, who has caught your eye, missy? Because by the look that you've got right now, let's say he doesn't have a chance of getting away. So where is the lucky guy?"

"He's the one with the dark green shirt sat at the bar. You see him?"

There was no way I could miss him. The guy must have been about six feet at a guess, with sandy bronze hair and dark stubble peppering his jaw. He was looking at my best friend in the same lustful manner as she was him. I guessed that her night was sorted. But it hit me just as he stood, and I could see his features clearer in the light.

I know that guy.

It was that idiot Julian Chambers. He was such an asshole during that meeting last week.

You'd think that someone whose family had amassed such a large and successful empire would at least know how to behave in a meeting.

"Son of a bitch," I muttered in contempt.

"What was that?" Ruby asked, still distracted by the jerk across the way.

"Nothing, hon. Just something to do with work popped into my head."

"I've told you, Serena, no work, not tonight. You hardly ever relax and enjoy yourself. I'm going to go to Mr. Temptation over there, and I want you to go and find a sexy guy and show him the hot stuff you are. And that's a birthday order!"

I wanted to dissuade her, but the last thing I wanted to do was get into it on her birthday. So, I swallowed my frustration and nodded while shaking my head.

"Yes, ma'am."

Lifting an imaginary hat off her head in salute to me, we both laughed, and I watched as she approached him.

I couldn't help but think back on my encounter with him last week. It was more than clear just what type of man he was. First, his assumption that I was an assistant and then the micro sexism that fell so freely from his goddamn mouth. It wasn't that I wasn't used to such statements, being a mixed-race woman who owned her own company, I'd heard plenty of them. But just because I'd experienced it multiple times throughout my life didn't make it any less frustrating.

The only good thing about his idiotic behavior was that it functioned as a decent distraction from seeing Rhett again.

I hadn't even noticed him when I first entered the room. Then, when I introduced myself and took in his face, I realized it was the guy from the garage. I had to lock my knees when recognition and shock slammed into me.

Seeing him again had set off that fire within me, and I didn't want him to notice his effect on me. So, I'd done my best to avoid his stare. Now and again, I'd watch him out of the corner of my eye. Even the flex of his arm in what I was assuming was a custom-made suit reminded me of that hot, wet dream, which, despite my attempts at clearing from my mind, seemed to be popping up more than I wanted.

I glanced over at Ruby and the asshole, and saw she was lapping up every single word he was feeding her. I sure hoped Ruby was only thinking of indulging in him for tonight. I couldn't think of anybody worse for her to start dating. Not that my opinion had ever played any part in her decision-making about the men in her life.

Taking a long sip of my drink, I welcomed the distraction of the warm burn of the alcohol as it trickled down my throat. I was out for Ruby's birthday, I would not let anyone fuck up my mood.

Setting my drink down, I went to the lady's room to freshen up.

"Girl, you're looking hot tonight. I better keep my man miles away from you," the woman standing next to me at the sink blurted out.

Despite my complexion, I managed to turn bright red in embarrassment. I could tell she was out having a good night, and by how she kept swaying, I was sure she was feeling reasonably buzzed, too.

"Thank you, but your man is the lucky guy."

I didn't know what else to say. The lady gave me a megawatt smile and swayed her way out of the restroom. After reapplying my lipstick, I ran my hands over my hair, which, to my amazement, had managed to stay in place despite all the dancing.

Leaving the bathroom, I headed to the bar, wondering how Ruby and Julian were getting on, but I couldn't find them. Walking through the dance floor, I scanned the room for Ruby and, on the off chance of spotting a hot guy and having fun. Just as I was about to start walking up the steps to our table, a firm hand grabbed my elbow. I turned around, ready to tell the guy to get lost, when I realized the piercing blue eyes staring so intently were those of Rhett Chambers.

Seriously, out of all the places and all the nights to bump into the man that had been haunting my dreams, it had to be tonight.

"Serena Parker, right?"

His voice sounded deep and authoritative.

"Yes, I'm surprised you remembered."

I tried to steady my voice as I could feel my pulse quicken. "Of course."

His hand still held my arm, and in any other case, I would have put a guy in his place, but something about him was keeping me from seeing any sense.

"So, are you here for a special occasion?"

He interrupted my thoughts, and I snapped back into the present.

"Yeah, I'm here celebrating my best friend's birthday. She, however, seems to have abandoned us in favor of your brother. What a small world."

I tried to hide my annoyance at the thought of his brother, but I wasn't sure if I'd done a decent job of it. I wasn't an idiot for not thinking there could be a significant chance of bumping into his brother after spotting Julian.

"Well, I hope he buys the birthday lady a drink and acts like a gentleman."

There was something in the tone and the way he spoke about his brother that made me wonder if he, too, thought he was a jackass. Hmm, the jury was still out on that one.

"So, can I get you a drink?" he offered.

"Sure, I'll have an Amaretto Cranberry Kiss."

Out of nowhere, a waiter appeared and took our order.

"Would you like me to bring the drinks here or onto the terrace, Mr. Chambers?" the waiter asked.

Huh? The staff knew his name. He was the epitome of a Manhattan bachelor.

"Would you like to join me on the terrace so we can hear one another, or are you needed back to your table?"

The look in his eyes made it clear which of the two options he'd prefer me to take. My brain was telling me to stay there, knowing it was not a clever idea to spend time alone with the arrogant guy, but my body had other ideas.

"I didn't know there was a terrace here."

"Then, why don't I show you? Shall we?"

He moved aside, and we started crossing the dance floor. With the speakers pumping out a deep, sexy beat, I felt myself moving to it unintentionally.

"But first, would you like to dance?"

Before he let me answer his question, I felt his hands glide smoothly down my dress and rest by my hips.

Despite the warning signs in my head, I let myself move to the music and the feeling of his tall, muscular body against my back. His hips rolled into me as I grind back against him. I was sure I could feel his erection hard against my ass. I hated to admit it, but the guy was hot, could dance, and was turning me on. We weren't dancing long before he leaned forward and whispered in my ear.

"We need some fresh air, and our drinks should be ready now."

Then he took my hand and walked us through the crowd of bodies dancing and gyrating with one another around us. He managed to get us to a discreet door opposite our VIP table. The entry was hardly visible, but the large security guy standing before it had made it impossible for anyone who didn't know of its existence to notice it.

"Your drinks are on the terrace, Mr. Chambers," the burly man said as he stepped aside and opened the door for us.

Rhett gave his thanks and handed the guy a hundred-dollar bill. Through the door, there was a dimly lit narrow corridor that led to another entrance, which led to a flight of stairs. He turned around and glanced at my feet.

"Will you be all right with these stairs in your heels?"

Ugh, men were clueless sometimes.

"Yes, thank you, I'll be fine," I assured him.

Finally, we got to what I hoped would be the final door. He opened it, and as I stepped outside, I was blown away.

Utterly Speechless.

The Terrace felt more like a rooftop haven than the little terrace I had pictured it to be. I could see all the high rises on one side and, on the other, the Hudson. The night was clear with hundreds of stars, and the moon was so bright it looked like a spotlight.

Looking around, I saw the rooftop had been decorated with beautiful exotic flowers and plants that filled the air with sweet scents. In the middle, there was what looked like a cabana you'd find on a beach in the Caribbean.

We made our way over to it, and I sat on the large red sofa that took up most of the space. In front of it was a glass table with my cocktail and what looked like a glass of either whiskey or bourbon, which must be for him.

Rhett unbuttoned his royal blue jacket, and underneath, he wore a crisp white shirt that set off his crystal blue eyes and blonde hair. He is so goddamn sexy. Taking a seat next to me, I quickly grabbed my drink and hastily sipped the delicious fruity concoction that I needed to steady my nerves, and moistened my mouth as it felt as dry as the Sahara.

"Well, this has got to be the quietest I have seen you since I've met you," he purred.

"Well, it's not every day you get to see the beautiful sights of Manhattan like this," I countered.

"Is that so?" he quipped.

I knew what he was alluding to, but there was no chance I would fawn over him and behave in the way I was sure most other women he met did.

"Yes, my work keeps me busy, and even when I finally have a window of time, I usually spend it at home relaxing or returning to see my family. Not all of us have the time or the luxury of seeing the city at its finest."

"Well, Serena, I'm not sure what you think I do, but I also find I'm very busy with work most of the time, but when I can, I like to indulge in the beauty that this great city offers."

He raised his eyebrows, and his eyes sparkled with mischief.

"So, does your family own this place?"

He frowned.

"Well, as you already know, my family's company has a large property and development portfolio over Manhattan and New York. The Mount, however, isn't currently one of ours. Julian and I were here because we're looking at using it to host our next event."

Oh, that wasn't quite the answer I was expecting.

"You seem surprised?"

He took another sip of his drink. I felt myself following his smooth and effortless movements.

"Nothing you or your family do surprises me. You seem to take what you want at any cost. Trust me, I learned my lesson back in college."

I look straight into his eyes to gauge his response. Finally, I felt like I was back in control and had taken the reins on how my body responded to him.

"What do you mean? What happened in college?"

There was no way I would dive deep into that can of worms, but I could see on his face that I wouldn't get away without answering.

"Let's just say I experienced the effects of getting in the line of fire with privileged families and the lengths they will go to both protect their own and control the narrative."

The firmness in my tone made it clear I wasn't going to be going deeper than that.

"Serena, my beliefs are very different from those of my family," he said with an edge of irritation.

So, I hit a soft spot.

Did he think I was that stupid and not know the type of man he was?

The type his family was?

I dealt with these wealthy, self-righteous clients every day.

He placed his drink back on the table and leaned his arm against the back of the couch, one leg bent and resting on the other as if opening himself up to me.

I found it unsettling, not because anything was intimidating in it, but because it made me notice his body again, and I'd been trying my hardest to suppress how much he physically turned me on.

"That's enough business talk. So, is your plan for tonight to celebrate your friend's birthday? Or are you looking to meet the man of your dreams? What is your true goal for the night here at The Mount?"

"I'm here celebrating my best friend Ruby's birthday. We've been friends since school, and I wanted to do something special for her. It does seem, however, that her night is now on a different course as she has spent the last hour flirting with your brother."

I didn't manage to hide my contempt for that fact entirely, and Rhett noticed.

Leaning in slightly, he picked up our glasses and, with a devilish smile, said, "A toast to Ruby's birthday. I wish her luck and good fortune, and that's just with my brother."

I couldn't help but smile. I clinked my glass with his and finished off my drink. The night had started to cool down, and the breeze was now chillier.

In the corner of my eye, I noticed him looking over my body with greedy eyes, and I felt my nipples harden to a peak.

Rhett also noticed it.

"It's starting to get chilly up here. Why don't we return, grab another drink, and find Ruby and my brother?"

Tentatively, I took his proffered hand and once again experienced tingles shooting from the tips of my fingers and coursing through every inch of my body.

Chapter 5

Serena

Making our way back into the packed club, I leaned over so he could hear me over the loud music, and the scent of his earthy, musky cologne sent a shiver down my spine.

"I'm going to go and try to find Ruby and make sure she's okay."

"Let me help you find her."

He didn't leave room for bargaining as he guided me around the perimeter of the dance floor. His hand is ever present at the base of my spine. Though the connection may only be slight, the warmth that spread through me was one of protective possession, and it awoke something buried deep within me.

Leaning against the wall, he waited for me outside the lady's room as I looked for Ruby in there.

"Any lucky?" he asked.

"No. I'm sure she is fine," I concluded.

Just then, a waiter passed with a tray with two shots, a bowl of limes and a saltshaker.

"Mr Chambers."

He grabbed the two glasses and turned back to me.

"Would you like one?"

Despite knowing how dangerous Tequila and I were together, I couldn't turn down his offer. Especially as I watched his brow lift in what I was guessing was his assumption of me turning it down.

Bypassing the salt, I grabbed the wedge of lime and toasted my glass with his. Maintaining eye contact, I watched his smirk as I managed to down the smooth agave without so much as a grimace, followed by the sour tang as I sucked down on the wedge of lime. His eyes tracked as my tongue caught the stray drops of juice. His pupils were blown, and his chest rose faster with each breath. Wanting to play into our little game of cat and mouse, I leaned forward and watched as his eyes bounced between mine and my mouth.

"I'm gonna go and dance," I whispered in his ear.

I could feel the deep exhale of his breath across my shoulder as I passed him.

As I walked past the throw of people on the dance floor, the deep base of Calvin Harris' *How Deep Is Your Love* pulsated through the room.

I let the rhythm flow through my body, adding to my heightened senses. My whole body felt like it was on fire.

Rhett gently pulled me back, and my back molded to his front.

Despite my better judgment and knowing I would regret it tomorrow, I let my body move.

I swayed and ground against him, getting lost in the music.

My skin felt damp from the heat of the room and my growing arousal.

My body purred beneath his touch as reason began to tumble into oblivion.

Everything felt majestic. His hands ran up and down my arms, keeping up with the music's beat and my dancing.

As I rolled my hips against his crotch, I could feel his hard cock straining profusely against his pants.

Running his nose along the back of my ear, I felt him take in the scent of my perfume.

I was unsure if it was my sweat or if he had licked his lips, but I felt their moisture as he parted them and ran them down the side of my neck.

He was not precisely kissing, more like nibbling his way down, and I arched my back to accept him better.

My pulse was racing, and my lungs felt like they were struggling for air.

The piercing strain of my nipples and the stimulation I felt rubbing against this man was bringing me to a state of evocative pleasure, which caused my eyes to start rolling to the back of my head.

Sliding his hands down my arms, skimming the sides of my breasts, he then wrapped his solid and supple hands around my wrists.

Spinning me around, he pinned my hands behind my back.

I broke out of my trance, realizing how close and intimate we were with one another at that moment.

My eyes flickered up, and I couldn't help but look first at his firm mouth, then focused on his striking blue eyes. Simply staring at them that closely, I got lost in an ocean of power, lust, and desire.

I could feel his cock throbbing against my belly button.

Slowly, he leaned his head down.

I knew where this was going.

My conscience screamed at me, knowing this was a terrible mistake.

Nothing good could come of this. But right then, my body was standing its ground.

It had been quite some time since I last felt this turned on, this hot and wanted.

Rhett lowered his head and rubbed the pad of his thumb gently against my lower lip. Giving me one last look. The carnal lust I saw almost made me scream.

He crushed his lips against mine, almost aggressively.

Then he let out a slight moan, and the passion of the kiss went in a completely different direction. One hand was at the back of my head, holding me firmly in place and slightly tugging on my hair as the other snaked around my body.

The feeling of his fingers running down my spine, exposed by my dress, sent feelings of exquisite lust through me. His tongue softly caressed mine. I bit his lower lip, and the most erotic sound escaped his mouth.

The kiss was no longer playful.

It was stimulating.

I began to feel slightly vulnerable.

At that moment, I remembered where we were. Standing in the middle of the dance floor of The Mount.

The other people dancing and enjoying themselves around us brought me out of the exotic bubble.

I felt dazed, almost as if I were in some hallucination.

I took a step back.

Rhett looked at me. His fiery eyes glowed with desire, but the look on his face also showed his confusion.

He tried to pull me back into his embrace, but I shook my head.

I needed to get the hell out of there. What was I thinking? First, he was a client. And secondly, he was different from the type of guy I wanted. He lived his life in a small, privileged bubble, so far away from my own.

I made my way through the crowd of bodies, men and women dressed to impress. Out for fun, drinks, and maybe something more if they were lucky.

My body screamed to return, but my head finally took the lead.

As I arrived at our table, Ruby's friend Lucy tried to talk to me. I couldn't hear her over the music and the loud sound of my heartbeat drumming in my ears.

I leaned in and could see on her face that she had a bit too much to drink. I steadied her arm, and she shouted over the music,

"Ruby told me to thank you for such a great night, and she's off for some one-on-one fun to end her birthday celebrations."

Shit.

"Did she leave with the guy she was dancing with?" I asked Lucy.

I hoped Rubs found someone else, but I knew in my gut I wouldn't like the news.

Lucy nodded and smiled like a Cheshire cat.

God, I should've warned Ruby about Julian. Why, out of all the guys there, did she have to go and take that asshole home?

I said my goodbyes to the other people at the table and left to hail a cab.

It had dropped a few more degrees since I was last outside, and my outfit was doing nothing to keep me warm.

I grabbed my phone from my clutch and pulled up Ruby's number.

I should call her, see if she was okay. Try to persuade her to avoid making a massive mistake. But as soon as those thoughts popped into my head, I dismissed them. She was a grown woman who could make her own choices. And mistakes.

I grinned, knowing that she'd probably come around

tomorrow with the mother of all hangovers and tell me how bad he was in bed.

Ha, now that would be funny—that stupid prick.

I logged into my taxi app and looked to see how far the closest driver was to me.

As my phone loaded the app, I ran my fingers across my lips, which felt sensitive. Almost as if they were going to bruise, instantly remembering the feel of his soft, firm lips as they fitted perfectly against my own.

What was it about that kiss?

Why did I let him kiss me?

I must have had too much to drink. I was sure he did, too.

Next time I see him, I must be as professional as possible to ensure he didn't get the wrong idea.

And if he had anything to say on the matter, that was his problem.

My phone beeped with the notification that my car should be pulling up. I looked up and saw a black town car roll to a stop at the curb.

I walked over and opened the passenger door, and to my surprise, I saw Rhett sitting in the back seat.

"Oh s-sorry," I stutter, shocked and confused.

"Get in. Let me give you a lift home," Rhett replied.

I could hear the slightest tinge of hesitation in his voice.

"No, it's okay. I've booked a car. I just thought this was it."

I tried to close the door with one hand when he stopped me.

"Serena, please, just get in. My driver will take you home. At least then, I'll know you got home safely."

I was just about to tell him I was a grown woman and could make my way home when suddenly I heard a voice behind me.

His driver.

"It is no bother, miss."

The tenderness in Rhett's eyes was my undoing, and I slipped inside the car. He closed the door behind me and walked to the driver's seat. Slipping inside the car, he asked for my address, plugged it into his GPS, and pulled away from the curb.

Looking over at Rhett, I thanked him for offering me a lift home.

"There is no need to thank me. A woman as beautiful as you should always get home safely. Plus, it's starting to get cooler, and there was no way I would leave you outside alone."

I wouldn't have noticed him glancing down at my dress as he spoke about the drop in temperature, if I hadn't been looking straight at him while he was talking.

That was when I noticed how my nipples were perked and visible through my dress. Fuck. Could this get any more awkward?

Wrapping my arms around myself, I tried to warm my skin, but it was my internal temperature that went up a notch, and it had nothing to do with the warmth of the car or the alcohol in my veins.

For the second time that night, I was near Rhett Chambers, and my body responded to him like an eighteen-year-old girl meeting her favorite movie star.

What on earth had gotten into me?

He must have sensed my unease, and to my surprise, he broke the tension.

"So, did your friend have a good birthday?"

I laughed a little.

"Well, I'm sure her evening will be ending eventfully. She left with your brother. They hit it off. Who'd have thought it?"

It wouldn't have been possible to put any more sarcasm in my voice.

"Oh, I see." He shook his head. "I hope she knows what she's gotten herself into?"

"What do you mean by that?"

I suddenly felt a sense of unease flood through me.

"Nothing that should worry you, it's just... well... let's just say my brother isn't the easiest person to get on with."

Now, that was an understatement.

"I'm guessing by that look on your face you agree with me?"

He flashed me his massive grin.

"Let's just say your revelation about your brother's character hasn't exactly floored me."

We both sat there and laughed.

It felt good.

"About tonight and..."

I knew he was going to talk about the kiss.

"Let's just... chalk it up to the moment," I said, hoping to bypass the whole issue.

Because I was not willing to go there.

That chapter of the night needed to get shelved and could be dealt with another day.

Luckily, as I looked out the window, we turned onto my street.

The driver pulled up outside my apartment and stepped out of the car.

Grabbing my clutch, I reached for the door when Rhett stopped me.

"I hope you and your friend had a lovely evening," he said, shifting in his seat. "I know what the highlight of mine was."

I willed myself not to look at him but failed. He had that sexy smirk on his face. My eyes were drawn again to his lips, and I was taken back to the memory of his mouth on mine.

Running my tongue across my lips, I could still taste him. I at once saw the effect it had on him.

He grabbed my hand, and I suddenly feared that he was going to pull me on top of him, and the way my body felt, I knew I wouldn't need much persuasion to fuck him right there in the car.

However, to my surprise, he tentatively kissed my hand, his eyes flickering up.

"I look forward to seeing you at our meeting next week."

Stepping out of the car, I smoothed my dress and managed to say goodnight. I walked into my apartment building and made sure not to look back.

As I stepped into the elevator and leaned against the cool marbled wall, all I could think about was how it was going to be seeing him again.

That was going to be an exciting meeting.

Chapter 6

Rhett

The muscles in my arms and legs were on fire. My lungs gasped for another gulp of air as the water rushed over me.

At the edge of the private pool, a reward of my penthouse suite, I paused, looking up at the clock—seven in the morning.

I'd been swimming for almost an hour straight.

My body screamed at me to stop for the last twenty minutes, but my mind needed the distraction.

I replayed every minute of that evening thousands of times in my mind. I wanted to remember every inch and curve of her body.

Picturing the sexy way she moved her body to the music.

Her full, luscious lips felt perfectly soft and plump against mine. It felt spellbindingly erotic as she ever so lightly nipped down on my lip, once again showing the two different sides of the woman that had gotten to me like no other ever had.

As I slowed the pace on my last length of the pool, I thought about the meeting I'd have with her at our office later that morning. I pulled myself out of the pool, glad for the privacy, as I walked across to the shower with a full hard-on.

Stripping out of my wet trunks, I welcomed the shower's warm water as it cascaded over me.

Instinctively, I reached for my cock, which was already pulsing with need. Wrapping my hand around the tip, I collected the pre-cum, which had already begun to bead.

Remembering the way Serena had been when in the boardroom, her skirt clinging to the curve of her ass, made my abs tense as my strokes grew faster. I imagined how good it would feel to trap her against the desk, bunching the material up, sliding my fingers over down, and finding her pussy already glistening with arousal. Squeezing my cock tighter, I bucked my hips into my fist. My chest tightened as I pictured the ripple across her ass as I pounded relentlessly into her.

"Fuck."

Wrapping her hair around my fist, pulling her head back and keeping her in place. Pleasure tingled up my spine, my balls tightened, and I squeezed the head tighter, imagining it was her pussy clamping down as she reached her climax.

"Fuck, fuck, fuck."

Spots dotted the edge of my vision as my cum shot out, hitting the tiled wall before being washed away down the drain.

Stepping back under the spray, I caught my breath. My muscles relaxed under the pounding water jets.

Having pushed my body profusely during my swim and relieving some of my tension in the shower, I wasn't surprised to hear my stomach rumble, informing me to fuel up for the day.

After a quick, healthy breakfast, I made my way down to the car, and for some reason, I found myself more aware and tentative of my appearance.

Attempting to shake off this adolescent behavior, I greeted Russell as he held open the door to the car.

By the time I'd gotten to the office, I'd already been inundated with emails and requests requiring my assistance, attention, and approval.

I knew that since my infancy, it had been planned that when my father finally decided to retire, I would inherit the business and continue to run it as my father, grandfather, and great-grandfather had.

My family's business managed to succeed and strive beyond most people's wildest dreams—I didn't have a problem with its success or history. I did, however, feel that it was time to change and adapt to the times we were living in. And that was one of the many hurdles I knew I would eventually face. Those that had been there for decades were incapable of change.

Their views were single-minded.

The future, the legacy that I knew one day would fall upon me, was never something I wished for. It was something I had always been told would happen. I had never been able to choose anything in my life for myself.

Not wanting to dwell on thoughts that wouldn't come to fruition for many years, I focused on the dozens of emails I needed to get through and prepare for my meeting with Serena.

Something I had been envisioning for days.

I finished sending the last few emails and correspondence when Charlotte buzzed in.

"Mr. Chambers, the team from Parker & Associates is set up and waiting in the conference room for your two o'clock."

"Thank you, Charlotte. I'll be right there."

So, she decided to still bring her team in with her. Interesting.

I wondered if she did that intentionally, worrying how things would be with us alone again.

I headed to the bathroom in my office, splashed some water on my face, and prepared to see the woman who had been haunting my dreams.

Walking into the conference room, a young man greeted me. He couldn't have been much older than twenty-five.

Despite his almost adolescent-looking face, he nearly towered over me when he approached me.

Jesus, he must've been about six foot nine!

"Good afternoon, I'm Brody Anderson."

We shook hands, and he introduced the other team members to the table.

Picking up the folder placed in front of me, I skimmed through the notes, eagerly waiting for her arrival.

"As you can see, we have retained three more agreements, and the settlements are currently being processed with the appointed lawyers. A meeting is scheduled next week with another of the abstentions as the owner is currently abroad, and they have arranged for a family member to attend and act as their proxy. Apparently, full requirements have already been discussed, and at the moment, things are looking good, so we will be able to come to an agreement with them as well."

As I waited for Mr Anderson to finish, I continued to scan the room, and the one face I expected to see was nowhere to be found.

"Is Ms Parker running late?"

I tried my best to hide the irritation in my voice, but I was pretty sure everyone could tell just how fucking pissed I was.

"I'm afraid she couldn't attend today's meeting. Something came up at the office. She hoped we could go over our progress so far and discuss what we still have to do and how realistic our timeline of getting everything done compares to yours. I hope that is not a problem, sir?"

Bullshit.

That was complete and utter rubbish that she couldn't make the meeting.

There was no way this didn't have something to do with me and what happened on Saturday night.

I regained my equilibrium and tried to erase the nervous and uneasy look that had started to creep upon Mr Anderson's face.

"No, that will be fine. Let's get on with it."

To my partial annoyance, the associates managed to keep up with my quick-fire questions, suggestions, and input.

I knew my foul mood wasn't their fault, but I couldn't shake the frustration that bubbled inside me.

Why didn't she attend the meeting, agree to go for a drink, and finally give herself to me?

She'd been driving me crazy for days, and now she expected me to endure this torture even further?

Well, she had another thing coming.

I concluded the meeting on a high note and praised the team's work.

With a newly lit fire burning, I motioned for Charlotte to follow me into my office.

It only took a few strides before I was at my desk and grabbing my briefcase when Charlotte entered.

"What can I do for you, Mr. Chambers?"

"I need you to clear the rest of my afternoon as I have some urgent business to address. Call Russell to bring the car round, and if anything requires my urgent attention, send it to me."

I didn't even wait for her to respond before I was headed to the bank of elevators, desperate to get out of the damn building and speak with Serena.

At the lobby, I saw, to my delight, Russell already waiting at the curb.

"I need to go to the office of Parker & Associates," I told him.

"Right away, sir."

Russell pulled the car into the flow of Manhattan's traffic.

Despite hoping otherwise, my frustration had quadrupled since I stepped into the conference room and realized Serena hadn't come.

It only took us about fifteen minutes, considering Midtown traffic at that time was quite impressive when Russell pulled the car over. Exasperated with how the entire day had panned out, I climbed out of the vehicle.

"I'm not sure how long this will take, so I'll call once I'm done," I clarified.

Russell gave a curt nod and got back into the car.

I straightened my suit and took a few deep breaths to regain my composure, then I entered her office block.

After being directed to the correct floor, I was greeted by the receptionist.

"How can I help you, sir?"

"I'm looking for Ms Parker. She is currently working with me and could not attend our meeting this morning. An important matter has come up, it's very time-sensitive and needs her urgent attention."

"What is your name?"

"Rhett Chambers."

"She's currently in a meeting, but if I take you to her office, you can sit there, and I'll pass on the message that you're here on an urgent matter."

"Thank you. That would be great."

She swiftly led me through the small but quaint office of Parker & Associates.

Pleasure ran through me as we walked past the conference room, and I saw her.

She wore a camel-colored pencil skirt, which fit her hips and ass perfectly. A three-quarter sleeve coral blouse set off her caramel skin in the most intoxicating way.

Her hair fell in loose waves down her shoulders.

As she bent over to pick up a file off the desk, my mind raced with other things she could do in that position.

Like being bent over my desk, clad only in panties.

Our eyes met, and a slight blush spread across her cheeks as recognition and realization hit. The receptionist turned and led me into Serena's office.

I mentally ordered myself to calm down as molten waves of pleasure crashed through me.

"I'll just let her know you're here. Is there anything I can get you to drink while you wait?"

"No, I'm fine. But thank you for your help."

As soon as she left the room, I looked around her office.

The walls were decorated with diplomas, certificates, and news articles of renowned successful cases.

No artwork, no memorabilia, no overly feminine touches.

I walked over to the window and saw the mundane view, blocked by a massive skyscraper next door.

It only took me a few paces before I was back at her desk.

That's when I noticed the pictures near her computer.

One frame held a picture of the two guys, one of which I recognized from the garage. I'm guessing they're her father and brother from the family resemblance.

Another photo was of a couple with two young girls, and the final was of her and another woman sipping cocktails on a beach somewhere.

Given the sparseness of her office, it was evident that the people in those pictures must mean a great deal to her as they were the only glimpse she showed of her private life. Was this her inner circle?

I put the picture back in its place and checked the time. It had been almost ten minutes since I was brought in, and she still hadn't come to see me.

Annoyance again burned in me, and I went to the door just as Serena walked straight into me.

Her smoldering eyes saw right through me. Her breasts brushed up against my chest, and her breath came fast, and again, a blush tinged her cheeks.

"Mr Chambers, you startled me."

She regained her composure, and I reluctantly let her out of my grasp.

"I was told you have an urgent matter to discuss?"

She dived around me and walked towards her desk.

"Please, take a seat," she offered.

I tried to gauge her physical reaction to my presence as she walked around her desk.

Despite her attempts to stay calm and professional, I noticed her eyes blinking more rapidly than usual, her breathing was short and clipped, and she continuously ran the palm of her hands down her hips as though to straighten her skirt, despite there not being a wrinkle in sight.

"I'm here, because I was made to believe that the meeting I had scheduled this morning was to be with you."

I did my best to hide my frustration, but how she raised her eyebrows showed she'd caught on.

"Well, as I'm sure my associates made clear to you, I had an issue that came up here that required my attention. Was there a problem in the meeting? Or do you have qualms with Mr. Anderson leading the meeting? If that is the case, he is one of my firm's best associates, if not the best. He is always prepared and is a keen, driven, and hard worker."

Well, it looked like my sexy little bundle's feisty side was out to play.

I wondered if she was as fiery in bed as she was in protecting her staff.

I couldn't help but grin, and when our eyes met again, I realized I wanted her now more than ever.

"No, Ms. Parker, Mr. Anderson did an excellent job, but I'm sure you can understand that in times of important business, unexpected changes such as getting others to take your meetings will have an impact. Especially as we are paying you for *your* expertise."

There, now, that should give her something to think about.

"Excuse me, Mr. Chambers, but I neither see your statement's importance nor meaning. Yes, I know my company's services are currently at your disposal because yours could not do the job, and we are. And even though we are a much smaller firm than most in Manhattan, we still deal with many cases, and you are not our only client."

There was a flush to her cheeks, and she kept digging her nails into her fists, seemingly to maintain her composure.

"I'm sure you are a man who's used to getting what he wants and how he wants it, but also, as someone with the business knowledge that I'm sure you have, *you* should by now know that things don't always go as expected."

I knew she was partially correct, but it was also clear that we weren't just talking about business. I still didn't believe her excuse and sudden distance were work-related.

I knew she was attracted to me. I could see it in her eyes despite her frustration.

I was desperate to uncover it. I just needed her to allow it. So, I guessed it was time to stop beating around the bush.

"It was never my intention to offend you, Ms Parker. It just seemed that your sudden detachment from our work—from me —was due to what happened on Saturday night."

I could see the shock and sudden embarrassment of me bringing it up on her face.

Turning in her chair, she looked out the window.

"I.... I'm not sure what you're getting at Mr Chambers," she stuttered.

Now, this was beginning to get ridiculous.

"Are you saying you don't remember our kiss the other night? Because there is no way you can tell me you were too drunk to remember. That would be an insult to both of us."

Her body was frozen in place. The sound of her taking a deep breath was the only thing I could hear in the room.

"I'm not saying I don't remember it. I simply don't understand why you're bringing it up here. It was a kiss. We were out, happened to bump into one another, we'd both been drinking, there was music, dancing, it's just something that happened in that moment."

"Bullshit!"

I scoffed, shaking my head, unable to hide the smile on my face.

"Excuse me?" Serena exclaimed.

"You heard me. I don't believe for one minute that the kiss was simply a fleeting incident that happened in a moment. Are you telling me that since then, you haven't thought about me? Thought about that kiss? Maybe what could have happened?"

She was still facing the window, and I took the opportunity to get up, walk around her desk, and lean back against it.

As she turned to respond, I could see the shock and desire in her eyes at my forward approach.

I studied her eyes, and I saw a change of emotions. One minute, she looked like she was going to bite my head off. The next, as if she were desperate to ravish me.

She swiveled her chair around so that she faced me, then crossed her legs in a deliberately slow and sexy manner.

God, she turned me on so much.

As I willed my body to control itself, I knew there was no hope. My cock was throbbing to the point of pain.

And she noticed, too. She glanced at the bulge in my pants. The corner of her mouth turned up with the slightest hint of a smile.

Her eyes traveled up my body. She ran her tongue across her lips, and it took all my strength not to pounce on her right there, right then.

Finally, she looked at me squarely and took a deep breath.

"Mr. Chambers, neither is it right nor appropriate for us to discuss this here. Yes, I had fun the other night. And yes, I will admit I find you attractive, but that is it. As you stated, we are working together, and therefore, things can't go any further, as it could result in things becoming complicated. Your presence here proves my point."

She was still rambling on about work ethics and such, her eyes once again straying down to my encased erection.

Hypnotized, I leaned forward, lifted her chin with my finger, and brushed my lips across hers. A gasp passed her lips as if a match had been lit. She stood from her chair, her eyes darting between my eyes and my mouth before her lips captured mine in a bruising kiss.

Passion and desire ravaged me.

My tongue invaded her mouth—massaging, stroking against hers. She let out a painted moan, which only fueled me more. Greedily, my hands caressed her body. One hand traveled down her body, over her thighs, and I finally reached her gorgeous ass.

Instinctively, I squeezed it, pulling her against me.

My other hand stroked the small of her back, then reached into her hair, holding her in place.

She tasted like the sweetest nectar, and I was hooked. I couldn't get enough.

Awash with sensations, I leaned her back against her desk.

My cock rubbed along her thigh, and the friction it created drove me insane.

She dug her nails into my back, encouraging me to carry on.

This is what I've been wanting. Needing.

Just as I was about to yank up her skirt, the telephone on her desk rang, cutting through the room.

She dislodged herself from me, freeing her just enough to turn and answer the phone.

"Yes, Sarah, what is it?"

The breathiness of her tone was impossible for her to hide.

I couldn't hear the response, but the fact that Serena was trying to put as much distance between herself and me made it clear that our moment had passed.

"No, that's fine, put her through."

For the first time since I leaned in to kiss her, I looked into her eyes, and I could see her desire fading as the strong and unwavering lawyer took over.

"Hello, Mrs. Cole, how can I help you?"

I walked over to the seat in front of her desk, adjusting my pants and straightening my jacket.

Looking up at Serena as I sat down, the expression on her face changed once again.

It looked as though she had seen a ghost.

"I'm so sorry to hear that."

Her voice was just above a whisper.

She covered her mouth with her hand and slowly sank into her chair. The hairs on my neck stood up as a sense of unease washed over me.

I leaned forward in an attempt to listen.

"Mrs. Cole... Raya, please, there is no need to apologize. Like I said, I am always here if you need me. Is there anything I can do to help?"

Another pause and a look of pure sadness etched on Serena's face. The sight of which felt like a punch to the gut.

"How long ago were you informed?"

There was a long pause, and I continued watching as she listened.

"Ah, I see... no, of course, I'm glad to help. I'll be right there."

Hastily, she put the phone down, straightened herself, and finally turned to me.

"I'm sorry, Mr. Chambers, but I've got to go. Something urgent has come up."

Once again, she turned away, giving me no clues about what was happening.

"Serena."

She bent down to retrieve her bag.

"What is the matter? What's happened?"

"That was one of my clients. Sadly, her husband passed away, and she has no other family, no one to talk to, and she needs me. So, I'm afraid I have to go immediately."

She tried to pass me to leave, but I caught her by the elbow, gently pulling her into me.

"Mr. Chambers."

"Rhett, call me Rhett."

"Rhett, I really must go."

Still holding onto her arm with one hand, I used my free hand to retrieve my phone from my pocket and dial Russell's number. He answered on the second ring.

"Russell, I need you to pull the car around immediately."

"Yes, sir, I'll be right there."

I put the phone back into my pocket and led the way out of her office.

"Rhett, what are you doing?"

"I've called for my driver, who will take you wherever you need to go. Let's call it a habit of mine. One I am coming to enjoy."

We just arrived at the bank of elevators, and I was half expecting her to go off on a rant dismissing me and my offer.

However, to my surprise, she glanced up at me with beautiful green eyes, murmuring, "Thank you."

Chapter 7

Rhett

We sat in the back of the car as Russell lowered the privacy window.

"Ms Parker, where would you like me to take you?" he asked.

"220 East 60th Street."

Immediately, I recognized it.

"Isn't that one of the addresses involved in our negotiations?"

"Yes."

She chuckled, but there was no humor in her laugh.

What the hell was going on? Why wouldn't she talk to me? My thoughts ran away with me, not knowing how to act or what to say.

The more time I spent with Serena, the more I felt control and understanding slip through my fingers. And I wouldn't say I liked it. I wanted this woman, but to my surprise, I struggled to get her. Unexpectedly, she broke the silence.

"Thank you again for taking me to her."

The slight shyness in her tone took me off-guard.

"There is no need to thank me," I retorted.

The slight furrow to her brow made me regret my choice of words. There was a long silence, which made my guilt feel even worse.

"I'm sorry to hear that your client's husband has passed away."

There was another pause, but I could sense the silence was affecting her, too. I was about to open my mouth again when she turned and rested her hand on my arm.

"I just feel so hopeless."

She bit her bottom lip to stop the slight tremble, her brows furrowed, and a look of complete sadness washed over her face.

"Raya Cole is such a lovely, caring lady. She and her husband, Isaac, had been through so much together. She was the apple of his eye. I remember I used to joke, saying how they didn't make men like him anymore. He was old-fashioned. Whether it was pulling out the seat for her, holding open doors, watching the games shows that he couldn't stand but she loved, or writing her love notes every day, simply telling her how much he loved her.

They did everything together. He even tried to persuade her to accept your offer on their property, they have the cafe and residence above. It was always her dream to have her place. She is one of the best cooks you'll ever come across and coming from the south, you know her food is delicious."

The smile on her face told me everything she said was true. And if it were under any other circumstance, I'd take this chance to take her there for food.

I also felt a pang of guilt, knowing my company was in the midst of an attempted takeover, and although I know it wasn't a hostile one, nor was there anything personal behind it. It wasn't as if we were kicking these people to the curb; it was business—

but for the first time, it didn't quite feel right, and I couldn't quite shake the feeling.

Tentatively, I placed my hand on her cheek, using the pad of my thumb to wipe away the stray tear that ran down her face.

With eyes that previously lit with fire, now all I could see was sadness.

Without breaking contact, she lifted the hand on my arm, placed it on my knee, and with the softest touch of her lips, gently brushed against mine.

Her kiss was feather soft, and I willed myself not to allow my desire to take over.

I kissed her back, not with the same yearning I had in her office, but cautiously, not wanting to ruin the moment or let her believe I was taking advantage of her in this situation.

Slowly, she deepened the kiss, one hand softly rubbing up and down my thigh, the other laced in my hair, almost as if she were holding me in place.

Adrenaline ran thick and fast through my veins. It wasn't the Manhattan heat making my body start to sweat. It was her.

She thrust her lush tits against my chest.

I could feel her pulse quicken.

I pulled her onto my lap as she hiked up her skirt and straddled me. She began to grind on my cock, lost in her senses.

Provocatively, she took my bottom lip between her teeth and lightly bit down.

My tongue greedily devoured her mouth, drinking her in.

My brazen hands grabbed her ass, urging her to keep rubbing herself against me. Her back arched to better accept me. I was allowing my erection to cushion against her panties.

Wild and fierce passion pushed me on. She clutched fistfuls of my shirt, gently pulling it out of my pants.

My hand traced up her rib cage, finding her breasts.

Without trepidation, my fingers began to work the buttons of her blouse.

Russell's voice through the intercom hit me like a bucket of ice water.

"Mr. Chambers, we are here."

Despite Serena's caramel complexion, her cheeks flushed to a deep rose hue.

I reached for the talk button.

"Continue driving, Russell."

My voice dripped with annoyance and frustration.

"No, wait..." Serena shouted.

Immediately, she climbed off me, readjusted her skirt, and fixed the buttons on her shirt.

Her eyes shot up to mine, they were open wide and full of panic. Her lips, which I had just been feasting on, thinned, and in the blank of an eye, those warm green eyes were cold with regret, and a mask of indifference slid over her face.

And I knew that look would go on to haunt my dreams. I clenched my fists by my side, and it was all I could do to reign in annoyance at the ever-ongoing cock blocking that was happening to me.

Now more than ever, I knew her body craved mine as much as I craved hers, yet she kept shutting things down.

Once she finally put herself to rights, she turned in my direction, not yet looking into my eyes. She was just about to speak, but this time, I stopped her.

"Go. I understand. You need to be there for her."

"No... I mean, yes, I do. But I would like you to come with me."

Her entire face softened, and I could see the slight pleading that shone in her eyes.

"Excuse me? That may not be the best idea. I've never met her before. As you've already explained, she is going through a horrific time. The last thing she needs is a random stranger hovering around."

"That isn't true. First, you're not a stranger. Your family is trying to buy her property."

Guilt was the first of many uncomfortable emotions that went through me.

"Hold on, I didn't mean that in a negative way. It would be comforting for her to meet someone from the company. Put a face to the name, especially at a time like this. It could be a good distraction."

I could see that she meant every word. But my gut was telling me this was a bad idea.

She rested her hand on my forearm.

"Trust me."

So, I did.

A little while later, sitting in a booth at the back of the eatery, I watched Serena run her finger around the rim of her cup of coffee. She was still talking to Mrs Cole, and it amazed me at just how many sides there were to this fascinating woman.

There was the alluring yet confusing woman at the garage, the no-nonsense attorney, and the sexy vixen who let her hair down. Now, I was drawn in by the support and tenderness she was showing to a woman who, by my definition, was her client but clearly meant much more to her.

Which was the real Serena?

The more I thought about it, the more I wanted to get to know all the different sides that made up this sensational woman.

Breaking my thoughts, Mrs. Cole placed a plate of food on the table.

"Thank you, Mrs. Cole, but this wasn't necessary."

"Don't be silly. You're a big young man, and you need to eat. And please call me Raya."

I looked at Mrs Cole's face, which was full of kindness, but the sorrow I saw in her eyes made me feel inadequate to be around her at this moment in time.

Then my gaze settled on Serena, and I didn't know what I was looking for. Permission? Reassurance?

The delicious smells from the plate before me made my mouth water. Serena handed me a knife and fork, our fingers only making the briefest contact. Instantly, I looked up at her, and my eyes locked with the piercing green of hers.

She promptly busied herself and continued the conversation with Raya.

I quickly cleared my plate of food. The pan-fried cube steak with brown onion gravy was a toast to Raya's understanding of southern cuisine.

The two talked about the last few days of Mr. Cole's life. The way Raya spoke of her husband told me she loved him. I tried to join the conversation but had not found the right words.

They both tried to tempt me into trying the house specialty —the peach pudding—but I politely declined as I was already aware that after today, I would have to put in an extra hour in the gym. And not simply because of the food.

Serena's phone rang, and she excused herself from the booth. I watched as she walked over to the glass front of the restaurant. My brain and body reacted as one as I was able to look and appreciate the stunning woman she was.

Raya sat herself down next to me, catching my line of sight.

"Feel free to tell this old lady to mind her business, but are you two an item?" she mused.

My arousal towards Serena and the embarrassment of Raya's question caused my cheeks to heat.

"We are simply working together."

The answer sent a pang of irritation through me.

"I know you two are working together, as you both explained earlier, and I have to say I am pleased to meet you. It would have been nicer under better circumstances, but it's nice to meet at least someone on the other side of these negotiations."

She pensively looked in the distance. All I could feel was sadness for this woman.

"I hope you understand why I haven't accepted the offer. Your offer is more than generous, but my husband and I put everything into this place. This building doesn't simply house our residence and employment. It's all we have.

Sadly, we weren't blessed with children, so twenty-seven years ago, we decided to gamble. We upped sticks and left Atlanta to make this our home. Here are some of our best memories. Isaac said we should sign the deal, pick a location from a hat, and retire.

But then he fell ill and working was the only way I could cope. I didn't want to give up on here as I feared it would result in me giving up hope in his battle. However, now he's gone, I'm scared of giving it up. What am I to do? What would I have left?"

Tears trickled down her face, and I reached into my pocket and handed her a handkerchief. Her words felt like a punch to my stomach. Guilt stuck to my skin at the thought that we were taking this away from her.

Yes, I had only just met the woman, and usually, I never let emotion cloud any business decision I made, but listening to her story made me start to think about things in a different light. And that was something that felt very odd to me.

"Mrs Cole—Raya, I am incredibly grateful that Serena enabled me to meet you. I'm so sorry for your loss, and I also apologize if our business involvement has caused any more strain or difficulty than you are already suffering."

"Mr. Chambers, there is no need for you to apologize. I understand this is business. This is what you do. And had I met you a few months ago, we may have had a different conversation. Let me say this though - I was lucky enough to find my soul mate, and even though my eyesight isn't the best, the tension and chemistry between the two of you is palpable."

I couldn't help the smile that crept across my face at her directness, and it amused me that despite the sadness she was suffering, she was still a strong and forthcoming woman.

"Despite your intuition being rather spot on, at least on my side, I have only met Serena a handful of times, and let's just say I'm finding her very difficult to read."

"I understand what you're saying. I have known Serena for a few years. We met her at a Black Rights rally in Washington and have been friends ever since. It was then a surprise to find out that by pure chance, she would go on to be the go-between, so to speak, in these negotiations. I have known her mainly on a personal basis. She is hard-working, driven, and kind, yet stern when needed, but she always fights for the rights of others. Things that have happened in her past, have pushed her to do what she does and how she does it. Keep in mind, it isn't as if she consults with me about her romantic life, but I will say that if you like her or are interested, take a chance. As you never know what life throws at you."

She cleared the plates on our table and took them into the kitchen.

I could hear Serena finishing on the phone and looked to see her watching Raya whistling away as she disappeared into the kitchen—a few things Raya said stuck with me. I could fully understand the importance of focusing on work. My passion and drive for work got me through every day.

The other thing that intrigued me was her comment about Serena's past. When I first met her, she seemed so at home, so settled and comfortable, and how she appeared around her father, I didn't get the impression of any trouble or strain. So, what was it that had caused Serena to be the way she was?

Just then, she returned to the booth and picked up her handbag.

"I'm afraid I have to get back to the office."

I could tell something was bothering her, and just as I was about to ask what it was, Mrs Cole came and joined us.

"Sorry, Raya, but I must return to the office. I wish I could spend more time with you. I'll be back in a few days, but you can always call me, okay?"

She walked over and hugged her. The look on Raya's face showed me it was exactly what she needed.

We said our goodbyes and then returned to the car.

Russell held the door open for us, and Serena climbed in first. Yet again, I was aware of our proximity to one another and that we were once again alone, with too many things unresolved. I pushed down the privacy glass to tell Russell to do two drops, first her office, then me back to mine.

Serena was seated entirely on the opposite side of me. This time, I could look her straight on, and maybe I would have a better chance at working out what was going on and where this could lead.

"I want to fuck you. I want to fuck you right here, right now."

Her mouth shot wide open, but I held up my hand to stop her response. I needed her to listen for once.

"I don't care what you're going to try to argue, but I know you want to fuck me too. We keep stop-starting, and I'm not sure how much longer I can hold myself back. I want to kiss you until your lips are swollen. I want to explore your body with my hands, stroking and caressing every inch of you. I want to gently roll one of your nipples between my fingers and suck on the other. I want to work my way down your body until I finally reach your wet pussy. I want to..."

"Rhett!" Serena shouted, interrupting me.

I took a deep breath through my nose, staying silent and letting her continue.

"I need you to stop talking. I won't deny I am attracted to you, and I would be lying if I didn't say that I would be interested in finding out what else you would like to do to my body, but fundamentally, I think..."

I watched as she continued to squeeze her hands in her lap, her eyes looking everywhere but at me. Her pause felt like it went on for minutes, although I knew it was mere seconds. Then, finally, her eyes landed on mine. She straightened her body and took a deep breath.

"No, I know it would be a mistake. The business that brings us together is delicate and challenging, so adding the potential intensity and awkwardness of a one-night stand will make both of our jobs harder."

"Who said I only want you for one night?" I countered.

"Rhett, come on, we are from two very different worlds. There is never a scenario that this could lead into anything more than one night, but even that is something we should avoid."

Her hands were clasped tightly in her lap, and her shoulders rolled in slightly as if she were trying to make herself as small as possible. Keeping her eyes cast down and hidden from view, I was unable to see the real truth behind her words, nor could I wrap my head around what she meant.

What did she mean by saying that we are from different worlds? We were both successful at an early age. I couldn't wrap my head around it.

"Serena, you want to fuck me, and I want to fuck you. We are consenting adults, intelligent, and can separate our personal lives from professional ones. So why don't you give me one chance? One date, one night? That's all I'm asking for. Then you can decide from there. And if you call it quits after that, I promise it will not cause tension when working together. I will even offer to assign others to take my place in any meetings to make you feel more comfortable if that is what you prefer. So, will you agree?"

She looked straight into my eyes, and for the life of me, it felt as if she could see straight into my soul. The feeling both bothered and aroused me.

She glanced out the window, and then a look of desire and longing seemed to settle across her face. Licking her lips, she leaned toward me, which sent a stirring of primal need within me. Watching her face, I saw her resolve settle over her.

She brushed her lips across mine like a feather. My eyes closed, and I could feel her tongue flick out between her lips, and she ran it along the corners of mine. She was teasing my lips apart, and I gladly accepted her. Wildness brewed beneath the gentleness.

Between kisses, she spoke with this sexy huskiness to her voice, which was goading me on more.

"Fine, Mr. Chambers. When. Will. This. Date. Be?"

I was so engulfed with her touch, the feel of her tongue, the taste of her mouth that it was only as she pulled herself away and sat down next to me that I remembered that she had spoken.

"So?" The teasing smile on her face was another reminder that I had never been this intoxicated by a woman before.

"Umm... I have to fly out to LA this evening and will be away for a few days, so shall we say as soon as I get back? How does Thursday sound? "

"Yes, Thursday sounds great."

I didn't even register that she had her bag in her hand, nor did I realize that we had come to a stop. It was only as Russell stepped out to open her door that I noticed we were once again outside her office.

Not wanting to give her any reason to doubt me, brazen hands reached the nape of her neck and pulled her in. The kiss I gave her was neither gentle nor tender, but I let her feel the brutal strength of the passion and want she made me feel when around her.

Chapter 8

Serena

Freshly showered, I sat at my dad's dining table and opened the takeout boxes, letting Dad and Roman serve themselves.

"Is there a reason why you moved to Manhattan when you just seem to be returning home continuously?"

The sharp edge to Roman's tone seemed to have come out of nowhere.

"What on earth do you mean? Am I not allowed to see my family?" I snapped.

I don't know what his problem was, but he'd been in a pissy mood since I arrived.

"Roman, Serena, please. Can we just sit and have a nice dinner together?"

My dad's eyes pleaded at me, reminding me of the millions of arguments he would diffuse when we were younger.

"I am having a nice dinner. Roman here seems to have a stick up his ass, and as always, we're the ones who have to bear the brunt of it."

"Of course. Ms Perfect is always doing everything right. Never stepping a foot wrong."

Roman groaned.

"What the hell is your problem?"

My anger was something I generally had reasonable control over, but there was no way I was going to let my brother act like a damn child and get away with it, especially as I hadn't done anything wrong.

"My problem is, you come back with your sad eyes, woe is me attitude when you haven't got a single clue what it's like actually to have real shit happen."

"Are you fucking serious, Roman!" I shouted.

"Serena language."

I looked over at Dad, and despite our age, he always had an issue with us swearing in the house. Taking a deep breath, I looked over at Roman as he sucked down the rest of his bottle of beer.

"I don't understand what I've done to you or why you're so annoyed at me. I've got some stuff going on. Work is crazy busy, and believe it or not, I love my family and enjoy spending time with them. I'm sorry if my arrival or mere presence makes you believe you have the right to belittle me or be your verbal punching bag. Get a grip. Seriously, I'm not in the mood."

"Of course, now you're making me out to be the villain. What a surprise," he barked back.

"Roman, that's enough!"

Dad rarely raised his voice, so hearing it always sent me back.

"No, Dad, do you know what is enough? The pathetic excuse that is my life! I'm sick and tired of it. First, mom doesn't think we're good enough, packs up her bags, and leaves. Then, my football career disappears -the one thing I was good at. The one thing that was mine, which caused me to lose Ruby, and now I'm stuck working in the shop."

Fuck this, I'm not letting him put the blame on everyone else.

"Firstly, you're not the only one Mom left. She left her husband and *three* children. Yes, your career got taken away from you, and for that, I am sorry but cut the bullshit. That's not what caused you to lose Ruby. You did that. You know she would have stayed with you no matter what. But no, you threw her away and broke her heart. And don't you dare say you are stuck working at the shop. You love working there. You're good at what you do, and you're lucky as hell you had something to fall back on after your accident, because I'm sure many people would have been in a far worse situation after losing their shot at the NFL who might have ended up homeless and broke. Dad has always and will always be there for all of us, and I will not sit here and listen to you wallow in self-pity, putting him and the rest of our family down because you are unhappy with your life!"

My chest was heaving, and I could feel tears stinging the back of my eyes.

I loved my brother, but there was no way I would sit back and let him get away with the things he said. Silence stretched for several moments, staring him down, his eyes the same green hue as mine. I watched as they glazed over with unshed tears. Shaking his head, he slammed the bottle onto the table, the sound echoing in the room, before storming upstairs.

I went to go after him, but Dad stopped me.

Together, we wordlessly cleared the table and tidied up the kitchen. I wasn't sure if Dad was simply letting me stew and reflect or if Roman's outburst hit him too.

As I looked at the clock on the wall, I saw it was 10:48pm. I grabbed a cold beer out of the fridge as Dad poured himself a bourbon. Neither of us made an attempt to turn the TV on as we sat on the couch. The deep sigh that left my Dad made my heart hurt.

"Are you okay?" I probed.

Taking another sip of his drink, I watched as he gently swirled the dark amber liquid in his glass and stretched his legs out onto the ottoman.

"Yeah, I'm fine."

But it was clear from the concern and worry that was etched on his face that it wasn't the case.

"Dad, you don't need to hide things from me. What Roman said was out of order, and I'm sorry he threw the shop in your face. You know he didn't mean it."

Once again, my frustration bubbled at Roman's stupid outburst.

"I know, but he's right."

The sadness in his voice made my heartbreak.

"He's just drunk and feeling sorry for himself."

"I know, but he has a point. After your mom left, I tried to do everything in my power to give you three the best life I could. I worked as many hours as I could, I missed a lot of family time. Then, after his accident, once we found out it had ended his footballing career, I just tried to keep him busy— distracting him with work at the garage."

He ran a hand over his face. I always remembered him doing it when I was younger, and it was usually when he was trying his hardest to keep everything together. And I couldn't bear seeing him like this.

"Seriously, stop this right now. You were working a lot, but I remember being at school, talking to my friends, and realizing how close we all were to you compared to them with their fathers. Dad, I have always said you are not just my dad but also my best friend."

And I meant it.

"Baby, you have always been my sweet little angel. I hope you know just how proud you have made me."

Seeing my dad's eyes full of unshed tears made me want to cry as well. I watched him lift his arm to the back of the sofa, and just like I used to when I was little, I leaned into his warm embrace.

"Now, you asked me if I'm okay... how about you? I love it when you come down, but it's never usually so close between visits. I know how busy you are at work, so I'm sure you can imagine how surprised I was when you turned up again yesterday. Honey, what's up? Is it to do with work?"

"Umm... not quite."

My face turned red as I had always hated talking to my dad about my love life.

"Oh, I'm guessing it's to do with a man?"

I could hear the curiosity in his voice.

"Yeah, sort of."

"I sure as hell hope you're not seeing someone who's mistreating you?"

The anger in his tone was palpable, and it made me giggle. My age didn't matter, he always wanted to ensure that any guy in my life treated me well.

"You have nothing to worry about. I'm not seeing anyone, and, come on, I would never let a man ever mistreat me. Why do you think I'm such an avid kickboxer?" I bragged.

My dad lifted his glass and clinked it with mine to toast. As I took a large swig of beer, I pulled my legs up, using my knees as a pillow and still avoiding Dad's face.

"So, if you're not seeing anyone, what's caused you to escape the city again?"

There was no way to hide the blush that crept over my

cheeks. And my fingers were busy catching the drops of condensation on the beer bottle.

"Remember the guy that dropped off the Mercedes-Benz 300 SL Gull-wing?"

"Yeah, what about him?"

"Well, his father's company is my newest client. And let's say his family is the complete opposite of ours. I had a meeting with his father. He was there, so was his brother and few others, and let's say it didn't go too well." I groused.

"What happened?"

"Well, his brother is a misogynistic bastard, and even though the Dad and the guy, Rhett, had been embarrassed by the brother's outburst and made him apologize to me, it just rubbed me up the wrong way."

Saying those words out loud made me realize just how much that interaction had truly bothered me.

"So, you're annoyed because an ignorant ass thought he'd be funny by putting down someone who is more knowledgeable and has more class than him?"

"No, the story doesn't end there."

Making myself more comfortable, I propped my legs next to Dad's on the ottoman. I took a big swig of beer before continuing.

"So, I'd met Rhett here at the garage, then again at the meeting. Then, on Ruby's birthday, I bumped into him again. We had a drink, he apologized again for his brother's behavior, and his brother ended up making close acquaintances with Ruby."

I stopped peeling at the bottle label and looked up at him.

"Dad, you cannot tell Roman about that."

"My lips are sealed."

I rolled my eyes as his face danced with amusement.

"So, we had a drink, and he told me about himself and his

work. He then asked about me and P&A. His driver drove me home, and that was it. Then, a few days later, he comes storming into the office, making out that I had been avoiding him, acting as if I'd been giving him mixed signals."

"Have you?"

"Um..."

I could feel the warmth spread across my cheeks, and my hands returned to peeling the label. My mind battled with coming up with the correct answer.

"Do you like him?"

"Yes... but... there is no point in even considering anything with him."

"Why? He's obviously fond of you and has good taste in cars."

My dad's chuckle was so infectious that I couldn't help but giggle.

"But we're worlds apart. His brother is an asshole, and technically he's a client."

"Honey, to me, it sounds like you're making excuses. First, you wouldn't be dating his brother, you'd be dating him. Secondly, if you're judging him based on his family's background, doesn't that make you just as superficial? And as it's his father's company, isn't it technically his dad that's your client?"

My dad might only have been a mechanic, but he could have easily become a lawyer. Boy, could he argue a case as good as the next guy.

"Legally, would there be any implications of you being involved with him? Would there be a conflict of interest?" he queried.

"No. I looked up the legalities and, as you said, his father is technically my client, so there wouldn't be a breach or conflict."

Dipping my chin into my chest, I wanted to hide my embarrassment that I'd already looked up something I was trying to pass as a reason for considering something with Rhett. I didn't have to look up to know he was smiling at me. I could hear it in his voice.

"Serena, why don't you just give the boy a chance? What's the worst that could happen?"

"Yeah, I guess," I muttered, as I mulled over every apprehension in my head.

After depositing his empty glass in the sink, he kissed me on the head.

"Just think about what I said. Goodnight, baby girl."

"I will. Night, Daddy."

Not long after, as I climbed into bed, my dad's advice ran through my head. Maybe I should give him a shot. Jeez, I knew I'd been wanting to fuck him since the moment I saw him in the garage. But that was something I didn't need to share with my dad.

So, as I let my body relax and succumb to sleep, I decided that the next time I saw Rhett back in the city, I'd at least have a drink with him.

The weather was hot and humid—pretty much the worst combination for my hair.

I swear to God, even though I was only a two-hour drive away from Manhattan, being in Franklin Park surrounded by hills and mountains on days like today, where it was over eighty-six degrees and overcast, and knowing the heavens could open at any moment, made me feel like I was trapped in a greenhouse.

I could hear Dad out back working on a gorgeous Ford Mustang, singing his favorite Stevie Wonder tune. I decided to keep myself busy by waxing and cleaning the cars ready for pickup.

As much as I loved Stevie Wonder, it was my turn to take control of the garage's sound system. Roman typically dominated the playlist, but not today. Soon, one of my favorite songs blared out of the speakers.

About twenty minutes later, my phone rang, and it was Roman video-calling me. Despite his shitty behavior the previous night, he was still my brother, and I loved him. Knowing he was most likely super hungover, I plastered the biggest smile on my face and answered loudly.

"Aww, are you a little hungover?"

"Don't tease him," Dad muttered as he walked past me to the tool shelf, but the grin on his face gave away his own amusement.

"Sorry, Ro. How are you feeling?"

"I'll survive. I'm starving, but I'm not sure eating right now is the best of ideas."

I felt sorry for Roman. I saw the sorrow on his face. It wasn't just the effects of a hangover. He felt lost, and last night's outburst proved it.

"I just wanted to call to say I'm sorry for last night. I didn't mean to upset you both. I guess I still have some stuff to sort through. Anyways, sorry, and thanks for filling in for me today."

"No worries. Besides, Dad seemed eager for me to help today, anyway. Maybe he's finally realized just how amazing I am and how lucky he would be to have me work here instead," I ribbed.

There was nothing ladylike in the cackle that left me.

"Mmh yeah, course that's the reason why."

There was something slightly unnerving in the glint of Roman's eyes, and I was just about to ask him what he was grinning about when he hurriedly said his goodbyes before hanging up.

Instead of trying to make sense of Roman's weird hungover behavior, I went back to work and focused on getting the cars cleared as quickly as possible.

I'd managed to get through five of the eight cars needing to be cleaned when I decided to take a break and head over to the cooler in front of the office to grab an icy cold bottle of water. Enjoying the cool down, I rubbed the cold bottle across my head, neck, and chest, desperately trying to cool myself down from this muggy heat. Downing the last of my water, I felt relieved.

Taking my hairband out of my pocket, I put my mane up and out of the way. Singing along to the track's final verse, I started backing up, returning to the cars, when I bumped into someone. As I turned around, apologizing, expecting to see my dad standing behind me, I froze when I saw Rhett.

Standing right in front of me.

What the hell was he doing there? I thought he was still in LA?

He stood there, looking as sure of himself as ever. He had his usual alluring smirk on his face. Yet again, it took me a moment to get my words out.

"What are you doing here? Shouldn't you be in California?"

I didn't mean to sound annoyed, but I was still shocked.

"Well, Serena, I'm here to pick up my car. What else would I be here for? Besides, my meetings ended up wrapping up sooner than expected. And I was keen to get back."

He spoke with such certainty. It used to be something that grated on me, but now I felt myself responding to it more as if it were an intriguing challenge. I looked around the shop, and low and behold, his Gull-Wing was sitting alongside the other cars, ready for collection. Dad or Roman must have finished it yesterday. I didn't know why I didn't put two and two together, and I wanted to kick myself for not realizing sooner that there was a chance I could bump into him there.

"As always, it's a pleasant surprise to see you here. Never in my wildest dreams did I think I would get my car and see you again on the same day. I must be a lucky man. Can I also have a bottle of that ice-cold water you so pleasurably enjoyed?"

This time, there was no way for me to be able to hide the blush that was covering my face. Walking over to the cooler, I realized he must have been standing behind me the whole time.

Damn it.

I literally must have looked like some music video wannabe rubbing that damn water bottle over myself and bending over to tie my hair. I wished the ground would swallow me whole right then.

He took the proffered bottle of water. I struggled to keep eye contact with him as I felt like I was ogling him as if he were one of those guys in the old Diet Coke adverts. Flustered, I pulled on my hair tie, more to distract myself from the direction of the thoughts in my mind.

I called for my dad to deal with Rhett and his car and cool the tension between us. I tried returning to work while watching Dad talk with Rhett in the office. But soon enough, I realized that trying to keep myself busy was fruitless. Giving up, I leaned against the car I was meant to be waxing and listened to the conversation between the two.

First, I heard Dad talk about the details of the work. Then, the conversation changed, and I heard my name being mentioned. I felt both embarrassed and intrigued. Dad looked at me with a knowing grin while Rhett talked to him. I didn't know who I wanted to kick more, me or Dad. Last night, when I told him about my predicament, he knew Rhett would come in today to collect his car. Now, I got why he was so eager for me to come in and cover Roman.

Rhett explained he had met me before, talking about how my company worked with him. I then heard Dad talk proudly about my passion for work and the company I had built up.

Hearing my dad talk with such pride filled me with such happiness. With everything we all went through, all I'd ever wanted was for my dad to be genuinely proud of me. I saw Rhett look over, and his face was full of appreciation and respect.

The look surprised me.

"Is Serena required in the garage for the rest of the day, sir?" Rhett asked as Dad rang up his bill.

"No, I can spare her, but I think you should be speaking to her, right? Also, please call me Elijah. Sir makes me feel old."

My dad smiled as he handed Rhett his credit card and put the chip and pin machine back on the counter.

With my interest piqued, I watched as he made his way over. My sexual attraction towards him instantly spiked once again.

"I'd like to take you out for a bite to eat, and maybe you could show me around. I want to talk to you about a few things."

"I'm not sure," I said. "I don't wanna leave my dad in the lurch."

My dad appeared from the office with the biggest grin, and my eyes turned to slits.

"Roman isn't in, and I haven't finished everything you asked me to do."

I was almost pleading for him to need me, stuck with the ever-conflicting feelings of what my brain was telling me and what my body desired.

"I'm only going to work on one more car before heading to

Dane's to watch the game. Don't worry, we're closed tomorrow anyway, so Roman can do it Monday morning if there's anything that still needs catching up on. You go enjoy yourself."

The smile on his face didn't soothe me, especially as he was aware of my feelings about seeing Rhett.

He kissed me on the cheek and whispered, "Hear the poor guy out. Remember what we talked about last night."

Chapter 9

Serena

My mind went a mile a minute as I got into his car. Still not having spoken one word, Rhett put the car into gear, pulled out of the garage, and started to drive down the road.

"What is it that you're so desperate to talk about?"

He looked over at me and started laughing a full-blown belly laugh.

"I'm a man that is never desperate. Eager—yes. Keen—I think we have established that. But desperate, I'm afraid, isn't one of my many qualities. And secondly, where's your spontaneity?"

Even though his tone was amused, it still bugged me that he hadn't answered my question.

Looking over at him, I raised my brows.

"And you're telling me you are the spontaneous type? I find that rather hard to believe."

I watched as he quickly glanced at me, the corner of his mouth pulled up in a smiling smirk. That look confirmed my suspicions.

"Okay, I'll grant you that usually, I have my schedule and generally stick to my routine. However, sometimes in life, I think it's important to take a minute and acknowledge when something unexpected comes your way and see where it goes."

There was a softness to his eyes I hadn't seen before, and I knew there was a deeper meaning to the words he said. But I still wasn't sure if he meant this pull that seemed evident between us or something else.

I didn't understand him. One minute, he was the aloof and self-assured bachelor I expected him to be, and the next, approachable, and joking. Which one was he?

"I need to quickly drop something off at the hotel I'm staying at and—"

"You're staying around here?" I interrupted him.

"Yes."

"Why?"

"As I said, my trip was cut short, then as I was about to book my flight back, I got a call from your dad that my car was ready, so I decided to fly to Philadelphia instead and had planned to pick up my car and then drive it back to Manhattan. But my flight was delayed, and by the time I landed, that garage was closed, so I thought, as I needed to stay in a hotel, why not stay for the weekend? Get out of the city. Away from work, life—all of it."

He looked away, but his facial expression seemed empty and almost a little sad.

The tension in the car was palpable. That didn't last long, though, as he broke the silence by announcing our arrival. He reached over to the back seat, his face only inches away from mine, and grabbed an envelope from his jacket pocket. Pulling back around, he gave me his cheeky, sexy smile and exited the car.

"Wait here," he told me.

He walked confidently and smoothly, almost strutting into the hotel lobby. I'd been reading emails on my phone as he opened my door instead of his.

"How about you drive? Show me something I haven't seen before."

For a split second, I thought he was making a sexual reference, and he seemed to have read my mind based on the panty-dropping look he was giving me. But he just winked and handed me the keys.

As I got out and walked around the car, his fingertips brushed against my hip, and I gasped. I tried to keep calm but checked my mirrors before taking the wheel.

We drove around town, and I was a nervous, rambling mess. A rarity in my professional field but seemingly frequent practice in the presence of the man who sat beside me. Where I clearly can't seem to hold idle chit-chat with him without my thoughts turning sexual, I try to fill the void with every ounce of knowledge I have of this place. And to my surprise, he listened and appreciated all I had to say.

We discussed which colleges we collectively attended and how we got into our careers, and to my surprise, I realized that he has a lot more drive and passion for his work than I gave him credit for.

"We can't drive further than here, we've got to walk the rest of the way," I said as I parked the car and turned off the ignition.

"Lead the way."

He stepped out of the car and motioned for me to lead.

We walked for a couple of minutes in comfortable silence before he spoke.

"So, this is the second time I have seen you working on cars. I will admit the first time I saw you, I was blown away, not only by your beauty but, I'll be honest, I'd never met a female mechanic. So I'm sure you can then guess my surprise days later when you walked into our office, and I came to find out you're a lawyer. So, what made you pursue law? Why not cars?"

I mulled his question over for a minute, carefully stepping over a broken branch that was across the path.

"I did. That is, when I was younger, all I wanted to do was become a mechanic. I remember on the weekends, Dad would watch Formula 1, and although the cars and the speed and technique of the drivers were impressive, what always fascinated me the most were the clips they showed of the mechanics in the pit stops. One year, for my birthday, I got a new helmet for my bike, and Dad specifically picked one that looked like the Stilo helmets they wear. Whenever I had to go with him to the garage, I always wore it, even if all I did was pass him a wrench."

I expected his look to be teasing or possibly even mocking, but his small smile was warm, so I continued.

"I still thought cars were the route I would take despite my brother and cousins always saying it wasn't for girls and how it was a man's job. That women wouldn't know what they're talking about."

I quirked an eyebrow in his direction as I knew that was what he most likely thought the first time he saw me. A slight blush crept across his cheeks, so I knew my assumption had been correct.

"Anyway, that was the plan until sophomore year."

"What happened then?"

"Well, I joined the debate team, and I realized I enjoyed the art of discussing and debating. The more assignments we had and events I would partake in, the more I was drawn in. But it wasn't until I watched a documentary on wrongful death row convictions that I started getting fascinated by the law.

Especially the effects and statistics on African Americans and minority groups. It seemed to ignite a fire within me, and all I wanted to do was fight for those who couldn't. So, I traded overalls and engines with law books and the gavel."

After that, I was slightly out of breath and couldn't help the pang of shyness that washed over me. I was passionate about it, but I was often met with ridicule or judgment. But as I stopped and looked into his eyes, all I saw was respect, even a hint of wonderment.

Feeling a tad vulnerable, I lightened the mood by telling him the story of my grandfather, how he built the garage from the ground up, and how my father took over from him.

A family legacy.

In a way similar to his, although nowhere near the scale and magnitude. Looking over at him, I'm surprised by his eagerness to find out about me. It's a bit off-putting.

"What about your childhood?" he questioned.

I hesitated to answer, mainly because I never knew how to answer that question. My childhood was such a mix of highs and lows. I hardly talk about it, but his earnest expression made me want to tell him everything.

"I've always been close with my dad. He has played such a critical role in my life. Constantly drilled into me that arduous work, determination, and integrity must be the foundation of all I do. Therefore, anything I want to do or achieve is possible."

"And your siblings? I remember you mentioning a brother and sister."

Smiling, I was impressed that he'd been paying attention.

"I have an older sister, Olivia. She's married to Calvin, and they have two daughters—Amelia and Eden. And then there's Roman, my brother. He's ten months older than me, so everyone called us Irish twins. Growing up, the two of us were super close, unlike Olivia and I. However, as we've gotten older, especially since having my nieces, we've been closer than ever. Anyway, Roman was always great at football. He was the quarterback all through high school, then got a scholarship to college, where he became captain. He went on to get signed by the Green Bay Packers, but on his way to training, he got hit by a drunk driver, and the injuries ended his NFL career before it even began."

I felt a lump in my throat, especially given the argument I had yesterday with Roman.

"It's clear how close you are to your father. And he seems like a good, hardworking, honest man. But you haven't mentioned a word about your mother. Are you two not as close?"

I didn't dare look at him.

My response is short and clipped. "My mother walked out on us when I was eight years old. I haven't spoken or heard from her since the day she left."

He seems to understand that it's a touchy subject and changes the flow of conversation. It takes me a while to gather my thoughts and adjust my mood, but he helps by distracting me as he opens up about his family.

"I'm the eldest of four. There's me, Kara, Julian, and Heather. Kara's always had a head for numbers and started her own business, specializing in partnering up with women-run start-ups. She is also on the board of many charities. She's married. Her husband, Austin, used to be a polo player but now is involved in the breeding of horses instead. Together, they have the only Chambers grandchild, Kai. I can tell you right now he's the most intelligent four-year-old I know."

The smile that lit up his face made me weak at the knees.

"Then there's Heather, who started her own bridal collection when she graduated from The Fashion Institute of Technology. She's been in Vogue's top ten most influential designers for the past three years."

"And finally, Julian. I guess his strongest attribute is that he can make most women he meets fall in love with him. And generally, does what he wants, how he wants."

He seemed to beam when talking about his sisters, but when he talks about his brother, there is evident tension and underlying anger. Plus, I didn't like the idea of Ruby becoming one of those women. That reminded me I needed to check in with her and see how things were going.

"I can't say I have the same fond memories of growing up. At least in the way you did." The clear dejection as he spoke surprised me.

"How so?"

"Well, I didn't spend much time with my siblings. Since infancy, I've been told what's expected of me—the life I was born to lead. I've always been told I would eventually take over the family business as my father and his father had done. It's not something I was ever asked if I wanted—I was just told it's what I would do. Everything has always been mapped out for me, and now, the older I am, I can see that was a lot of pressure when I was young."

A somber look crossed his face, and it felt like a tender moment.

"Anyway, I spent most of my time with nannies and tutors and was always too busy with endless school clubs, tutoring and meetings with my father where he'd explain the ins and outs of Chambers Industries as he felt the earlier my training began, the better. So, I didn't have time to seek close friendships or mess around. I was too busy being molded into being the future CEO, continuing to make it grow and flourish, just as my father and grandfather had done."

He laughed, but it was hollow and had a real sadness to it.

It felt like he repeated a declaration that'd been engrained into him. One he's recited countless times.

"That sounds lonely. I'm sorry I don't mean that in a rude way."

"It's fine. It is what it is. I know I'm more fortunate than most."

What struck me was how casually he talked about his family's expectations of him.

"You know, I think this is the most I've spoken, to anyone, about my family who isn't interviewing me for a news article. Something about you makes it easy for me to talk."

"Yeah? Why is that?"

I couldn't hide the blush that took over my face. There was something that felt powerful that a man as well-known, affluent, and at the same time guarded—open up to me like this.

"Well, I...."

I look up to see why he's fallen silent and realize we have reached our destination. Or, as he put it, a place he's never been.

We were standing at a rock's edge, and the view in front of us overlooks the town in all its glory. Behind us lies a small waterfall leading down to a stream.

"Today's cloudy weather isn't the best for the view up here, but you said I should take you somewhere you wouldn't have been before. And although you seem to keep popping up in places I least expect, I'd be astonished if you told me you've been here before." I couldn't help but giggle. I could see he wanted to come out with some joke, but as he looked out again, he responded, "Serena, it's beautiful."

The simple honesty in his response makes me feel a pang of guilt. Maybe my Dad was right. Perhaps I have been judging him too soon, too hastily.

"We can't stay long as the clouds are getting darker, but

when the sky is clear, it's my idyllic place to come to. Especially at either sunrise or sunset."

"How did you find this place?"

"When I was younger, I would come up here if I felt upset or just wanted to think. I come here when I need a break from the city or after a tough case. Even though I love my job and family, sometimes I want to switch off and get away."

He walked around and then paused by my side, my eyes never leaving him as he looked at the view.

I notice him take slow, deep breaths, opposite my fast-shallow gusts.

Tentatively, he moves closer, reaching out and pushing a curl that came loose from my ponytail out of my face and behind my ear, then resting his hand behind my neck.

Unintentionally, I lick my lips. I watch as his eyes dart from my eyes to my mouth.

Trustingly, I lift my chin, and it's all the invitation he needs.

His mouth plunges into mine.

My breath hitches at the feel of his soft, firm lips against mine, and I whimper as his tongue strokes against my lower lip, coaxing my mouth open. I can feel his groan vibrate through his chest as his tongue captures mine.

The feel of his hands all over me is intoxicating. Molten waves of pleasure began crashing through me.

He pulls me into him, rubbing my body up against his.

I can feel the bulge of his solid and muscular arms as my hands travel up his arms and around the back of his neck. I was utterly lost in the sensation of him consuming me.

We are all teeth, tongues, and lips, biting, sucking, and devouring each other as if a dam has broken wide open.

I'm not sure how long we kissed when suddenly tiny drops of rain fell upon us.

Those few drops turned into a full-on downpour within less than a minute.

Letting out a frustrated grunt, he breaks our kiss, slides his hand down mine, and takes my hand, entwining our fingers.

"Looks like we're going to have to head back."

Even though he chuckled as he spoke, I could see the frustration of the interruption.

Holding hands with one another, we jog back down the path. The rain has turned into a torrential downpour, and the sky is lit with lightning and thunder.

Knowing we needed to get inside to safety as soon as possible, I suggested we take shelter in a country inn just a few minutes down another path instead of the thirty minutes it would take us to walk back to the car.

Chapter 10

Serena

We managed to make it to the Inn but were both soaked to the bone.

Upon entering, we were greeted by a lady in her late sixties. She had salt and pepper hair, with her roots being more white than gray, with a warm smile and kind eyes.

"Looks like you two got caught out in the storm. Welcome to Spring Falls Inn. My name is Ann. How can I help you?"

Rhett approached the desk, shaking raindrops from his thick hair.

"Is there anywhere we can go to dry off and wait for the storm to pass? I'll pay whatever the room's rate is."

"I'm afraid the only room left available is the Royal Suite. The charge is $185 a night."

He doesn't hesitate.

"That would be great."

He gives her one of his charming smiles.

"You wouldn't, by any chance, have any clothing I could purchase for us to change into?"

"We have sweats that our guests can buy as souvenirs. Would that be okay?"

"That would be great. Thank you."

Rhett could clearly charm all women, no matter their age, and I couldn't help but smile.

He paid for the room and the sweats, which had the Inn's logo emblazoned.

Handing him the garments and the room key, Ann directed us to the Royal Suite, situated on the first floor, and informed us of what they'd be serving for dinner, adding that we could choose to eat either in the dining room or to have it sent up to our room. With amusement, I watched as he gave her his thanks and a hefty tip.

It was clear by the look on her face that tips like this weren't a regular occurrence. We walked down the hall, and as we entered the room, it felt like we'd been transported back to the 1960s.

The room had been decorated as though JFK would have been an expectant guest.

I walked around the suite, taking in my surroundings. On the other hand, Rhett headed over to the side table, which housed a variety of spirits in decanters.

Lifting a glass, he turned. "Do you have a preference?"

"I'm good with anything."

A drink sounded good as I shivered in my still wet clothes. I should change, but I began to feel shy for some odd reason. I could go to the bathroom, but something about taking off my clothes with Rhett in the next room made me pause.

One minute we were kissing so passionately that I would have had no reservations about fucking him right then and there in the outdoors. The next, we were laughing and running, trying to get out of the rain.

Now, I found myself alone in a bedroom with Rhett, not

knowing how long we'd be in there, and I wasn't sure exactly what to do.

Having poured me a drink, he casually made his way over, his body oozing confidence and sex appeal, and handed me my glass.

The simple touch of his fingertips against mine feels like an electric shock. Our sexual attraction seemed to get stronger and more intense with each encounter we had with one.

I shivered, watching his back muscles flex beneath his soaked shirt as he walked to the bathroom.

"Would you prefer a bath or a shower?"

His voice interrupted my wayward thoughts.

I pause momentarily, thinking how good a hot bath would feel, but decide on a shower instead, as having a bath felt too romantic.

"I'll have a shower, thanks."

He came back out, announcing that the water was ready.

"You go first," I tell him. "I'm going to finish this drink."

He looked into my eyes, and it felt like he wanted an answer to an unspoken question. But instead, smirked before walking into the bathroom.

"I'll be quick," he said with a wink before closing the door.

While he was in the shower, I went around the room and took in all the different ornaments decorating it. There were old black and white photographs of famous guests who had stayed there and an array of various artworks scattered around.

The room housed an array of items, styles, and colors. It would be too much in any other setting, but everything together gave the room more character.

As I heard the bathroom door open, the room's telephone rang. I reached over to answer it.

"Hello, dear, it's Ann from reception. I just wanted to inform you that the highway patrol called, and that the main road has been closed off as a tree got struck by lightning and a fallen branch has blocked the road. They said it should be clear and open by the morning, but in this current storm, there is no access back to the main road, and all guests are advised to stay inside until the storm has passed."

"Thank you for letting us know."

I put the receiver back.

My mind raced a million miles an hour as the realization of being stranded here, with Rhett, at this Inn, in this room, for the night, really hit home.

The thought made me down the rest of my drink.

The sudden sound of his voice behind me almost made the glass fall out of my hand.

"Is everything okay?"

Bringing my breathing back into check, I turned around to relay the information Ann had given me when I was struck at the sight of him.

With just a towel wrapped around his waist, his hair damp with water droplets falling down his wet, glistening torso, my mind flashed back to my dream.

His body was almost a replica of what I had imagined. Better, in fact. There was a potency to his presence. And I was hit with an onslaught of raw physical desire.

My nipples began to peak with arousal. My tongue ran along my lips. I felt myself almost salivating at the incredible physique and sensual masculinity of the man standing before me.

Shaking my head, I cleared my throat and looked into his eyes.

"We're stuck here for the night."

His face turned into a grin, reaching from ear to ear. I was unsure if it was because he caught me ogling him or were stranded there.

Taking the empty glass out of my hand, he walked over to the sidecar and poured us another drink.

"I'll have mine after I shower," I shouted over my shoulder and told myself not to run into the bathroom.

"Take your time. I have a few calls to make."

As soon as I entered the bathroom, I stripped off my wet clothes and entered the hot, steamy shower.

Mentally, I pleaded for my body to calm down. My craving for him was increasing by the second.

As I lathered my skin with the lavender and citrus body wash the Inn supplied for its guests, I reflected on our conversations.

It was as if Rhett showed a whole other side to himself today.

The more I got to know him, the more he surprised me. But not only did it surprise me, it intrigued me.

He was increasingly the opposite of the man I thought he was.

Yet, despite knowing we were both mature, consenting adults who were attracted to one another, I couldn't seem to be able to come to a rational decision whether to sleep with him or not.

Was it purely the differences in our backgrounds? Was it his brother?

A few years ago, Ruby suggested I start speaking to a therapist as she was worried I was suppressing too much. I'd been seeing Dr Michaels on and off for almost four years. One of the things we had been working on or, as she said, 'working through' was my struggle with letting people in, which apparently was connected to my abandonment issues from my mother leaving at a young age.

Was that what was making me question any and every little thing with Rhett?

I couldn't put my finger on what it was, and honestly, I was getting tired of arguing with myself. I wanted the man, didn't I? It was as simple as that.

Whatever happened would happen.

As I washed the conditioner out of my hair, I realized there was no point in avoiding the inevitable.

I got out of the shower and ran my hands through my hair, squeezing the excess water. Wrapping a towel around myself, I took one last look in the mirror before returning to the room.

Sitting on the chair by the desk, I could see he was on the phone. He abruptly ended the call as he turned and noticed me standing in the bathroom doorway.

With his drink in his left hand, he picked up mine with his right and swiveled around to face me.

"Would you like your drink now?"

The husky timbre of his voice caused goosebumps to prickle my arms.

Slowly, I approached him, taking in the tension and desire flowing from him.

I retrieved my glass, not breaking eye contact with him, and downed every last drop.

As the liquor left a warm, burning sensation down my throat, I watched as he followed suit.

Still maintaining eye contact with him, I retrieved his glass and placed them both down on the desk.

I ran my hand through his damp hair, tugging ever so slightly on it, mirroring what he did to mine earlier.

I followed that by faintly ghosting my lips over his. Running my tongue along his lips, I placed feather-light kisses upon him.

A guttural growl escaped his throat, which spurred me on. Straddling him, I could instantly feel the friction of his hard cock rubbing against my sensitive clit. Which had been wanting and waiting for him for an eternity.

He skimmed his hands across my back, leaving a trail of fire. It was as if the hunger within both of us had been released, as there was almost a devouring ferocity in how we kissed one another. He ran a trail of kisses down my neck, behind my ear, across my collarbone. Kissing and licking his way up my shoulder and then gently biting down on the soft skin pocket. Simultaneously rocking and rubbing his cock against my now soaking wet pussy.

"I... can... feel... you're... soaking... wet..." he whispers.

"You've... drenched... through... both... your... towel... and... mine."

Every word he uttered made me crave him more and more.

Then, he lifted me as though I weighed nothing and carried me over to the bed. Wrapping my legs around him, I plunged into a deep kiss, softly biting down on his bottom lip. Coming to a halt, he detangled my legs from around his waist. I could feel the cool oak of the large four-poster Edwardian-style bed against the back of my thighs. I broke the kiss and reached for the knot in my towel.

Seeing his pupils dilate and focus solely on me, I undid my towel and let it drop to the floor. I watched as his eyes greedily looked down every inch of my body. His thumb trailed down my neck across my chest, over the swell of my breast.

My nipples were erect into high peaks as he tenderly rolled one between his thumb and forefinger. The moan I let out came from deep within my soul. There was a brutal strength to his passion. I felt my arousal reaching dangerous heights, my body teetering on the precipice of pleasure and pain. Taking his left hand away, I whimpered in protest, but he instantly replaced it with his hot mouth.

His tongue licked and sucked my nipples, swirling the tips

and sucking it into his mouth. Working for minutes, hours, God knew how long, then pushed my tits together so both nipples were in his mouth when he bit down hard on them and sent my body into an explosive orgasm. Every follicle on my skin lit up. Fireworks filled my eyes, and searing heat rolled through my body from the top of my head to the tips of my toes.

He softly pushed me back, effectively sitting me on the edge of the bed. Spreading my legs wide open, he dropped down to his knees.

Never in my life had I been so glad to be a regular at the wax salon.

He slid one finger softly into me, and my fight to keep quiet was becoming fruitless.

"You are so wet. You're dripping onto my finger."

As he licked and sucked my clit, he pushed two fingers inside my pussy. I could feel myself stretching to accommodate them.

His mouth left my clit. "God. Your pussy is perfect."

If my body weren't building up to another orgasm, he'd have made me blush with that statement. But instead, I was lost in the shocking waves of pleasure that sizzled over me, making my body shudder with desire.

Beginning to build into a rhythm, I could feel my body climb higher and higher, almost at the precipice of another orgasm, when he suddenly stopped. With my eyes partially dazed, I looked down at him and saw him rise to his feet. I could see his cock, largely tenting beneath his towel.

Sitting back, I watched with excitement and slight trepidation as he reached for his towel and let it drop to the floor. My eyes slowly scanned him from head to toe. My line of sight only enabled me to see just past his knees, but that was more than enough. Tremors of excitement raced through my body.

Our eyes locked with one another. And I was lost in the

narcotic-like power of those crystal blue eyes that seemed to perceive and understand my every desire. Reaching out my hand, I ran my fingers across his bare chest. The feel of hard, solid muscles beneath my fingertips showed that the man kept himself in great physical shape.

As one hand ran across his supple chest, I used the other to prop myself up. He watched every move I made, his eyes never breaking contact with mine.

Running his tongue along his mouth, licking up the juices that glisten his lips. It was as if he didn't want to let a single drop go to waste. Watching that unbridled hunger flare in his eyes turned me on even more.

Lowering his head, bringing us face to face. Finally, his lips once again brushed against mine. Greedily, I licked his bottom lip, tasting myself. The salty sweetness of my own arousal, mixed with his primal passion and want for me, made me moan with deep satisfaction.

My actions must have set something off within him as he then branded his mouth upon my own, capturing me and enthralling me deeper and deeper.

He rained rapid kisses across my mouth. Then, my shoulder. His primitive maleness sent ripples of pleasure through me. Mounting the bed, Rhett leaned over me, his arms on either side of my head, his cock cushioned between my thighs. Quivering awareness shot right through me. I could feel the hot, pulsing heat of him at the apex of my thighs.

He looked at me, his eyes narrowed, and his face went serious for a split second. His eyes sought my consent. Staring back into the depths of his stunning blue eyes, I nodded. Yes, this was what I wanted. I wanted him. All of him.

Leaning over the bed, he retrieved his wallet and grabbed a condom. My nipples were stiff peaks, and my chest rose and fell in quick succession as I watched him rip the packet with his teeth, then slowly roll it over the broad mushroom tip that was already leaking with pre-cum. His large hands only emphasized the size of his mouthwatering girth.

Fully sheathed, he leaned back over me, running his nose along mine before his lips once again devoured mine as he entered me slowly. It had been quite some time since I'd last had sex, so my body needed to stretch and accommodate him. Molten waves of pleasure rippled over me. An onslaught of raw physical desire overwhelmed my senses.

I wrapped my arms and legs around him, feeling the flex of the muscles in his back and legs. His hips raised, and he surged into me, causing me to arch my back to accept him better. Like that, I felt every inch of him deep inside me. With one hand, he began kneading my breast, teasing my nipple. His other grasped my hip. He tilted me at a slight angle, which caused my clit to rub against him with every thrust.

His body pounded deep into mine in a relentless rhythm that sent my mind reeling. Feeling my body build up with another orgasm, my pussy tightened, gripping him deep within. Neither his power nor his pace faltered as I screamed out his name incoherently.

"Rhett... yes... oh god... yes... yes... yes."

My climax was still rearing on, as I felt him swell even larger. Before he let out a deep guttural roar, as he found his own release. Focusing on the euphoric sensation taking over my body, I was taken aback as he greedily devoured my mouth.

As we allowed our breathing to steady and slow down, he rolled over to one side, taking me with him. Our bodies were molded intimately against one another.

Both of our bodies spent.

~

The stirring movements and the tight arms wrapped around me woke me. As I lay there, slowly allowing my body to awaken, my mind began to go into overdrive.

Stretching my limbs, I could feel the slight soreness between my legs. Rhett shifted, his arm pulling me back into his back, subconsciously, as he was breathing heavily and still fast asleep.

As I tiptoed to the bathroom, I realized how sore I was. I turned the shower on to heat the water and to mask the sound of me desperately peeing.

Once I stepped in and the hot water cascaded over me, I reflected on what had been going through my mind just before I fell asleep.

We'd finally stopped around three a.m. Both our bodies were utterly spent. It was as if now that we were finally unleashed, we couldn't stop.

He'd fucked me twice in the bed before we showered again —this time together where he got on his knees and made me come twice more. I gave just as good as I got. It was as if a fuse went off, and we couldn't stop. We'd gone three more rounds, once on the desk, then the sofa, and finally again in the bed.

I had just had the best and the most intense sexual experiences in my life. Despite my mind still in a foggy, jubilant state, I knew I hadn't just come so intensely and frequently simply because of the sex. All the tension and desire that had been building culminated in the feelings I knew I had been suppressing about him.

That was when it sank in that my feelings for Rhett were much more profound.

At first, I felt his persistence and charm towards me were superficial. But on more than one occasion now, he had proven to be able to look and appreciate things for their more profound value.

Yes, I could admit my feelings for him were growing more potent, and I could also appreciate his skills in bed. But there was so much more to him than that. I could see the handsome, hypnotic, and powerful man everybody did. But I could also see a tender, enthusiastic, and delicate man. And that was what was drawing me in more and more.

I still wasn't sure if I wanted this to lead somewhere. And, if so, to what? With how I'd brushed him off in the past, I could fully understand if he felt I only wanted a one-time thing. But why now, thinking of it not happening again, am I left with a sour taste in my mouth?

As I exited the shower, I resolved to play it by his actions.

With that in mind, it was no surprise that I was shocked, if not a tad disappointed, to see him out of bed, sitting by the desk, and talking to someone on the phone.

"I see, so there is nothing left from breakfast. No, no, that's fine. Ah... brilliant, thank you."

The disappointment in his voice was unmistakable.

"Who was that?"

I startled him slightly, based on his reaction, as he turned around.

"Good morning. That was Ann from downstairs. I was trying to order some breakfast, but we overslept and missed it."

At his mention of food, I felt my stomach begin to rumble.

"How are you feeling?"

Looking into his eyes, I tried to gauge whether he was being silly or serious.

"Fine, thank you. And yourself? Did you sleep well?"

I didn't realize I'd been holding my breath, waiting for him to respond. I was still struggling to get a good read of his facial expressions, but all I could see was a look of relaxation and an unguardedness shining from his eyes.

"I feel great. I don't remember the last time I slept so well."

I was still trying to decipher what his angle was. I wanted to know if he was trying to mislead me.

But seeing his shy, genuine smile settled my anxious thoughts.

"Thank you for last night. It was special. I mean it."

I must have had a look of doubt across my face for him to feel the need to convince me his words were truthful.

Instantly, I felt terrible.

Walking over to me, he gently took my face in both hands and brought his lips to mine. The kiss was soft and gentle, miles away from the intensity of how we kissed last night, but I could still feel the connection and desire there.

On both our parts.

"As I never got to take you out for food last night, I wanted to arrange breakfast in bed, but as it's already eleven thirty, we missed breakfast here. How about I take you for lunch? Ann said the road had been cleared. You hungry?"

It was evident from the look in his eyes that he was keen to spend more time together, and I couldn't help the smile from spreading across my face. In the same breath, I couldn't believe how long we'd slept in. I needed to return to my dad's sometime this afternoon, but my stomach answered for now.

"Lunch would be great."

Chapter 11

Rhett

We had a fantastic lunch at this small Cajun food truck she recommended. Then I decided to park the car at my hotel and walk as the weather was perfect.

I didn't know what it was about her, but she mesmerized me.

Last night was incredible. I spent hours watching her after she passed out, taking in every inch of her stunning face, not even daring to breathe too hard for fear of waking her.

I kept having flashbacks of the way she walked out of the bathroom last night. Slow, sexy, and wet. She had been everything I'd hoped for and more.

I could still remember the taste of her arousal on my lips, the feel of her full plump breasts, and her amazingly tight, wet pussy. It took all my self-control not to pounce on her, yet again, as my cock began to thicken in my pants.

All morning, I'd been trying to work her out. She was such an enigma to me. Her words told me one thing, her body another. Despite the doubtful look on her face and the vain attempt at a polite brush-off this morning, I knew she was interested. Well, at least her body was.

Throughout lunch, I could see how her body responded when our fingers touched as I passed her a glass of water or when my fingers brushed along her shoulders.

If only she knew the enjoyment I got in watching her eat and appreciate her food. Man, this woman just oozed sex appeal. Yet, she managed to make everything look and seem effortless.

Walking back to the hotel, Serena played the role of tour guide, reciting stories and memories from growing up there. She pointed out certain buildings and stores and even introduced me to people we met along the way.

We met this old couple who owned a florist. Mr. and Mrs. Bailey. They must have been in their late sixties but were still in great shape. I offered to help as he was lifting a large garden vase. It must have weighed over 130lbs. But he politely declined my offer and took it inside with ease. Looking back at Serena, I could see Mrs. Bailey listening and talking to her with admiration, warmth, and pride. Those looks of kind-hearted love were instantaneously washed away as she set her eyes on me.

They were cold and assessing as if she were warning me. When at work, I always had a clear head, but there, with her, around her, I couldn't quite keep myself in check. And it was starting to bother me.

By the time we arrived in the lobby of my hotel, it was just after four o'clock. The atmosphere had changed entirely, and I didn't know what to do or say to make her stay.

Stepping in front of her, I slid one hand over her shoulder, down her arm, and then held her hand within mine. I was cupping the side of her face with the other. The pad of my thumb softly grazed the line of her jaw, brushing across her full bottom lip. My wanton needs and desire for her erupted like a volcano gushing from a pit in my stomach. Her eyes, such an enchanting, vibrant green, made emeralds look plain.

She placed the palm of her hand just by my navel. I'm not sure if she's holding on or steadying us. One thing I did know was that I wanted to kiss her. I needed to kiss her.

Serena softly and slowly ran her tongue across her upper lip, and my cock twitched in response. I leaned in to devour that delicious full mouth and...

"Rhett! Rhett... Rhett."

My body instantly became rigid. At first, I thought I had misheard someone shouting my name. Nobody knew me there. But then I realized I knew that voice. My palms began to sweat, I could hear my blood pumping through my ears. A knot in my stomach formed.

"Rhett... Rhett, I'm so glad I found you."

The unwelcome voice of Verity Lancaster cut through the white noise of the guests and staff who were busy talking, walking, or just simply getting on with their day. It didn't take me long to follow the sound of her voice and see her walking towards me from the reception desk.

She was the girl next door but on steroids. Her family was almost as affluent as mine. Though not as wealthy, they still had a good, privileged life.

We used to date back in college, and I knew both her family and mine wanted nothing more than for us to get married and for our families to unite and continue their retrospective legacies.

Though we had broken things off in college, I'd seen an increase in Verity's presence at family and business events, dinners, and galas. And should my parents host anything, they always put her next to me or on my table.

She spent more time with my mother than I did.

Focusing back on the now, I looked back down at Serena and saw the confusion in her eyes. She took a step back. The space was just a few inches apart, but the disconnect and distance felt much more. I felt as if a dam was about to burst through between us and I didn't know what to do.

Verity finally reached us and stood by my side. I watched as she eyed Serena from head to toe, enjoying that her heels gave her a few inches of height over her, enabling her to look down at her.

"Hello, I'm Verity. And you are?"

She offered Serena her hand, and to my surprise, Serena straightened her back, rolled back her shoulders, and shook her proffered hand.

"Nice to meet you, Verity. I am Serena."

"Verity, what are you doing here?"

I tried to suppress the annoyance in my voice.

"Rhett, I thought I'd surprise you. Your brother told me you came down here to collect your car yesterday, but you didn't return due to the storm, and I wanted to come and see if you were okay. Plus, your mother is having a family dinner this evening and said it was important for you to attend."

The woman was damn well overstepping her boundaries. She took no care nor interest in my apparent disregard for her and bypassed me and spoke to Serena.

"So, how do you know Rhett, or do you just work at the hotel?"

"No, I met him at my father's garage. We repaired his car, and—"

Verity interrupted her before she could continue.

"Oh, what a wonderful service. You repair and deliver. Rhett, make sure you give the nice girl a large tip."

And with that, she turned her back to Serena, effectively

shutting her out, then tucked her arm into mine and pulled me away.

"We must get going and make our way back. Luckily, I got my hair blow dried this morning, but I still need to get ready. After all, your mother said it was important for everyone to be there as there's to be a big announcement. I believe she wishes to announce our engagement."

"What?" I snapped.

I couldn't believe what she had just said. My eyes flashed over to Serena, and the person I was looking at wasn't the woman I had gotten to know deeply and intimately over the past twenty-four hours. All I could see was anger, hurt, and pain.

"Serena," I began because all this had become a nightmare. "It's not true. It's..."

She looked at me as if I was a stranger and shook her head.

Clearing her throat, she turned to Verity.

"It was lovely to meet you, and congratulations on your engagement."

Verity smiled and nodded at her.

"Mr Chambers, please call the garage for any further issues with your car. And congratulations on your engagement."

She turned and started making her way toward the large glass doors. I could not believe what was happening.

"Wait, Serena, let me explain."

Running after her, I grabbed her hand. Her skin felt like it was on fire, and I was not meant to touch it. She instantly pulled out of my grip, and her eyes were the darkest green I had ever seen.

"I don't want to hear it. I can't even bear to look at you. How dare you! I should have listened to my gut instincts about you. God, I can't believe I was so stupid. I wish you and your fiancée all the best. I hope she knows what kind of man she is marrying."

"Serena, I am not engaged to her. Listen. Let me talk."

"Okay, so you're planning to get engaged. That's semantics. Please leave me alone, there's nothing more to say."

Steeling her spine, her gaze darted to the exit doors, and she turned to leave.

"No, I can't let you go. This is a complete misunderstanding, if you give me a minute to explain things."

"Rhett, no! I don't want to hear what bullshit story you have concocted to justify lying to me. I didn't ask anything of you. You were the one who wouldn't drop it. You're the one who kept pushing for me. All the while, your girlfriend—fiancée, whatever you want to call her, is sitting at home, thinking she has hit the jackpot with you. I cannot believe I let myself think you were a decent guy. My biggest regret is believing that Julian was the lesser brother. How wrong was I?"

Those words cut like a knife. I knew how and what she thought of my brother, it was exactly what I thought of him. And now she thought I was worse than him. I didn't know how to come back from that.

I watched as she ran out the door, her head bowed and shoulders shaking. My body hummed and vibrated with anger as I tried to understand everything that happened in the last two minutes.

With balled-up fists, I started walking towards the main entrance. As I scanned the sidewalk, I couldn't see her amongst the small crowds walking by. Verity was shouting my name and began following me.

"Wait, Rhett, what's going on?"

"No. Stop. First, we are not and never will be engaged. Secondly, how messed up is this? What the fuck is wrong with you? We are not together. Yet, you busy yourself with my family and chase me down on some haphazard pursuit of what? And what is this whole thing about an announcement from my parents? I know even they would not try to announce an engagement I am not having. So, what is it? Has something happened?"

Verity looked away, which infuriated me more.

Frantically, I grabbed my phone out of my back pocket to call Serena. Only then did I realize I didn't have her number.

"Fuck!"

I ignored the outraged looks of the passersby.

"I don't know why your parents have asked for this dinner. I don't know what is going on. They are, after all, your family, remember?" Verity lamented.

"So why did you say they were announcing our engagement? Where did you pluck that from?"

I was doing everything I could to speak calmly to her, and that was becoming a fruitless task as she seemed to grate on me more with every passing moment.

"You know how our families would love to see this union happen. I know we shelved things after college, but you were young and immature and needed to let loose a bit and get that single-life mentality out of your system, which you have. Your mother and I..."

"Don't bring my mother into this."

"I was led to believe that an engagement was what we were all working towards, and it was suggested you simply needed a little push."

"Are you kidding me right now? Verity, I know I'm a busy man, but don't you think I would want to be in an actual relationship first if I were to get engaged? It is my life. Not my mother's. Not yours. Not your family's. I decide what I want, how, and when I want it. Do I make myself clear?"

I looked her square in the eyes, and it was no surprise that she looked away, pouting, and started playing with her hair.

I had no idea where to find Serena. I knew her father's shop was closed as it was Sunday, and I had no idea where her family lived, so until I could get hold of her, my best bet was to reach her back in the city. Knowing there was no way to get there, I knew I needed to leave.

My hands were shaking with anger. I couldn't believe that, once again, my family had interfered where they weren't welcome. I heard her heels clicking along the tiled floor, following me as I walked towards the elevator.

Hitting the call button, I turn around. "Verity, you are not following me upstairs. I will shower, pack my bag, check out, and then go to my parents' house. I think it would be best if you returned home now."

I didn't want to see her. I needed to get away from her.

"I can't. I had a driver bring me here, and it wasn't for a return trip as I thought you would be driving us both back."

She had planned this whole goddamn thing.

"Fine, wait here, and I'll give you a lift."

Right on cue, the doors opened, and I stepped into the awaiting car. Waiting for the doors to close, I could feel myself losing self-control. When the doors finally closed, I let go—slamming my fist into the metal door.

Despite the hard contact, I couldn't even feel the pain in my knuckles over the pain I saw etched in Serena's eyes.

I stared at the dent I made in the door as the car stopped at my floor. I needed to speak to her. I needed her to know this was all a genuine big mistake.

Despite it being a Sunday, I dialed Charlotte's cell.

"Good afternoon, Mr. Chambers. Is everything okay?"

"Sorry to disturb your weekend, but I need you to get me

Serena Parker's personal cell number. Not her work extension. And I need it immediately. It's an urgent matter."

I knew it seemed dramatic, but I couldn't wait. I needed to speak to her, see her, touch her skin, and fix this colossal fuck up.

Chapter 12

Rhett

ours later, I pulled into the long, winding driveway of my parents' estate. As always, I was greeted by my mother as if I were an adolescent.

"Oh, Rhett, darling, I'm so glad you could come. Ah, Verity, I'm glad you were able to bring him. What would I do without you?"

I went to respond, but there was a cold, almost sad look in my mother's eyes. I'd never seen that look on her face, so I dropped it for now.

I didn't know what felt more uncomfortable, the almost three-hour drive with Verity or how much she saw Verity as one of the family.

We went inside and found everyone else waiting for us in the lounge. On the large Chesterfield sat my younger sisters, Heather and Kara, and next to Kara, her husband, Austin. Their son, Kai, ran out from behind the couch.

As he collided with me, I grabbed him and threw him high up into the air, which made him squeal with delight, but Kara always complained.

"I see you finally decided to show your face."

Even though Kara was younger than me, she always acted like the older one, forever talking down to me.

"And it's good to see you too, sis."

I kissed my nephew on the cheek, said my hellos to Austin, and handed him Kai.

Leaning down, I kissed Heather on the cheek as well. She barely acknowledged me as she continued debating my father about the merits of free college funding. A conversation that sounded like it had been going on for quite some time. I made my way over to the bar and greeted my father.

Only then did I notice two figures seated on the bar stools. One was my brother, and the other was his date. We made eye contact at the exact moment, and it took me a second to realize where I had seen her before.

It was Serena's friend. Oh fuck.

And with how she looked at me now, I could tell she's spoken to Serena.

I greeted Julian, and to my surprise, he stood and properly introduced us.

"Rhett, this is Ruby Tanner. Ruby, this is my brother Rhett."

"It's a pleasure to meet you, Ruby. I do believe I was at The Mount on your birthday. I hope you had a good evening?"

Her eyes were profoundly assessing, and for a moment, I wondered whether she would shake my hand or simply leave me looking a fool.

Luckily for me, she shook my hand. And despite her small size, her grip was firm as she dug her nails in.

"Yes, how could I forget? You were looking after my best friend, Serena."

Her intelligent eyes bore right through me. She didn't need to say anything. I knew exactly what she meant.

I glanced over my shoulder to see Verity's reaction and could see she was about to say something, but for once, she read my facial expression and stayed silent. Now was my opportunity to tell Ruby the truth about Verity.

Still, before I could, the housekeeper alerted us that dinner was ready, and my father walked over to say hello.

"Come on, son," he said, patting my shoulder, and I followed him into the dining room.

Could this day get any worse? There was still no word from Charlotte on retrieving Serena's number. And now I had to endure this unnecessary family meal with Verity and Serena's best friend present. I didn't want to think about the version of this evening Ruby would portray to Serena. I needed to speak to her.

My mother always had to make a song and dance at family dinners. It couldn't just be one dish we all tuck into, share, and enjoy with our family. Instead, it was a four-course meal cooked by their private chef.

The food was delicious, but I couldn't appreciate it. Not with Verity beside me, constantly flirting and trying to reminisce and dredge up family stories. And on the other side of the table, I had Ruby silently watching my every word and movement, not even trying to disguise her disdain for me. Her coldness seemed to spur Julian on more, and he lapped it up.

My phone vibrated in my pocket, and as I looked at the message, I saw Charlotte had managed to obtain Serena's number. I needed to call her. Now.

"I'm sorry, but I've got to go; something important has come up. Thanks for a lovely dinner."

I went to get up and leave when my mother shouted, "Rhett, sit down!"

"Excuse me?" I queried, my brow raised at her unexpected outburst.

"Rhett, please, we don't want to do this during dinner. Please wait until we are all finished and talked, then you can make your way. I'm sure whatever it is can wait."

"Mother, I'm afraid this cannot. Now, if you'll excuse me."

The sound of her slamming the table with her closed fist brought everyone to a stop.

"Your father is dying! Is that important enough for you to hold out on whatever is causing you to rush off?"

I froze.

He what...?

"Alice."

My father reached over and took my mother's hands, then leaned in and kissed her temple.

The taste of bile came up my throat.

"Dad, is this true? What the fuck is going on?" Julian pleaded.

My sisters started crying and shouting. My ears felt as though I were underwater. Everything sounded faded. Disconnected.

Looking into my father's eyes as he went to the drinks cabinet and poured himself another drink, I was waiting for him to refute the bomb my mother had just dropped. I watched as he walked back to his seat at the head of the table and rubbed the bridge of his nose.

"I'll explain, but first, let's see that Kai has something to do." He called in the housekeeper and asked her to take Kai into the kitchen.

I watched as he looked around at us all, and all I could see was the shell of a man. When had he gotten so thin? Had he always looked so pale?

"A few months ago, I went to see my doctor as I had been having terrible headaches. He ran some tests on me there and then at the hospital. Then, a few days later after my round of golf, he called me and asked me to come in for my results. As soon as I sat down in the chair in his office, I knew the prognosis wasn't good. I've got Glioblastoma multiforme."

"What does that mean?" Heather spoke in almost a whisper as tears fell down her cheek.

"It means, sweetheart, that I have a malignant brain tumor."

"Surely, there is some sort of treatment for this?" Kara demanded. "We know some of the best doctors and surgeons in the world. You need to get a second opinion. There must be something that can be done."

Unlike Heather, Kara was angry.

"Kara, I've since seen five of the top specialists in the country, and all have given me the same results."

The room went silent. The only noise coming from my mother and Heather's crying. Austin was trying to comfort Kara, but she wasn't interested. She walked over to the bar and poured herself a large scotch.

Julian's voice broke the silence.

"How long have you got left?"

That question made me focus back on my father. I could see the tears in his eyes.

"Eight months at the most."

My stomach flipped. I felt as though I was going to be sick. I took deep breaths and kept swallowing hard.

Kara let out a primal scream from where she was standing. Her glass fell out of her hand and smashed on the floor.

Everything seemed to go in slow motion.

Austin ran over to her. Heather and my mother hugged, crying, and consoling one another. Verity walked over and joined them. Looking over at Julian, all I could see was his head hung in his hands as Ruby rubbed his back, and from the look on her face, it was clear that she didn't know what to say. Just then, she looked up at me. No longer were her eyes full of anger and annoyance. Instead, they were reflecting sorrow and pity.

I couldn't stand this anymore.

I stood and walked towards the door.

My mother looked up at me, her eyes awash with tears. "Rhett, why must you always walk away? How can you leave? Now? With everything that your father has just told you. We are meant to be a family. Does that mean nothing to you anymore?"

I knew her words came from her hurt and sorrow, but I was not going to sit around and allow myself to be her metaphorical punching bag.

"Alice." My father spoke softly and embraced my mother. "This is a shock to everyone. Let him go. We must all deal with this in our ways."

I turned to him, and by his gentle nod, I knew he understood how I felt. I had never been one to show my emotions openly. Many might see me as selfish, cold, or unloving, but it was how I dealt with things. He knew I couldn't process everything that I had just heard.

Giving him a nod back, I reached for the door and left.

My plan to drink myself to sleep wasn't working. I was halfway through my bottle of Delamain de Voyage, hoping to feel numb and make everything that had happened disappear. I wanted to be in a black abyss. But instead, with each glass, my temper grew.

I was angry at my father. Angry that this was happening to him. His whole life had been dedicated to family. His eye for business helped us grow and prosper tremendously. We'd always been a well-known and prosperous family, but after my father took over the company following my grandfather's death, he worked and pushed us to stay at the top. And I'd been trained to do the same, eventually.

But I never expected it to happen like this. I knew my life was about to change substantially, and everything that was expected of me would now be coming to fruition much sooner than I could have ever expected.

My father was expecting me to take over from him, continue to prosper, and drive the company into the ever-changing markets, but that always seemed like such a faraway thought. He always took me under his wing and let me make mistakes when needed, allowing me to learn and grow from them. He never held a grudge or condemned me for actions and decisions made in the office.

For the past eight years, he had given me a large amount of the company to run myself. But he was always there should I need his advice or guidance.

His leaving was never meant to happen so soon.

He was only sixty-nine, for fuck's sake.

How could this be happening?

What was my mother going to do? How was she going to cope? Losing Dad was going to destroy her.

How was Kara going to manage this? She always struggled when something terrible happened, even when we were kids. And then there was Heather. Unlike Kara, she never hid her sorrow or worries. She wore every emotion on her sleeve. She was always quieter and more subdued than Kara.

We were never a super affectionate family growing up, but one thing I remembered was how, at dinner times, we would all be together, and Father would check in with everyone. It became our routine. Everyone would give him a run down on how their days were, whether it was things that happened at school, or my sisters complaining and gossiping about their group of friends.

And even though my mother usually sat back nursing a glass of wine, she always filled in anything important that we'd forgotten to mention. Or reminding Father of which functions they had to attend that week or appointments he needed to remember. They worked together as a team. Between the two of them, they managed to have it all—do it all.

It was only when I was older and working myself, did I realize just how well he balanced his work and family life. We were never an afterthought. I had no idea how he managed it.

How was I ever meant to live up to that?

The thought that I was expected to fill his shoes made me feel physically sick.

I retrieved my phone off the table and tried to call Serena again. I had called more than forty times since leaving my parents' house. I left dozens of messages. Why wasn't the one person I needed to see right now not answering? Why wouldn't she hear me out?

It felt like the walls were closing in on me.

Feeling dazed, I reached for the decanter and poured myself another drink.

It had been ten days since I last saw Serena and found out my father was dying. I had continued my attempts to call her every day. Each time, it rang through to her voicemail. Most of the time, I wouldn't leave a message. However, when I'd call her in the evening after I'd drowned my sorrows, I often felt the need to leave one. They varied from *please answer, hear me out, what Verity said was a complete mistake, and God dammit. Why won't you answer? I did nothing wrong!*

I knew I was becoming desperate. The previous week, we'd had two meetings with her firm about issues with the takeover. Both times, she had sent her associates. There was another meeting scheduled for today, and unlike the other two, the heads of finance, legal, and PR were also attending. I knew that compared to the others, this one was more important. I desperately hoped that she would attend this one.

Surely, it was too important for her to miss? But deep down in my gut, I knew she was hurt. And despite me knowing the truth, she, however, didn't and instead thought I was a liar and a cheat. But it wasn't the truth.

Our meeting was scheduled for 4:30, but I had already found myself sitting ready and waiting in the boardroom from 4:00. I made Charlotte re-arrange the last appointment I had lined up for the day in the fruitless hope that she would show up.

I needed time. Time to explain. Time to talk. It was time to make her want me again because I knew I needed her.

The door opened, and Mike from Legal, Daniel from PR, and Tim from Finance walked in. They were all busy talking about the two new interns who had started working in finance that day. Instead of listing the attributes they brought to the company, Tim tried debating which was better, blonde or brunette. The other two were happily engaged in this ridiculous conversation, and their voices were already setting my teeth on edge.

They were shocked to find me seated at the head of the table, waiting for the meeting to start. I gave them a stern look, and they shut up. Charlotte entered, handing everyone the notes for the meeting, and in an attempt to block the other guys out, I put my head down to skim through the file in front of me.

It wasn't until I registered the sounds of stilettos clicking that I looked up and saw Serena walk around to the far side of the table.

My body reacted instantly as my eyes fell upon her. I drank in the very sight of her. She wore a gray top, with a short black blazer. It wasn't until she walked out from behind that I saw she had on a black leather pencil skirt. She was even more beautiful than I remembered. If that was even possible, but it wasn't her body I missed the most. It was how she made me feel.

She made me happy. I liked who I was when I was around her. She made me feel free and even gave me hope that I could change the narrative of my life. She was someone I could turn to who I could open up to.

She conducted most of the meeting, giving updates on progress and the offers that some owners were putting forward and pointing out issues we faced that no one from PR or Legal had brought up yet.

The meeting lasted almost forty minutes, and she avoided eye contact with me. Whenever I asked a question or directed the conversation towards her, she either looked down at her notes or spoke generally to the other people at the table.

I was not going to put up with this anymore. I'd tried to talk to her, reaching out and getting her to give me a chance, and she had given me nothing. I had to take a chance. I didn't care anymore.

"Ladies and gentlemen, Ms. Parker has given us much work to get on with. I think it's best if you all go and get on with it, especially Mike and Tim. And let's not make it a habit of letting others find gaps in your work."

"Yes, sir."

They all got up and left the boardroom with obvious embarrassment etched across their faces.

As soon as the door closed behind them, I stood and went to where Serena was packing her files.

"Serena, please, will you give me just five minutes? I need to speak with you," I pleaded.

"Rhett, no. Everything that needed to be said has been said. It would be best if you stopped calling. I don't even know how you got my unlisted number. Like I said at the beginning, let's keep things professional. You are my client. You are engaged to be married. There is nothing more to say."

I watched as she continued packing her things away, still avoiding my gaze.

"For fuck's sake, how many times do I have to say this to you? I am not engaged. I never have and never will be engaged to Verity Lancaster."

"I don't know what kind of games you two play, but I don't want any part of this."

"Serena, please just hear me out."

"What for? What happened with us was a mistake. A slip on my part, it shouldn't have happened. Trust me, it won't happen again. Now I have said all I need to say."

Her eyes never left her bag as she picked it up and went to walk out.

I grabbed her by the waist, spun her around, and looked straight into her beautiful eyes.

"Verity tracked me down. We dated in college, but I broke things off years ago. Her family and mine have been friends for decades. She, along with the help of my mother, has tried to get us back together. I have never given her any reason to imagine anything would come of it. She is, however, used to getting her way. And I think she felt that if she pushed the idea of an engagement to my mother, I would eventually give in."

"So, what was the announcement at your parents' house?"

Part of me was surprised. First, because she'd allowed me to talk, and secondly, that Ruby didn't tell her about what my father had said at dinner. To which I was both grateful and respectful.

"Ruby didn't tell you? My father wanted to get us all together to tell us that he had a brain tumor. Serena, my father is dying."

Chapter 13

Serena

"**O**h my god!" I gasped.

I instantly felt terrible. Poor Rhett. Why didn't Ruby tell me? Goddamn, now I feel awful for not answering his calls.

Fuck!

Why hadn't I given him a chance to talk? He called me every day. But I knew why. For days, I hated him. I hated that he had lied to me. I hated that he made me feel like a cheap side piece.

What kind of woman was this Verity? Seriously, who did that?

All this time, I'd been angry and ignored him, and he'd been dealing with the terrible news of his father. I might not have known Rhett for long, but I could see in his eyes that he was telling the truth.

The man standing in front of me was hurt. He wasn't the robust and in-control bachelor that was a regular feature on page six. He was a man used to control and things working to his advantage, yet now he was facing something out of his control. And I'd only made everything worse.

"I am so sorry. I don't know what to say... how are you doing?"

"To say I am dealing with it would be a lie."

"How long has your father known?"

"He'd found out a few weeks before telling us. I guess he was in shock. I know I would be if I had been told I only have months to live."

I let out a gasp and covered my mouth with my hand.

"Rhett, I'm so sorry. Is there anything I can do?"

I knew I couldn't do anything about his father's health, but it just felt like one of those things you're meant to say.

There was a long pause, and I watched as his hand slowly reached out tentatively caressing my face. The feel of his hand on my cheek made me weak at the knees. With the pad of his thumb, he wiped away a stray tear that fell down my cheek.

"You're already helping. You're listening to me. You are probably the first person ever truly to listen. I've never had that before."

It was with the gentlest touch he brushed his lips across mine. Being so close to him, I could smell his heady masculine scent. That's what tipped me over the edge. Deepening the kiss, I wanted to taste and savor him. His tongue massaged mine. The yearning for this man instantly awakened.

My hands reached into his hair, gently pulling him closer. His hands drifted down my body, and I could feel his palm on my ass through my leather skirt, making me want and need him more. I started to rub my hips against his and could feel his cock getting hard against my thigh, making him more rigid and engorged.

I could taste the salty tears on his lips. His groans of desire and the hot need from his mouth drove me on, and my eyes closed, reveling in the ecstatic feeling. I felt lost in him, lost in this moment and my connection with him.

All too soon, we were reminded where we were as his secretary knocked on the door and entered. Pushing myself away from him, I was panting, trying to bring my thoughts and breath back. Had the secretary seen us? Did she know what we were doing?

I was utterly embarrassed. I was there on a professional matter, not personal. I didn't want her to think I was that kind of woman. Looking over at her, I expected to see a disgruntled, judgmental look cross her face. But instead, she gave me a warm, shy smile.

"I'm so sorry to interrupt, Mr Chambers, but I have Fiona from HR and her team waiting outside. They are scheduled for a teleconference here in twenty minutes and need to set up."

Putting his hand on the small of my back, Rhett led me to the door.

"It was a pleasure seeing you again, Ms. Parker," Charlotte spoke softly, but I genuinely felt she meant every word.

"Please, call me Serena."

I extended my hand, and she shook it, once again gracing me with her smile.

Seconds later, we were standing by the bank of elevators.

"We should talk. Or...."

I could see the desire in his eyes. But everything felt so... overwhelming. And this wasn't the time or place to talk. Or kiss.

"I should go," I said, watching his face fall. "But if you don't have any plans later, let's talk over dinner or drinks.

His face lit up like a child on Christmas morning. I struggled with the thrill his reaction gave me.

"That sounds great. Why don't we do both? I'll make the reservations. What time should I come to pick you up?"

I couldn't help but smile at how eager he sounded.

"Okay, how does 8:30 sound?"

"I'll be there at 8:30 sharp."

He pressed the call button for the elevator.

As the elevator doors began to close, I did my best to remain calm. I tried to keep my eyes down as the doors closed, but unintentionally, they wandered up his body. He unbuttoned his jacket, and I saw his prominent bulge straining against his slacks. Without realizing it, I bit down on my lip, trying to tame my desire.

To my utmost embarrassment, I looked up at him and saw that he had been watching me. The grin on his face said it all.

I didn't leave the office until almost seven, so I had to grab a cab home to ensure I'd be ready.

Once home, I had the fastest shower and made sure my hair was kept dry under my shower cap. I'd had it wrapped in a chignon all day, so luckily, when I took it out, it fell in loose waves past my shoulders.

That was just going to have to do.

I was putting the final additions to my makeup when Ruby called.

"Hey, babe, what you up to?"

Putting her on speaker to continue getting ready, I shouted, "Umm, I'm getting ready for a date. And he'll be here in fifteen minutes, so I don't have time to chat."

"Wait, you never told me you met someone. Who is it?"

I paused. Ruby was my best friend, and I tell her absolutely everything. But suddenly, I wondered how she would react to me telling her I was going on a date with Rhett. Especially since I'd been shooting her down every time she mentioned his name.

"I'm meeting Rhett."

She paused for so long that I thought we'd been disconnected.

"Ruby, are you there?"

"Yeah, sorry, wow. I wasn't expecting that. Jeez, what happened? Last week, you wouldn't even let me say his name, and now you're going on a date."

"It's complicated, but I saw him today at work. We talked and... well... I changed my mind."

Walking over to my jewelry box, I grab my favorite piece. When I started my company, my father gave me the necklace— a rose gold chain with a coral gemstone pendant.

"But why?"

I explained the situation with Verity and how that woman is determined to snag him. I also told her what he said to me about his father.

"Ruby, why didn't you tell me?"

"I'm sorry. After what you told me about what had happened, I thought you were done with him. Plus, how he reacted when their father told them all, Serena, he just left. His mom and sisters were distraught. Julian was devastated. Rhett, on the other hand, didn't say or do anything. He was like a robot. He just got up and left."

My heart hurt for him. Somehow, I understood the need to not break down in front of people.

When I learned my mom had left, I wanted to get on with things—not wanting or needing anyone and just wanting to be alone. And I was only a child at the time.

"But when I told you how he wouldn't stop ringing me, you should have said something then. I feel awful. It's bad enough he's dealing with the news his father's dying. Add to that, me completely blocking him out and ignoring every attempt he made to contact me."

"Babe, I don't know what to say. I truly am sorry."

As I finished fastening my necklace, I continued filling Ruby in on what happened.

"After he told me everything, I looked into his eyes, and I knew he was telling me the truth. And then he kissed me."

"And..."

"And his PA walked in. He invited me to his office, but I needed to return to work, so I suggested we go for dinner this evening."

"Hold on, so you asked him out? Look at you."

"Rubes, we live in the 21st century. I run my own company. I'm capable of asking a man to dinner.

"You mean a date?"

She laughed.

"Whatever."

I couldn't help but laugh.

"So, since you're in such an asking mood, will you invite him back to yours at the end of the evening?"

"No! That will not be happening."

"Oh, come on, I know you wanna fuck him again. After how good you told me he was, even I want to."

"Ruby! You're dating his brother."

"I know. I know. I'm just kidding."

"I gotta go. I need to get dressed, and Rhett'll be here in ten minutes."

"Okay, have fun, call me tomorrow and tell me every detail. Oh, and don't do anything I wouldn't."

"Oh, yeah, because that leaves me with so much."

"Hey, enough with the cheek. Love you."

"Love you."

Hanging up the phone, I went to the bed, where I had laid out my outfit. I picked a green sheath dress with capped sleeves and my favorite nude Valentino Rock stud pumps. I kept my accessories minimal, with just my necklace.

My phone buzzed, and I saw a message from Rhett.

Looking at the time, and just as he said, it was 8:30 on the dot.

Taking one last look in the mirror, I took a deep breath, grabbed my keys, clutch, and jacket, and went down.

~

We were cocooned in a corner booth at Masa. When the waitress took our starters away, we were back in our private little bubble. With the dim lights and soft sounds of the other patrons in the distance, this felt more intimate than any other date I've ever been on.

When we'd first arrived, it seemed neither one of us wanted to address the elephant in the room—the whole misunderstanding about Verity and, most importantly, his father's diagnosis. But even when I asked him how work had been, I could see the fear and anguish in his eyes. So, I wasn't going to bring it up or push him to talk until he was ready. Instead, sticking to easier and safer topics.

"I know you've said before your main hobbies are cars, both driving and collecting them..."

I couldn't refrain from giving him a playful eye roll before continuing.

"But there must have been other things that piqued your interest over the years?"

He slowly rolled the tumbler of whiskey around in a slow circle, and my eyes zeroed in as his thumb caught the stray drop that had started to trickle down.

"I've always loved swimming. When I was younger, it was

just the excitement of being in the water. Then, as I got older, and we'd go on vacations, the water drew me in. My father realized I was fast, so I set myself up to join the swim team in high school and did the same during college. I loved the water, but more than that, I liked that it wasn't a team sport. I didn't need to rely on others. If I worked hard enough, swam fast enough, pushed when I thought I had nothing left, I'd come out on top."

Once again, I realized how much of his life he had spent alone. At times, he reminded me of a deserted island in the ocean. Strong enough to withstand the tumultuous waves and elements yet isolated through those around him.

He'd never mentioned any close friends or any kind of inner circle—besides his father. I can't imagine not having Ruby, Roman, or even Olivia, who had continuously been there and supported me throughout various times in my life. The sound of his voice broke me from my thoughts.

"It also became a release of sorts. The more I was studying or being taught the ins and outs of the company, the more time I would swim. On some days, I would get up at four, head over to the pool on campus, and swim till I needed to leave for class at seven. At one point, I even got approached by a scout from the US Olympic Team, wanting to arrange a meeting, but that was shut down quickly as it wasn't in the plan."

A sadness in his eyes accompanied the bitterness in his tone. I couldn't even fathom how it must have felt being that good—seemingly without even trying and being told you were good enough to compete, yet your family that had planned your whole life out for you put a stop to it.

A seed of resentment began to grow within me with just how much they controlled and manipulated him—never allowing him anything for himself. Always them. Always the family—the business—the expectations.

"Anyway, I guess it became engrained within me, and now

I try to do at least an hour every morning before work. It's one of the reasons why I picked that apartment, as it's the only one with a full Olympic-sized pool. Enough about me. I know you said you came top of your class at Columbia. Tell me, were you ever a wild child at college? Joined any sororities? I want to know the most memorable thing that happened."

My pulse increased, and I knew he was hoping for a funny and entertaining anecdote from me, but all my mind went back to the one thing that went on to taint my whole college experience.

My knee-jerk reaction was to brush it off and say how boring I'd been, but this felt important. And I knew if I were giving him a chance, I'd have to truly open myself up, and maybe, just maybe, it might allow him to understand why I was the way I was.

I waited for the waiter to finish serving our mains and leave before taking a big gulp of wine and ripping the band-aid off.

"Sororities were never something that interested me. Something about them always reminded me of cults. All I wanted to do was keep my head down and focus on my studies. I joined a couple of clubs and organizations, but they were mainly ones that were in some way connected to my degree."

Giving myself a moment, I ate a couple of bites, and as I looked over at Rhett and saw his eyes were focused on mine, it was as if he knew I was about to say something important. The recurring nod and smile he gave me was all I needed to feel safe to continue.

"During college, I only ever dated casually, never wanting or looking for anything serious. Most of the time, I was too busy with papers, deadlines, and extra credits. But then I started seeing this guy. We hit it off straight away. He was really sweet, charming, and attentive. His family came from a rather affluent background. He could speak four languages and would often tell me how horrible his family was and the pressure he always felt under them."

I looked up and watched his adam's apple move up and down.

"Anyway, we spent more and more of our time together, and I started thinking he could be someone I'd have a future with. Given everything he'd told me about them, I didn't find it weird initially that I hadn't met his family. But the more time that passed, the more things started niggling at me. One day, I found a second phone of his. One I hadn't seen before. And there wasn't a password on it. It turned out he was only with me as he'd always had a fetish for being with a woman of color. He and his friends had made a WhatsApp group whereby they had a spreadsheet and would rate and review the physical and sexual attributes and differences of women from different ethnic backgrounds."

The words came out of me in a rush.

"When I found out, I confronted him. He said he would never be able to be with someone like me seriously as I didn't fit into his family and didn't have the correct pedigree. I had tried rallying the other women who were in that group and being exploited, but where the guys involved all came from money and powerful families, it was covered up, and the guys only got a slap on the wrist. Their families made donations to the school for counseling for the women and then gave the option to either make a second donation towards a charity of each woman's choosing or to pay for their tuition."

There was a slight tremble in my hands when I reached for my glass of water, but Rhett covered it with his own. His thumb ran soothing circles across my palm.

"What was the guy's name?"

Despite the low volume, his anger seeped through his tone.

"It doesn't matter. It's done and in the past. But it cemented my lack of trust in men. As I found myself continuously doubting their true intentions. That was until I met you."

Slowly, I raised my eyes, and my breath caught in my throat as I saw the thanks and tenderness on his face.

Wanting to liven the mood, I changed the subject and began peppering him with questions about his travels and his love of food.

Later, we moved on to a private member's bar at the top of a hotel overlooking Central Park. I'd have thought we'd have run out of things to talk about by now, but he was so warm and open I felt I could tell him anything, and I did.

There were no awkward silences, no long pauses between topics. I felt utterly at ease with him, just as I had when I took him on the walk to the lookout.

I was slowly nursing a whiskey sour, and Rhett enjoyed a Bourbon.

At dinner, I'd gotten carried away with how much wine I drank. And, there at the bar, I was on my second drink, so I knew I needed to slow down. I didn't want to get drunk. I knew the more I drank, the more turned on I got.

Alcohol always did that to me.

"So, back to cars," I jested and couldn't contain the smile that spread across my face before continuing.

"Besides the Gull-wing, what others do you have?"

This time, a smile lit up his face, and I could tell this topic significantly interested him.

"Growing up, I always loved the classics my father and older relatives drove. Once I got my license, my father gifted me his Porsche 911. I know what you're going to say, spoilt rich kid. Well, yes, I was more fortunate than most, and I loved that car. It was an amazing drive, and the girls loved it."

I couldn't help rolling my eyes and laughing.

Rhett chuckled, then continued, "But I loved it most

because it had been my father's. When I was younger, I remember the few times my dad took me out in it. When we were on the open road, he'd drive it so fast it felt like I was on a roller-coaster. It'd always been our little secret as my mother always hated my dad going fast, especially with me in the car. So, it was from there that my love of cars evolved. Now I have the Benz Gull-Wing, a 1971 Ferrari 246GT Dino RHD, an Aston Martin DB5 Vantage, a 1968 Mercedes Benz 280 SL Pagoda – Manual, and a 1952 Jaguar XK120 Supersonic. But my absolute favorite is my 1966 Red Ford Mustang 289 Convertible."

"You can't get more classic than that," I said with a smile.

Most of those he listed I had seen in my dad's shop or at the car shows he used to take me to. One thing was for sure, you needed to have real pocket change to have those in your collection.

"Well, I have to say, I am extremely impressed. You clearly have more of an interest in the older collection of classics. But with your busy schedule, how do you find time to enjoy them all?"

"There are times when I'm stuck in meetings, and my mind does think about how I would prefer to be out on the open road. Luckily, I have my cars at mine and my family's various properties, so whenever I can take a few days off, I head out there and enjoy them. You know, you're the first woman I have met that I can have this conversation with and not be bored senseless."

Over my glass, I give him a shy smile.

"I'm not boring you, am I?"

There again was the doubt etched across his face.

"No, of course you're not boring me. It's refreshing to have this conversation with someone under the age of fifty. Most of the customers at my dad's shop are older, and they have this way of talking to me about cars as if I came from another planet. I do love the surprise on their faces when I quickly put them in their place. Just like I did the first time I met you."

Retrieving my drink, I finished it off with a flourish. I couldn't tell if he was laughing at me or with me. And as I was feeling the buzz from my drink, I didn't care.

"Guilty as charged. You took me by surprise. I'm unsure if it was your quick understanding of what was up with my car, how hot you looked, or your beautiful singing voice?"

Jesus, how embarrassing. I hated people hearing me sing. With family, it was OK. But not strangers. I grew up singing along to our favorite songs in the car with everyone. God knew how often Ruby and I would think we were American Idol finalists, belting out Whitney or Mariah as we were getting ready for a night out.

But now, knowing Rhett had heard me, that felt too intimate. As if he'd seen a part of me, I never showed in public.

"There's no need for you to blush. You have a lovely and sexy voice. Is there anything you can't do?"

Now, I was beginning to feel uncomfortable. This was getting too much. Especially as I was getting increasingly turned on by him, every time he ran his finger along the rim of his glass, licked the drops of whiskey off his lip, or rubbed his hand along his thigh, I couldn't help but be turned on, drawn in. He seemed to sense my unease.

"Would you like another drink?"

There was a cautious apprehension as if he knew me saying no would bring the evening to an earlier end.

For a moment, I deliberated the idea in my head. But then sense kicks in.

"No, I'm fine thank you."

I expected him to try to convince me otherwise, but he accepted my answer without complaint.

A half-hour later, we were back in his town car, his driver

heading toward my apartment. All my nerves and senses seemed hyper-aware. It's as if my body was completely attuned to his. We made light conversation, but I knew he felt just as I did. We both wanted to fuck. But both knew we shouldn't.

The car pulled up in front of my building, and my body was already beginning to feel a sense of regret.

Rhett stepped out of his side and walked around to open my door. As I got out, our bodies moved closer together. My breathing came fast.

"Thank you for a lovely evening. I have truly had a wonderful time."

He looked deeply into my eyes, searching for confirmation that I meant the words I had just said.

"I assure you the pleasure has been all mine."

I wanted to kiss him. I needed the feel of his soft mouth against mine. I gently leaned my body into his, slowly raising my head as I caressed my lips against his.

Instantly, a fireball erupted. Our tongues invaded each other's mouths, laving and coaxing one another. His hands dug into my hips, grinding my body against his. Taking his lower lip in between my teeth, I gently nipped on it. Causing him to let out a deep moan. The sound that escaped went straight to my pussy, I could feel myself getting wetter and wetter with each passing second. I held on tightly to his solid and supple biceps, not wanting to lose my balance.

I knew I needed to break the kiss.

If I let it carry on, I'd ask him to come up. And I knew the best thing for us was to take it slow. Especially after everything I had told him.

Gently, I released my grip on his arm, driving the kiss to an end. Finally breaking for air, he rests his forehead against mine.

"Thank you again for a wonderful evening, Serena."

I steadied myself on my heels and waited as he bent down

and retrieved my clutch from the car. Needing to keep my distance, I took a step back. He handed me my clutch, watched, and waited as I walked through the door.

Taking one last look back at him and couldn't help but smile.

Chapter 14

Serena

The smell of popcorn and red wine filled my apartment. Ruby was over for movie night and a catch-up.

I didn't care what anyone said, there was no better Friday night than a movie, wine, and gossiping with my best friend. I felt terrible that I hadn't seen her in over three weeks.

Between work and Rhett, my schedule had been hectic. We had four significant cases going on that required the use of all my associates and interns. Although Chambers Industries was my biggest client and took up most of my attention, they weren't the only ones. I was currently running on a tight and full schedule.

It also made me feel guilty when I agreed to go on a second date with Rhett on the only night I had free last week.

We'd decided on the classic Dirty Dancing as our movie of choice, and Ruby set out the popcorn as I poured the wine.

"So, I know I said I'd wait, Serena, but I've been here for more than ten minutes, and I'm dying to know what is happening with you and lover boy. Have you fucked him again?"

"Ruby!" I couldn't help but smile, shaking my head. "No, I haven't slept with him again."

"But you've been seeing him? What's holding you back? He's hot and, by my recollection, and I quote, was the best sex you had ever had, so why are you not screwing him senseless?"

"Because... after everything that happened, I want to take it slow. I can't listen to my body."

"Why not? That's what normal people do."

This time, she couldn't help her giggles.

"Well, he isn't exactly a normal guy. Plus, whenever I'm around him, it's like he's this sex god that my body feels automatically synchronized to. He makes me want to lose my inhibitions and pounce him."

"That's a no-brainer. Most women who have met him or just seen a picture of him would want to jump him. And yet here you are trying to deter that? I love you, S, but you're nuts."

"Hey, I am in the room, you know. I'm not nuts. I'm being cautious. The man loves being in control, deciding when, where, how, and who. But so do I. You know I can't give up total control. It needs to be give and take."

Ruby had been my biggest support after what happened at college. Whether it was sending me care packages, coming on surprise visits, or just listening as I cried over the phone, she knew how much it knocked me. My self-confidence. My self-worth. And especially being able to trust a man.

And given that my ex and Rhett came from similar backgrounds and lifestyles, I knew she'd understand my apprehension deep down.

"So, the last time you saw him, how did you put out the flames? I can't see him giving up on you. Especially after you told me how your date ended."

In a vain attempt, I tried to hide my embarrassment by taking a large sip of wine.

"Something happened! You've seen him. Spill."

"Well, on Wednesday, I had a crazy, hectic day at work. It was gone seven before I noticed everyone in the office had left, and it was only me and the cleaning crew. So, I'm preparing my final notes for my meeting the next morning when I get his call."

Ruby leaned in, eagerly waiting for me to continue.

"Anyway, he called to ask if I had any plans for the evening. To which I responded that I was finishing up at the office. So, he asked if I would like to go with him to this jazz bar, as there was a band he loved playing that night. At first, I was apprehensive to say yes, but I knew I could do with a drink, and I didn't have Rhett tipped to be the jazz bar kind of guy. So, I was intrigued."

I readjusted myself, getting more comfortable on my corner sofa.

"Oh, my gosh. If you don't get on with this story, I swear to God..."

I couldn't blame her because I knew I was dragging it out, but it was more so I could re-live it again. Putting her out of her misery, I gave her a thoroughly detailed run-through of the evening.

"So, you left him hanging again?"

"I didn't leave him hanging. We had a nice evening, and we kissed goodnight. Wouldn't consider that as being nothing."

"I'm starting to feel sorry for the guy. You're going to give him the worst case of blue ba—"

I cut her off before she could say it. My body had also screamed at my brain as I lay in bed that night. But I needed to make sure that the next time I slept with him, my head and my body were as one.

"So, when are you seeing him again?"

"He asked me to dinner tomorrow night."

"At his place?"

"Yep."

My body began to feel hot. And I was guessing by the look on my face Ruby could tell what I was thinking.

"You're so going to get laid," Ruby said almost in a singsong-like tone.

"Depends on how the night goes, I guess."

I smirked as I emptied my glass of wine.

"Oh, come on, it will depend more on what you wear. So, what have you decided on?"

"Who says I've decided on anything?"

"Serena Parker, if I was the saleswoman at Nordstrom, I might believe your answer. But I am not. I have been your best friend since we were babies. Now spill, what have you decided on?"

"The red lace dress we brought for my birthday last year that I didn't wear."

Grinning, I knew her response before she even said it.

"Well, I think it's safe to say you are getting laid tomorrow."

And we both couldn't hold back our giggles.

"Listen, I know you're anxious, and knowing you, you're probably analyzing every minute detail, dissecting every word uttered. But I'm telling you, you need to stop comparing him to Sebastian. If there was a single part of me that thought he was in any way similar, I promise you'd be the first to shut this down. I know it's scary putting yourself out there, and I mean really putting yourself out there, but you need to give yourself a chance. You deserve it. Don't let that pompous asshole keep holding you back. I truly think it'll be worth it."

As much as I hated to admit it, I hoped she was right.

All morning, I nursed a slightly sore head. Ruby and I consumed two bottles of wine before she decided to call it a night at around one A.M. I'd done my usual Saturday ritual - read the paper, went to my spin class, and did my laundry. I fit in an hour of work, called my dad, did some reading, and then started getting ready.

I always liked to take my time when getting ready, whether it be a date, event, or even work. My hair alone usually took me two hours, especially when I wanted it to look perfect.

My car would be there in half an hour. My hair and makeup were done, I had my lingerie on, and despite living in my apartment alone, I wasn't trying to kid myself into thinking I was a supermodel, so I had my favorite silk robe covering me.

I'd made myself a martini to steady my nerves and gain liquid courage. What was it about him that always made me feel so nervous? Musiq Soulchild was crooning in the background, and I was trying to work out why it was taking me so long to finish getting ready.

Knowing I needed to fully accept giving him the benefit of the doubt and another chance, I had to do it wholeheartedly. Or end things before they progress any further. He'd messaged me earlier with his address, and despite knowing the street, it wasn't until my car pulled up in front of his building that I put two and two together.

It wasn't as if my apartment was mediocre in any way, but I knew this block's residents were among the city's wealthiest. And Rhett sure fitted that bill. I arrived at the lobby reception and greeted the man behind the desk.

"Hello, my name is Serena Parker. I'm here to see Mr. Chambers."

The man gave me a once over, and I guessed I met his approval as he offered me a warm smile.

"Yes, Ms. Parker. If you take the elevator around the corner on the left and punch in this code, it shall take you straight up to the penthouse."

Of course, he lived in the penthouse. I gave my thanks and took the piece of paper. I did as instructed, and in no time, I stepped out of the elevator and walked to the single door occupying the floor. Raising my hand to knock, the door opened before I could touch it.

He stood before me in blue slacks and a crisp blue shirt that perfectly matched his eyes. He looked hot. His eyes raked me from head to toe before he finally spoke.

"I'm so glad you could make it. Please come in."

As I walked in, I was mesmerized by the floor-to-ceiling windows that wrapped all the way around.

"Let me take your coat," Rhett offered.

Slowly, I unbuttoned it and watched as he watched me.

Sliding it off, I saw his pupils dilate, and the way he looked at me made me feel even sexier. He took my coat and walked away to hang it up somewhere.

I saw him checking me out in the reflection of the glass. Ruby was right about the dress.

"You look incredible. I'm glad I've already plated up, I'm sure I'd burn myself with you distracting me like that."

I couldn't help but run my tongue along my lip. He knew just the right words to say.

Handing me a glass of wine, he guided me to the table that had been beautifully laid out. It was just the perfect balance of simplicity and luxury. My body craved him. But my tummy craved the delicious food I smelled.

After a quick toast, he gestured for me to start. And I wasted no time in tucking in.

"Have you always enjoyed cooking, or is it something you save to impress women?"

I lifted my glass of wine to my lips to hide my smile.

Putting down his cutlery, he lifted his napkin, wiping the corner of his mouth.

"No. I haven't always been interested in cooking. Growing up, I don't think I ever saw my mother even cook as much as an egg in the kitchen."

The way he raised an eyebrow at his statement made me want to laugh, but I rolled in my lips, nodding for him to continue.

"We always had chefs or caterers if there was an event or someone important over."

The flickers from the candles he had laid out between us and the soft hum of the music in the background cocooned me in a cloud of intimacy. And I didn't remember the last time I felt both so comfortable and turned on simultaneously.

"But I've always enjoyed food from different cultures, and when I was at college, I spent a lot of time trying every food truck or pop-up cafe within a five-mile radius. There was this one particular Vietnamese stall that I went to every Friday for lunch, and the old lady who ran it said I stopped by so often that I might as well be in the kitchen."

His eyes shone with fondness at the memory.

"So eventually, I asked her if she could show me how to cook some of them, and she did. That became a habit, and now and then, I'd ask or watch how the different vendors prepared and cooked and started practicing them at home on my days off. I'm sure you can relate to working long hours, and it isn't always possible, but I try to mix things up. So, I'm not always getting takeout."

Listening to him open up always felt like I was privy to a

glimpse no one else saw. And it sent a warm feeling right through me.

"Besides, I don't know if you've noticed, but I don't spend much of my free time with others. I've always been used to my own company."

I felt a pang of sadness, and I remember him telling me how much time he spent alone despite having a larger family. But I wanted to keep the energy positive and not dwell on the negative.

"Well, I've seen you frequently in your spare time. So, you can't say it's only your own company you keep."

I gave him a megawatt smile, letting him know I was teasing.

"But that's because you are special and important."

He clinked his glass with mine, and I bit my lip, holding back my smile, and continued with my meal.

I wasn't ashamed that I finished every single morsel. The guy really was an amazing cook.

"Dinner was delicious. I'm extremely impressed. Is there anything you can't do?"

I threw his words back at him.

He'd made a gorgeous warm Thai salad, followed by a Miso Cod Fillet with sautéed green beans and sesame Pak Choi. He'd taken note of my love of Asian cuisine.

"I remember going to Thailand in my early twenties and falling in love with the food there. Luckily, there are now amazing Asian restaurants here in the city. And some of them offer cooking lessons to their regular customers."

"You are full of surprises."

And I meant it. Whenever I thought I had him worked out, he would do or say something unexpected.

"Well, I'm glad you enjoyed it."

Taking our drinks, he headed towards what I presumed was

the lounge. With everything being open planned, I wasn't sure what to call it. I sat on the plush couch as Rhett walked over to the glass door in front of us, which led out onto his balcony. The view was breathtaking.

"Let me know if you feel cold, and I'll close the door."

"I'm good. The view here really is incredible."

He sat next to me, one leg propped underneath him and his arm resting along the back of the couch. His hands are just millimeters from my shoulder.

We'd been talking for quite some time, comparing embarrassing college stories and funny incidents at work. There was no pressure. Simply two people getting to know one another.

"Unlike you, I never really had a dream career or job."

"What? Not even when you were little? You didn't want to be a firefighter? Astronaut? GI Joe? Rock star?"

He laughed, but there was no humor behind it.

"I guess where I'd always been told what I was meant to do, who I was meant to be, I never spent any time wondering... thinking of anything else."

"Come on, there must be something. If you could pick anything, with there being no repercussions, anything in the world, what would you be? What is your passion?"

I don't know why, but I really wanted to know. I was so eager to discover what he would pick—without the restrictions or restraint shackled to him by his family. Pulling my legs beneath me, I turned, eagerly waiting for his answer.

"If I had to pick something I'm passionate about, I guess it would be something with cars."

The belly laugh that burst out of me was so unladylike, and I couldn't help but roll my eyes.

"I'd find something involving classics and vintage ones. Whether it would be as a collector, driving them for stunts in movies, or even just opening a museum."

I watched as he rubbed his hand over his cheeks, trying to hide the blush creeping in. At that moment, I realized I was probably the first person he'd ever told that to. The feeling was one of privilege and sadness.

Unsurprisingly, he changed the topic of conversation back to me, and I understood the need for that.

"So, Serena Parker of Serena Parker and Associates, how is a woman as young as you able to break into the field of law and have your company, though smaller in comparison to others, be one of the most sought-after ones in the city?"

I knew that was a question he would eventually ask, but it still always set me back slightly.

"Well, after I finished law school and passed the bar, I was lucky enough to get a job at Goldheim & Steiner, and within three years, I had worked my way up to associate. It wasn't an easy task. I worked hard, but luck also fell my way. I was given a few important cases, and our clients walked away happier and with more money than they had hoped they would. I always made it a crucial factor of mine to have honest communication and relationships with my clients. After a while, my bosses noted that and sought me out by giving me the cases other associates struggled with."

I took another sip of wine and could see I had his undivided attention.

"I was handed a case where a mother was suing the NYPD for the wrongful homicide of her son. She and I became very close. He was the only family she had, and the loss she suffered through his death would break most people. But she was adamant to fight and so was I. The officer was found guilty of homicide, and she was rewarded eighteen million dollars in damages. The settlement was so high due to the lengths the officer had gone to in covering up his crime. Sadly, just a few months after we won the case, she died of a stroke. I was the only person who attended her funeral. There, I was told that she had left everything in her will to me."

"You really must have meant something to her."

I could feel my lip tremble, and taking a deep breath, I had to look up to the ceiling as my eyes began to water. I tried not to well up as I often did when explaining that story. I didn't want to do that in front of him.

"As you can imagine, I didn't know what to do with that money. At first, I considered giving it to charity, but then I thought about helping my father out and giving him the choice to retire early. To which he straight up shut me down. My bosses at G&S also had many ideas, but how they discussed it, with no regard for where it came from, made me realize I could no longer work for them. They were a typical large legal machine—case after case through the door, with no afterthought. I decided to use the money as capital to set up my firm. I used it to hire and train other lawyers who didn't just want a job but wanted to make a difference. So now, even though we practice general law, we specialize and take an interest in cases that other firms would class as too much hassle."

"So, you fight for the underdog?"

"I guess, in a way, you could say that."

I was also lucky as some of the clients I had worked with previously only wanted to work with me, so they broke their contracts with G&S and signed on with me.

"So why take us on as clients? We don't fit the bill of your ethos."

"You're right, your company doesn't. But the apartment owners and tenants do. And I want to be able to deliver what your company wants while also making sure the residents get the best deal they can."

"I admire you. To do what you've done and continue to do

takes a strong, hardworking person. Many people would have taken the money and lived a life of leisure and luxury. Yet instead, you work twice as hard and with more drive than anyone I have ever met."

I couldn't help but blush. I guess he really did understand why I did what I did.

Chapter 15

Serena

Ever so softly, his fingertips ran across my shoulder and neck. The simple touch at the soft spot of my neck sent tremors through my whole body. I could feel my nipples peak.

Slowly, I turned towards him, wanting to savor every moment. Trying to go in softly and keep my composure, I leaned in, but as soon as my lips touched his, I felt wild with the need for him to have him touch every inch of my skin.

Eagerly, I began rubbing my body against his. My breasts felt full and heavy and my nipples ached as they rubbed against my satin bra. I could feel my panties getting wetter by the second. I continued pressing against his erection, prolonging the ever-increasing pleasure that seemed to forever emanate with every encounter I had with this man.

With one hand, he held my head in place. The other ran over the lace of my dress until he reached my ass. He dug his fingers in and kept me against him, allowing me to rub our bodies together gently.

I was about to lay myself fully on him when he lifted me,

carrying me away from the sofa into his bedroom. He made sure not to break our kiss. I wrapped my legs around him, causing my dress to ride up, exposing my ass.

Untangling my legs from his waist, he gently lowered me to the ground. I could feel his fingers deftly begin to unzip my dress. Once he fully unzipped me, I stepped back.

His eyes were a dark, stormy blue. After he had taken off his shoes and socks, I led him to the wing-back chair in front of his king-size bed, gently pushing him down until he was seated. Taking my time, I did a striptease for him.

I wanted to make sure he was as turned on as I was. As my dress pooled at my feet, he let out a primal grunt. I glided my fingers across my silk and lace bralette down to the matching silk thong.

Sliding my hands behind my back, I unfastened the hooks and slipped the straps down. My breasts spring free and hang heavy with my desire.

Leaning forward, he pulled me closer and began nipping along my hip and across my stomach. His fingers slid along the thin silk of my panties, and he delicately pulled them down. As I stood there in my nude heels, I began to massage and toy first with my right breast, then my left.

His eyes never broke contact with mine.

Running my hands along his shoulders until I reached his collar, I unbuttoned his shirt. I could feel myself picking up the tempo and my need to be filled by him growing higher and higher.

Pushing his shirt off his shoulders, I got down on my knees and kissed his chest, working my way down to his slacks. As soon as I unbuckled his belt and opened his slacks, his hard cock sprang free through his briefs. Lifting his hips, he helped me pull both his briefs and slacks off at once. His erection was swollen, thick, and ready.

Sliding myself between his thighs, I rubbed my breasts against his cock, and then, as I took him between my lips, he let out a hiss of pleasure.

It took some adjusting to fit him in my mouth comfortably and get into a good rhythm of licking and sucking, working both my mouth and hands. Tasting his pre-cum surged me on. I picked up my pace, savoring the taste of him along with the groans of pleasure that escaped his lips.

Suddenly, he pulled me back by my shoulders.

"Stop. I can't come yet. It's my turn to taste you now."

Once again, he was lifting me, but instead of putting me on the bed, he placed me on the glass table in the corner.

The coldness of the glass against my burning-hot skin almost made me scream. This time, he kneeled as he spread my legs wide open. His lips licked and parted my folds. I was already soaking wet for him.

One hand kneaded my breast, the other gently rubbed circles over my clit before sliding first one and then two fingers in.

I could feel my orgasm build and could no longer control the moans and cries of pleasure escaping me. He slipped in another finger, rubbing just that right spot and making me feel complete. His lips kissed and bit my inner thigh as his fingers worked to their own rhythm.

"You. Taste. So. Sweet. It. Is. True. What. They. Say. The. Darker. The. Berry. The. Sweeter. The. Juice."

He kissed me between every word.

My legs began to shake as waves of pleasure rushed through me. When I thought I couldn't take anymore, my body exploded into a million pieces.

My eyes squeezed so tight they began to hurt.

"I love the feel of you squeezing my fingers tight as you come."

My head sagged back as my body recovered from that mind-blowing orgasm.

"And I'm only getting started."

It's almost an evil promise. And I knew he meant every word.

He kissed his way up my body as he got to his feet.

My nipples felt sensitive as he grazed over them with his teeth. As he brought my mouth to him, I could taste my arousal on his tongue.

After sheathing himself with a condom, I felt him rubbing his cock along my wet cleft, lubricating himself.

Inch by inch, he pushed into me before finally burying himself to the hilt. Once fully in, he waited a moment, allowing me to stretch and accommodate him.

Starting with slow thrusts, he rocked into me. Urging him on, I didn't want him to go slow.

"Harder... yes..."

That was all the direction he needed before he fucked me hard and deep.

Our bodies grew slick with sweat. Once again, I felt the pressure building within. He was perfectly attuned to my body. The angle he was taking me perfectly rubbed against my G-Spot. I could do nothing more but hold on to his muscular, supple arms as I came once again screaming, knowing nobody could hear.

Still riding through my climax, I wasn't aware that he lifted me, never breaking contact, still driving into me. I could feel the soft cotton of his sheets beneath me.

Draping one leg over his shoulder, he continued what now felt like leisurely torment.

As one orgasm rolled into another, my head became awash with pure pleasure.

His thrusts got more brutal, and I could feel he was near his own release.

Taking one nipple in his mouth, he sank deeper into me.

At the precipice of pleasure and pain, he buried himself balls deep and groaned deep from his chest as he came.

My whole body felt numb. I winced as Rhett gently eased himself out of me.

I knew I'd feel it tomorrow.

His mouth captured mine, and his kiss was a complete contradiction to the rough, raw passion he'd just given me. It felt soothing and warm as our bodies were coming down from the spiral of pleasure we had just experienced. His hands softly caressed my skin.

"You are the most beautiful woman I have ever met."

My mind, still scattered with senses and emotion, needed to lighten the mood.

"You're not too bad yourself."

His shy laugh made me feel closer to him than ever. Our bodies were wrapped and tangled with one another. Reaching down, he pulled the sheet over us and kissed me once again.

After a few minutes, his limbs became heavier, his breathing slower, and I knew he'd drifted into a deep sleep.

Looking at his gorgeous face, I felt unbelievably happy and content.

I enjoyed my time with Rhett. As my body gave into fatigue, it was with a cloudy head. Where did I want things to lead with him? Did I risk allowing myself to enjoy this? I could feel myself becoming addicted to this man.

Chapter 16

Rhett

I was pile-driving through work like it was going out of fashion. My body vibrated, full of energy as if I could conquer the world.

For the first time, I felt a genuine sense of freedom in God knew how long.

I stayed focused, especially during meetings. I knew it wouldn't do any good walking around with a smile plastered across my face, especially as most staff were now aware of my father's condition.

I didn't need anyone to think I was happy about my family's heartbreak. But I could honestly say that if it hadn't been for Serena, God knew how I would get through everything now.

She was like a beacon of hope for me. After the night at my place, I thought I wouldn't be able to have a day go by without seeing her.

Sadly, our busy schedules often made meeting up a next-to-impossible task. We did manage to fit in an impromptu lunch mid-week.

I remembered watching how her hips swayed as she entered the restaurant. Unbeknownst to her, every man in the room was checking her out. That's what made her even more attractive. She was not aware of just how beautiful and sexy she was.

Most other women I knew used their looks to their advantage and often as a weapon. But their beauty quickly faded. On the other hand, Serena went about her day, unaware of the attention she drew. Lucky for me, I was not only able to admire her from afar, but I got to devour her.

As we said our goodbyes at the restaurant, we both had to restrain ourselves. It turned me on knowing she wanted me as much as I did her.

At various points in the day, I thought back on the night she had come over. The feel and taste of her. The sweet way her body responded perfectly to mine.

Those thoughts required me to prolong one or two meetings when my dick was too hard, thinking about her on her knees, spread open for me, on my bed. But it wasn't just how much I was physically attracted to her. It was also how she made me feel.

How comfortable I felt opening up to her and talking about everything and anything. I had spoken more to her than anyone else ever in my life, at least on a personal level.

Something about her made me want to try new things. I found myself eager to impress her—something I didn't think I had done since college.

Somehow, I managed to control myself and got through the next four meetings I had. At the end of the last one, I found Charlotte patiently waiting outside. My final meeting had run over, and I knew she was meant to have finished almost an hour ago.

"Is everything okay?"

I suddenly worried there might be something about my father.

"No, sir, everything is fine. Ms. Parker called while you were in your meeting and asked if you could call her back. And I wanted to ensure you got the message, as I know you sometimes leave without returning to your office."

She was a Godsend of a PA.

"Thank you, Charlotte. Here go and enjoy a drink, you deserve it."

I handed her a hundred dollar bill, and before she could protest, as I knew she always tried to, I eagerly returned to my office.

Grabbing my cell, I pulled up Serena's number, and luckily, she answered on the second ring.

"Hey, have I caught you at an inconvenient time?"

"No, I'm just picking up some groceries. I tried to call earlier, but Charlotte said you were in a meeting. I wanted to ask if you had any plans for Saturday during the daytime?"

I quickly skimmed through my calendar and saw that I was meant to have a round of golf with some of my business associates, but I knew they wouldn't mind me canceling rather than taking an ass-whooping through eighteen.

"Nothing important. So, what would you like to do with me?"

I tried my best to leave the double meaning hanging in the air. If only she could see the thoughts going through my head.

She let out a small laugh.

"How would you like to join me at the Sunningdale Car Show? I usually go with my dad every year, but he can't make it. I thought to myself, who else do I know that appreciates great cars, tasty food, and great company?"

My girl had good taste. The Sunningdale Car Show was amazing. Not only was it an excellent place for car enthusiasts to view and show off their cars, but they also had a silent auction, which I usually monitored online.

Another date with Serena and the possibility of finding something to add to my collection. How could I say no?

"Sounds great. What time shall I come and get you?"

"It starts at midday, so shall we say ten?"

"Perfect. I look forward to seeing you then."

"I'll be ready at ten sharp."

I couldn't help but laugh as she used my words against me again.

Saturday came around in no time. I'd decided on having Russell drive us there first because I wasn't sure if we were going to be drinking but also because there was a chance I'd be making a purchase.

When we picked her up, she said she was surprised I wasn't bringing one of my cars. Little did she know I was more than content with her on my arm and every man dying with envy, showing her off.

By the time we arrived, the show was well underway.

There was every car you could wish for, from a vintage Sunbeam 30 HP 90 Tourer to every Ferrari and Aston Martin from the early 1960s.

I bumped into a few family friends and business associates but only spent the required time making pleasantries without seeming rude.

I was somewhat taken aback when we bumped into an old friend of my grandfather's, Mr. Fitzgerald. He had been my grandfather's best friend, lawyer, confidant, and go-to guy. He greeted us both and briefly reiterated his sorrows as he had not long learned of my father's deteriorating health.

His wife extended a warm welcome to me but outright blanked Serena. I didn't know if she fully clocked onto it or put her down as being a grumpy old lady. But her behavior got my back up.

Serena excused herself as she had just seen a family friend. I was about to do the same when Mrs. Fitzgerald's dainty arms rested on mine.

"I am sorry to hear about your father. As you know, we have known him since he was an infant. We see him as one of the family. Our families have always been close."

She paused and then looked me square in the eye. "That is why I feel the need to express my concerns."

"Your concerns about what exactly?"

"I know you're a young man, and I'm sure you have a flurry of women desperate to land a ring on their finger. But as I'm sure your mother taught you, don't let yourself be swayed by the wrong kind of woman."

"I beg your pardon?"

I wasn't sure how I managed to hide and keep my voice down.

"I can appreciate that she is an attractive young lady, but surely you can see that families such as yours that have strong, long lineages in our society must maintain certain standards."

I couldn't believe what I heard. What century does this woman live in? It took every ounce of my patience to rein in my growing temper.

How dare she?

"I appreciate your concerns, but I can assure you Serena is a remarkably successful attorney of law with impeccable grace and standards. Many would say I do not live up to her moral standards. After all, as you said, I was a free and single man for quite some time and did a lot you would disapprove of," I condemned.

"But she isn't one of us," she snapped.

"You mean she isn't white?"

There was no way for me to control my anger anymore. I pulled my arm away from the woman I now utterly detested. Her husband did his best efforts to make amends.

"Rhett, I'm sure you've misunderstood what my wife is trying to say."

His pleading tone did nothing to calm me. Mrs. Fitzgerald turned her nose up and looked away, despite clearly wanting to say more.

"I think what she meant to say was we see you as family, son. And we wouldn't want to see you taken advantage of."

Despite being a man I grew up with, seeing him as almost a surrogate grandfather figure, and having always admired him, I now pitied him.

"As I have already told your wife, Serena is a very accomplished and successful woman. She has built up her law firm, which, to your surprise, we hired out, as our legal team was insufficient in doing the job themselves."

With my blood at boiling level, I turned my full attention to the vile woman.

"I want to make myself very clear. Who I see or have a relationship with is of no concern of yours."

"Your mother can't be too happy about this."

Anger blinded me even more at the mention of my mother.

"My mother has no say in who I share my bed, time, or feelings with."

I turned to Mr. Fitzgerald, gave him a slight nod, and looked for Serena.

I couldn't believe what had happened as I passed through the crowds. Despite how wrong those prejudices were, I might not be as surprised if we lived in the 1800s. The world had changed. It was a fucking joke that people dared to still have those opinions.

How was this even a topic of conversation? I was so glad Serena wasn't around to hear the terrible things from that woman's mouth.

As I searched through the crowds of people, I didn't want to let what happened ruin my day.

By the time I found her talking to the owner of a beautiful 1964 Ferrari 250 GT Lusso in the main tent, I'd managed to get control of my emotions.

"There you are," she said. "I was about to send out a search party."

I took her head between my hands and kissed her, needing to connect with her again.

"Sorry, I got caught up talking to an old family acquaintance. Did you catch up with the person you spotted?"

"Yeah, it was my dad's best friend. We usually bump into him here as well every year. I explained why Dad couldn't make it, and he told me how he'd brought his current girlfriend here to show her a fun day. Unlucky for him, she's not too keen on cars. He's been keeping her drink topped up instead."

She covered her mouth as she laughed.

"Well, I guess I'm just the lucky guy whose date isn't only sensationally beautiful but probably knows more about cars than I do."

I took her hand and felt as she looked down at the gesture of it. We returned to the gentleman she had been talking with, and he gushed at Serena's knowledge of this car.

A slight blush crept across her face, and she said, "It's my favorite car. I've always loved it. I remember the first time I saw one. It was at a car show I went to in Chicago, and I instantly fell in love. I was only nineteen, but I knew I would own one, one day."

I was somewhat taken aback.

"Why haven't you gotten one yet? I know you could afford it."

"A car like this can't just sit in a garage. It must be properly looked after, driven, and enjoyed on the open road. You know how busy my schedule is. Unlike you, I'd struggle to have my dream car sat somewhere without being regularly driven by me."

She gave me her devilish grin. She was right. It also gave me an idea.

We said our thanks to the gentleman and continued to look around. I was on my fourth drink now. I managed to nurse one for the first hour we were there. But after that encounter, I knew I had to seek refuge in alcohol.

Serena looked terrific. Which was not helping me in any way deal with my lust for her. She wore a lilac dress that wrapped around her body, seamlessly melting onto her gorgeous curves. She wore wedges and had her hair down in long, flowing curls. She looked like the ultimate mix of her two worlds.

The dress was elegant enough to wear in a meeting, but I loved that she wore her hair naturally.

Walking hand in hand, we went to where the auction was held. I got her to find us some seats and excused myself under the pretense of needing to make a call.

Hurriedly, I put my plan into motion. I couldn't wait to see the look on her face.

I made it back just in time.

Car after car got sold. As the auction went on, the price of each lot increased, and so did the atmosphere in the tent.

"So, are you planning on making any purchases today?" she whispered.

"You'll just have to wait and see. I like a few lots here, but I'll see how it goes."

There were only a handful of cars left to auction off. They announced the next lot, and it was the Ferrari Lusso.

I watched as she subtly leaned forward, looking around and watching the bidding progress.

I listened as the auctioneer boomed through the mic.

"Commission bid is currently at fifty thousand. Do I hear seventy?"

A gentleman behind us bid.

I watched as Serena looked at him and tutted her disapproval. He had an oversized fur coat on despite it still being late summer. He had a cigar in one hand and a glass of some dark spirit in the other. Next to him stood a woman who looked no older than eighteen. Peroxide blonde hair. Fake tits hung out of her dress as she smirked and batted her eyelashes at every man who looked her way.

"See, this is the thing I hate about these auctions. You have people who love and understand cars that buy works of art like that car. Then you have others who will buy anything with a large price tag. To show off that they can."

I knew she didn't mean the statement about myself, but I couldn't help feeling slightly guilty for having done such things in the past.

"Commission against you, sir, at eighty thousand. Do I see a hundred?"

The man behind us shouted, "Yeah, I got a hundred."

Everyone was becoming entertained and started paying attention. Finally, the bidding went to a hundred and fifty. And it seemed the gentlemen had admitted defeat. The car finally sold on a commission bid for a hundred and fifty.

Serena turned to me.

"I'm glad someone outbid him. I hope they appreciate it."

We waited and watched the final two lots be seized up.

As the auction concluded, and we were making our way out of the tent, she said she wanted us to go to the stands by the track as there would be a race of some vintage race cars.

"We'll go in just a minute. I want to show you something quickly."

I grabbed her hand and returned to the temporary sales desk they put up.

As we started walking in that direction, the auctioneer spotted me and immediately made his way over.

"Congratulations on your bid, Mr. Chambers. The paperwork is being sorted out as we speak. Do you wish to have the car delivered, or would you like to drive it from here?"

I watched her brow crease in confusion. And couldn't help but laugh.

"Please be sure they have the ownership papers and registration made out to Serena Parker. As the car is for her."

I heard as she coughed on the sip of the drink she had just taken.

"Wait, what?"

"Excellent, sir. I'll have everything drawn up for you at once. I'll be sure to have everything ready for when you leave."

The auctioneer shook both our hands and left us.

I turned and saw she still hadn't moved a muscle.

"So, do you like it?"

"You just spent a hundred and fifty thousand dollars on a car? A car that you want me to have? Why?"

Her eyes were wide with alarm, and I watched as her chest rose and fell faster with each breath.

"Well, first, I thought you'd just say thanks and might feel obliged to show your gratitude somehow. I would greatly accept."

I laughed as my eyes raked down her body.

"I... I... I don't understand why?"

"Seeing how much you loved and appreciated this car, I couldn't help myself. Besides, the cost isn't an issue. If there had been one I wanted and there had been a bidding war, I still would have made sure I won. No matter the cost. Don't you like it?"

"I do. I love it. I can't quite believe it."

She looked deep into my eyes. I wasn't sure exactly what she was looking for, but I could only smile.

I wanted her to have this car. I knew it would mean a lot to her. And I wanted to be the one giving it to her. I wasn't trying to buy her affection—quite the opposite. I knew Serena couldn't be bought. It was one of the many things I cared and appreciated about her.

The more I got to know her and the more she let me share and experience her life—the more I could see just how selfless she was. She continuously put others' wants and needs above her own. Whether it be the cases she was working on, her family, friends, or even strangers who passed her on the street.

It wasn't something I was told to do. It was something I wanted to do. I knew it would make her happy, and as each day passed, that was becoming a greater pull of what I wanted to do.

She must have found whatever it was she was looking for as she suddenly lunged at me, wrapped her arms around my neck, and kissed me deeply. Her kiss was neither soft nor gentle. Our mouths crashed together. Her tongue massaged mine, hands through my hair, tugging and pulling me deeper in. Feeling her soft breasts rub against my chest, and her hips sway and rock against me, I felt myself getting hard.

Reluctantly, I broke the kiss.

"If you carry on rubbing your body against me like this, I

can't guarantee I'm going to be able to stop once I start. And I don't care that people surround us."

"I don't think I care either. Let's get out of here."

I wasn't going to protest.

We made our way to the collections area. Once we collected the paperwork and keys, a staff member showed us where to collect the car.

I handed the keys to Serena.

"Like I said, the car is yours. Plus, you're still within the legal limit. Looks like you're finally going to be able to take her on the open road."

Once again, she granted me another delicious kiss. This time, she stopped before things started heating up once again.

Chapter 17

Rhett

Sitting in the passenger seat and watching Serena drive with such ease again fueled my desire for her.

We went the same route back to the city, with mile upon mile of open road for her to drive this baby. When she turned down a long dirt road, I wondered if she was lost and had taken the wrong turn.

Not wanting to distract her, I stayed quiet. She pulled the car up and cut the engine. We were in the middle of nowhere. All I could see was an abandoned farmhouse in the distance.

"Don't tell me you've brought me here to kill me?" I joked.

"No, I've brought you here to say thank you. And to fuck you on the hood of my new car."

Her eyes narrowed. Her lips formed a sexy, seductive pout.

I followed as she stepped out. The sun began to set, and the sky was awash with red and orange hues. She climbed onto the car's hood and gently pulled her dress up. Pulling on my belt, she brought me between her legs.

I watched as she unfastened the buckle and then deftly unbuttoned my jeans. I knew it would have been hotter to watch her take her time, but my body couldn't wait any longer. I pulled down my jeans and briefs in one swift motion. Reaching down, I ran my fingers along her panties, feeling how wet she already was.

Not caring about being a gentleman, I ripped her panties off, carelessly discarding them on the grass. I watched her as she ran her hand across her chest, sensually inviting and teasing me. Wildness brewed beneath the gentleness. My eyes completely and utterly focused on her every move, not wanting to miss a second.

Needing to get my fill of her, I didn't waste any time with foreplay. Her pussy was wet, and her arousal was dripping down her thighs. In one swift move, I was buried deep inside her.

Her eyes rolled to the back of her head, gasping and moaning my name.

Having her in this position gave me significant leverage and allowed me to see every part of her.

Looking into her eyes, the hunger I saw within caused me to increase my pace. The sound of my hips hitting her ass every time I pounded deep inside her echoed all around us.

Pulling my mouth down to hers, she kissed me as if her life depended on it. She bit down on my lip, teasing my tongue with every touch and swirl of hers.

I needed more.

I wanted more.

I needed her to scream at the top of her lungs. Sex with Serena was electric. Every inch and fiber of my body felt like it was on fire for her.

Lifting one knee onto the car, I slid up her body, bringing us closer together while staying balanced. Freeing her breasts out of her bra, I take a straining nipple into my mouth, whirling my tongue around, biting down as I increase the tempo of each thrust. I was teasing and caressing the other between my fingers. Then her pussy began to tighten and squeezed my cock.

Knowing she was on the edge of coming, I moved over, paying attention to her other breast.

This time, I increased the pressure, and my body surged into hers, and she let out a guttural scream as she came. She was clenching me like a fist, bringing me to the precipice of my own release. I bit down on her nipple harder. Tingles ricocheted down my spine as my cum exploded inside her.

I feel utterly euphoric.

Her in that field, at that moment, still being inside her, kissing her full juicy lips, I knew I had found utter bliss. Gently easing myself out of her, I put my jeans back on, retrieved a tissue from my back pocket, and handed it to her. Then, I took her hand and helped her off the car.

"You may have tempted me to buy you something every day just to get that kind of thank you again."

Kissing the corner of her mouth, I walked her to the driver's side door.

"As much as I'm still in both awe and shock by your amazing and thoughtful gift, I never want you to feel like you ever have to buy me anything."

Peering over, I was surprised and confused to see her face swimming with uncertainty. I thought she was happy about the car.

"I'm confused. I thought you were happy about the car. I thought it was a nice surprise."

Turning, she grabbed my hands, her eyes darting between mine.

"Of course, I'm happy. It's amazing. I just... I guess I'm a little overwhelmed. It took me by surprise. And a part of me doesn't understand why."

"What do you mean why?"

"Why did you get me the car?"

"Because I wanted to."

"Rhett, this isn't dinner, or a cake or a book. This is an expensive car!"

I didn't understand why her face was full of anguish. There was a sadness in her eyes that I couldn't understand.

"So? I don't understand why you are making it into a big deal. I knew you would like it and wanted to buy it for you. It's as simple as that."

A heaviness that hadn't been present suddenly filled the space around us, and Serena turned her head, gazing out of the windshield, avoiding looking at me.

What the fuck was going on? With my thumb and index finger, I gently pulled her chin back, lifting it slightly so I could see her. Her eyes looked muted, almost haunted, and I couldn't fathom what had caused such a change in events.

"Please talk to me. Tell me what's wrong. I thought I was doing something good. Something to make you happy?"

"You are. You have."

I watched her as she took a deep breath and closed her eyes. When she opened them again, a slow smile crept across her face, and she leaned forward, kissing me softly. Then, resting her head against mine, our noses softly rubbing against one another, I listened as she spoke just above a whisper.

"I'm sorry, I really am grateful. It just really overwhelmed me and I panicked. I thought maybe you were sending some hidden message or something. My mind went back to what happened at college and how carelessly money had been thrown around to cover things up. I started to panic—waiting for you to tell me... I don't know that this was a parting gift. Or like you were trying to buy something from me."

Shaking my head to refute this, so leaned forward and kissed me again before pulling back and continuing.

"I'm sorry, Rhett. I know you weren't trying to do that. Please don't let my insecurities spoil the amazing things you've done for me. I'm so so sorry. I didn't mean to spoil our day."

"You didn't."

She stared straight into my eyes, and for the first time, I had to work hard at hiding how much her words hurt me.

She didn't seem to notice my inner turmoil and wrapped her arms around me, squeezing me tightly.

"I'm sorry," she whispered, peppering kisses along my neck.

I knew she meant it.

But that didn't help silence the fact that she had thought of me in the same regard, dammit, in the same bracket as those assholes and what they had done. Even if it was only for a split second. I was nothing like them, and I thought she knew that.

Soon enough, we're back driving on the freeway. Neither she nor I had spoken for some time. I suspected, on her part, it had more to do with her driving her dream car.

But I couldn't get Mrs. Fitzgerald's words out of my head. Nor the fact that Serena had worried that I had an ulterior motive. I was sure the Fitzgeralds were at the auction, and it wouldn't surprise me if they found out I had bought a car, probably even found out I gifted it to Serena. I could only imagine the face that they would have pulled. Allowing herself to believe her statements were correct.

That was what bothered me. Serena didn't ask me for it. She hadn't asked me for anything besides going there on this date. Unlike other times when I had bought things for women to either get laid or as a farewell gift so I could move on to the next woman, there was never any thought behind it.

Things were different with Serena. I knew she could have afforded the car herself. I knew she was someone that couldn't be bought. I know she wasn't drawn to me because of my money.

In some ways, I thought she'd prefer if I didn't have the money, the name, and everything most other women eagerly wanted from me.

I bought that car for her because I wanted her to know I understood what it meant to her and that my physical need and desire for her didn't just blind me. That I both listened to and respected her.

As we got closer to the city, she broke the silence by rolling off various stats and details about the car. I couldn't help but smile. Nor could I help by being turned on by her once again. We continued talking the rest of the way back.

She dropped me off at home after grabbing a bite to eat at a fantastic little hole-in-the-wall tapas restaurant she knew. I didn't offer for her to come up, as I wanted the offer to be made by her.

Plus, I didn't want her to feel she was in any way obliged, especially not today. It felt weird having her drop me off and kiss me goodnight.

But I was beginning to get the feeling that things with her would always be more complex than I would expect them. And for the first time, that was a thought I very much liked.

The following week flew by in a blur. Wednesday night, I went round to Serena's for dinner. Her apartment was different from what I had expected. She had lofty ceilings, and the layout, although also open plan, had raw wooden beams running through it, which gave it a modern and rustic edge.

For dinner, she'd cooked up a Bajan feast. She was a fantastic cook. We talked about cars, work, sports, and everything in between. I had come straight from the office, so I was still in my suit.

Taking our glasses to her couch, we discussed the various places we had traveled worldwide. I could sense she was becoming a little restless, and I wasn't sure if it was the wine or something else. But it was making me wonder what was bothering her.

"Is everything okay? You seem like something's bothering you."

Taking another sip of wine, I waited for her response.

"Well, I have two things I need to ask you."

My mouth went dry, so I hastily took another sip.

"Go on."

"My aunt and uncle are having their annual BBQ this Sunday. I was wondering if you would like to come. I understand if you're too busy or have other plans. I don't want to be taking up all your free time, I know you're a busy man."

I let out a small breath of relief.

Why was Serena so nervous about asking me this? Did she think I wouldn't want to go? Or was she worried about how her family would act upon meeting me?

I knew I could be stern and maybe, at times, a bit moody, but that rarely happened in my social life. I usually kept those feelings at work.

"I would love to come. That is only if you genuinely want me there?"

"Of course. Why would you say that?"

"You just seemed a little cautious when asking."

"I guess it's just a girl thing. I don't want to come across as needy or demanding."

"The only time you are either needy or demanding is when we fuck. And I have no problem with that."

I leaned over and kissed her. I could taste the wine on her lips.

"And what was number two?"

"Excuse me?"

"You said there were two things you wanted to ask me?"

"Oh, yes. I wanted to know if you wanted to stay the night. It's getting late, and I don't want you to be tired at work tomorrow."

I would have taken her words more seriously had she not mounted me as soon as she said them.

"I will be getting less sleep staying here than I would if I were to leave," I said as I began kissing down the column of her throat.

And this time, I showed my gratitude as I flipped her on her back and had my way with her on the couch.

After that, we showered together before going to bed for round two. This time, it was her time to have her way with me. And boy, was I one lucky guy.

Russell had dropped us off at her aunt's house about an hour ago, and I wasn't going to lie. I did start feeling a little nervous the closer we got. But as soon as we arrived, I couldn't believe how warm and welcoming everyone had been.

Well, almost everyone.

There were tables filled with delicious food that had my mouth watering the second we stepped foot out there.

It took us about twenty minutes to go around as I was introduced to everyone. And I was trying my hardest to remember everybody's names.

I also hadn't spoken about such a range of topics in such a short period of time.

Her Uncle Dane was telling me some impressive stories from his annual fishing trips in Barbados. Then, her cousin Lewis joined us, who's over in the States on holiday as he lived in the UK. He was a mechanic for Maclaren.

I tried to catch a race whenever I had to head over to Europe for work, and Serena burst out laughing when I told her that I got my PA to try to coincide my business meetings with the racing calendar.

She hadn't left my side since the moment we arrived, and I knew at first it was her way of easing me in, but the longer we were there and the more I relaxed, her touch changed from one of comfort to both of us simply wanting to always stay connected.

As this was the first time I was meeting her family, I made sure to remember to keep everything PG, but I didn't miss any chance I had to kiss her shoulder or feel the goosebumps on her skin as I ran soft ghostlike touches across her bare skin.

She did get me back whenever she bit down on her lower lip, a movement that always sent all the blood rushing straight to my cock. And with the smirks she gave me after, she knew exactly what she was doing.

But I can honestly say this was turning out to be one of the most relaxing and enjoyable get-togethers I had ever gone to.

Looking over the garden, I found Serena's brother, Roman, deep in conversation with the guy Serena had introduced me to as Antony, their cousin, and the son of our hosts. Just as I went to take a sip of my beer, both looked up and slowly made their way over.

"Serena, Mom asked if you can quickly help her with something."

Anthony preened.

"And why can't you help?"

I watched in amusement as she glowered at her cousin, both standing in some silent deadlock.

I gently rubbed the back of her arm, and she glanced over. We both knew her brother and cousin had come over to say something—to me, at least, and I knew I'd be okay with whatever was sent my way. So, I gave her a slight nod, my eyes softening, letting her know I'd be all right.

Lifting onto her tiptoes, she gave me a quick kiss on the cheek before huffing and walking toward the patio doors.

After about a couple of seconds of both guys staring me down. Roman broke the silence.

"I'm not going to beat around the bush. My sister means the world to me. She's been through a lot. I know she seems tough and strong to most—and she is those things, but she's also got a gentle heart. So, if you fuck her over, I will come after you."

Their cousin Anthony grunted in agreement.

Now, I was not going to lie to myself, the guy had a serious physical presence. At a guess, I'd say he's about three inches off my six-three, but he still maintained a strong football build.

"I understand and respect that."

I'd always felt the same way with both my sisters. Even after Kara got married to Austin, I still reminded him that should he ever hurt or seriously upset her, I would kill him.

I reached out my hand to shake his. He eyed it for a split second before shaking mine, and I didn't miss how he smirked and tightened his grip slightly.

Then Anthony reached his hand out, not wanting to miss out on the action.

"So, now that we've put that to rest, I gotta say I was impressed when Serena sent me the pictures of the Lusso you bought her. I know how much she'd always loved that car. It must have cost a pretty penny," Roman said.

"It was worth every cent. Just wait till you see her drive it."

Even I could hear the pride in my voice. And as I watched Roman's face light up, I knew he did too.

"Well, as you seem to like giving generous gifts, I just thought I'd give you the heads-up that it's my birthday in a couple of weeks."

Anthony beamed.

I couldn't help but laugh as Roman rolled his eyes and punched him in the arm.

"What? I'm just saying. Now that he's been welcomed into the family, he should know the most important days of the year."

Anthony groaned.

Roman continued shaking his head, but my mind was still focused on the word *family*. As I continued to roll the words over in my head, I realized how much I enjoyed the sound of that.

We were interrupted by the arrival of Serena and her Aunt Sylvie, who came loaded with even more food. And when she introduced me to her, I was pulled down into a great big hug, and my eyes bulged when I felt her hand going perilously close to my ass.

"Well, aren't you a handsome piece of white chocolate? I'm so happy Serena has finally met someone and with such big and strong shoulders too!"

I was momentarily lost for words, and as I caught Serena's eyes, I wasn't sure who was blushing more, her or myself.

"It's a pleasure to meet you, Sylvie."

I managed to detangle myself gently and saw Anthony bent over laughing and Roman trying but failing to hide his own laugh.

Serena grabbed my hand and hastily led me away.

"Jesus, I am so sorry about her. I swear the woman has no filter."

Wrapping my arms around her, I gave her a squeeze, and she finally looked up at me.

I bent down to whisper in her ear.

"I have to say I've never been called white chocolate before, but I think I like it."

The way her face lit up as she laughed was one of the most beautiful things I've ever seen. The smile on my face was genuine and relaxed, and I couldn't believe how utterly different this was from any get-together my family had ever had. Her uncle and aunt went all out. The spread of food could easily have fed a small army.

I spoke with her father about cars and Serena's work. He also mentioned the car I had gifted to her. I was surprised when he, too, thanked me for buying something that meant so much to her.

Her sister, Olivia, was the opposite of Serena. She was much more stern and always found something to tell her poor husband Calvin off about. But I could see it was just their playful banter, as the way they looked into each other's eyes, it was clear they loved one another.

I also ended up becoming a human climbing tree for her two nieces. They seemed interested in making me their token pet horse, barking orders at me and climbing on my back, sending me round and around in circles. I didn't mind, I always loved seeing my nephew, Kai, and playing with him.

On the few occasions we got a few moments to ourselves, we struggled to keep our hands off one another. But as always with Serena, every look, every touch, and every whispered word seemed to hit so much deeper.

It was almost seven by the time we left, and I could honestly say I had had a wonderful time. And as soon as we got into the car, I took full advantage of the privacy window, which allowed me to have my fill of her as Russell drove us back.

It was the day after the BBQ, and I was out having dinner with my father, Julian, and Carter Rutledge, my father's best friend. Where it was only the four of us, I decided now was as a good a time as any to tell them about my relationship with Serena.

"Hold on. Have you been seeing her this whole time? What about Verity?"

My brother always had to throw a spanner in the works.

"Nothing is going on with Verity and there never will be," I retorted.

I finished off my bourbon and called the waiter over for another.

I was half expecting my brother to make another stupid remark, but it was my father who spoke.

"I already know."

"Excuse me?"

My head snapped back so quickly that I was surprised it didn't roll right off.

"Rhett, I love you and your siblings dearly, and I know it can't be an easy time for the whole family now. But despite everything that is going on, for the past few weeks, I have seen you be even more in control of yourself. At work, you're always focused and hardworking, but you're never usually desperate to get out of the office, especially during the week. Like I said, I know you, son. Plus, I also got a phone call from Walter Fitzgerald a few weeks ago."

At simply the mention of the name, my anger began to creep up.

"And what did good old Walter have to say?"

"That is of no importance. The only thing that matters is whether she makes you happy."

The reverence and sincerity were evident on his face.

"She does."

I couldn't help but smile. And the smile my father gave me back let me know that whatever Walter said to him didn't matter. I knew I could rely on my father. That was what made the thought of losing him so much more heartbreaking.

Julian cleared his throat.

"Hold on a minute, surely there's something wrong with all this? She works for us."

"As if that's ever stopped you before, Julian."

Right now, Julian reminded me why I only associated with him because he was my flesh and blood.

"But surely, it's a bit convenient that she suddenly takes an interest in you when she begins working for us, finding out our net worth, then knowing you'll soon take over the family business. The words gold digger come to mind."

I shot up to my feet. My fists were clenched, ready to deck him.

"Rhett, please don't. For me. Please."

I searched my father's eyes, and I couldn't bring myself to cause him more stress and hurt than he must already be feeling.

"You, Julian, will apologize to your brother. And if I ever hear you utter one more ill word about Serena Parker, I assure you I will take it as a personal insult. So, choose your words wisely from now on."

Sitting back in my seat, I watched Julian polish off his glass and clink it with mine. He muttered the word sorry under his breath and he then ordered himself another.

"Julian, I don't know exactly how much time I've got left. I want to spend as much quality time with those I love and care about. I also need to know that things between the two of you will be okay once I pass. You seem happy with Ruby, and that brings me such joy. Don't you want Rhett to have the same happiness with Serena?"

"Whatever you wish, Father."

Julian didn't even have the decency to look at our father as he spoke. He was a pathetic excuse of a man. If it weren't for my dad, I'd have battered him to a pulp already.

The more my father spoke about his plans over the upcoming weeks and months, the larger the pit in my stomach grew. I was a grown man who understood what was happening. That didn't alleviate my fear of losing the man I always looked up to and saw as my hero.

Chapter 18

Serena

Work has been manic. I'd already had one court case, which the judge ended up adjourning, sat through two depositions, and was wrapping up a meeting with my associates.

Gathering my folder and papers from the meeting room, I wasn't concentrating when our receptionist suddenly appeared at my side.

"Sarah, you startled me there."

"Sorry, I thought you heard me knock."

"Not a problem, today has just been one of those days. So, what can I help you with?"

As I turned around to give her my full attention, I saw the large bouquet in one hand and a card in the other.

"These came for you. The courier gave specific instructions to make sure they were hand-delivered."

I returned my folder and papers to the desk and took the flowers and card from her. As I opened the card, I saw Sarah standing there hovering, eagerly wanting to see who they were from.

"Thank you, Sarah. That will be all."

I wasn't sure if she knew I heard her huff on her way out. She was a good receptionist and always did her job well. But I was also aware that she was one of the biggest gossips, she loved to know everybody's business.

Opening the envelope, I read the card inside.

Dear Serena,

I hope you like the flowers. I wasn't sure what your favorites were, so I picked those I felt best suited you.

I want to invite you to be my plus one at the Lexington Hospital's Annual Benefit Fundraiser on Thursday evening.

It's a black-tie charity ball, so there will be lots of food, wine, and donations.

Yours,

Rhett

X

A warm and fuzzy feeling enveloped me, and my pulse leaped with excitement. I hadn't even put the card back in the envelope before I was working out what I could wear.

I'd gone to a few fundraisers before, but never to one as big as I was sure this one would be. It really was sweet of him.

My thoughts were interrupted by the ring of my cell phone.

"Hey, Ruby. I was actually about to call you."

"Really? Must be sixth sense. I was calling to see if you wanted to check out this new barre class I keep hearing about. But now I'm more interested in what you wanted to talk about."

"Well, yes to checking out that class. That is depending on when you want to go. But I was going to call as I just got the biggest bouquet from Rhett along with an invitation to the Lexington Benefit."

There was a momentary pause followed by a squeal of laughter.

"Oh, that is one of the biggest fundraising events in the city. Literally, Vogue do a four-page spread on it every year."

"How on earth do you know these things?"

"Um, because I know everything. Seriously, Serena, surely you should know this after all these years of friendship."

Her teasing tone made my eyes roll.

"But seriously, it's actually one of the better functions. They raise a shit ton of money, there's full press on the red carpet, and fashion wise, it's almost as coveted as the Met Gala."

"So, in other words, a seriously big event? That's what you're telling me?"

Suddenly, my excitement turned to nerves as I took a seat at my desk.

"Yes, that's what I'm telling you."

I could hear the taps of her typing on a keyboard as she spoke.

"Also, apparently, Rhett hasn't brought a date with him for the past five years that he's attended."

"How on earth do you know that?"

"There's this thing called Google. You should try it."

Her cackle did nothing to calm me.

"So things must be getting serious if he's inviting you to this. How are things going with you guys?"

"Well..."

"Come on, I'm your best friend."

"Things are going good. We're spending most of our free time together. And you know that he bought me my dream car, and I filled you in on how the BBQ went, and I guess since that

Verity curve ball, things have been going well. Good. Things are good."

"First, don't even get me started on that bitch. And secondly, why do you keep saying good? That's so mundane. I can't imagine your boyfriend would enjoy hearing you describe your relationship as merely good?"

"I'm not exactly sure how else to describe it. We've been seeing each other for several weeks. He's met my family. I haven't met his, besides his father and brother, but that's in a work capacity."

"Ah, I see," she said.

"What do you mean you see?"

I anxiously waited for her to enlighten me on what apparently she could see that I couldn't.

"You're apprehensive about the relationship and don't want to admit your feelings because deep down you're still hurt about what happened during college. I'm sorry to tell you this, but you do this every time you start seeing a guy. You always compare, looking for every possible flaw. And it's understandable, given what you went through, but I can promise you now Rhett isn't like that douchebag. If he was, I would have told you. The fact that you haven't met his family isn't because he doesn't want you to. It's because, like you've told me, both of you have crazy work schedules."

"Wow, you're just laying it all out there, aren't you?"

"That's what best friends are for."

Leaning my head back, I took a deep breath, accepting that everything she had said was right.

I was scared.

I was scared of being hurt again and with how much I thought about Rhett and what he meant to me, the fear of being hurt by him terrified me.

"Listen, I love you, but you over-analyze everything. The

fact that he's inviting you to this fundraiser should show that he wants everyone to know you guys are together. Don't get caught up thinking about the past. Enjoy the present. And enjoy this fundraiser. So now tell me what you're gonna wear?"

I let her words soothe my trepidation, and I mentally started going through the potential dresses I could wear in my wardrobe, but nothing felt like it would be right.

"I have no idea. I think I need to buy something new. And I may need your help."

Ruby's cheers burst through the phone, and I laughed as she was a serious shopaholic.

"Okay, how about tomorrow after work? We'll do shopping followed by dinner?"

"That sounds perfect."

As we said our goodbyes, I remembered I hadn't yet responded to Rhett. With my phone still in my hand, I rushed out a text.

Thank you for my lovely flowers. They are beautiful. My receptionist was eager to know who they were from...Regarding your invitation, I would love to go with you. I am looking forward to Thursday. What time should I be ready? X

I left work early on Wednesday and met Ruby in Saks Fifth Avenue. Having spent most of the previous evening ransacking my wardrobe, looking for a dress. I was utterly annoyed that I couldn't find anything.

I needed the perfect dress, and I knew Ruby would be the best person to help me find it.

"Oh, my God, you look beautiful."

Ruby clasped her hands together when she saw the lovely Balmain gown I had on as I twirled in front of the three-way mirror outside the dressing room. Yet, I couldn't help but feel that the dress was too sexy.

"Rubs, I'm not sure."

"What do you mean? The dress is gorgeous and you look beautiful. What's wrong with this one?"

"Nothing's wrong with it. It's beautiful. But..."

"But what?"

I could feel her growing impatient.

"I don't think it's appropriate for a hospital gala."

"Oh, come on, I've been to loads of these kinds of events, and I've seen women in much less than that countless times."

"I know, I know, but I don't want people to judge. I'm nervous enough as it is going with Rhett to this thing, let alone having New York's elite just thinking of me as cheap and easy."

"First, you could never look cheap. And I remember you wearing a monstrosity you found in a discount bin that would have made most other women look like they worked the pole for a living. But no, you look frigging stunning. Plus, the salespeople wouldn't appreciate you calling that dress cheap. Have you seen the price tag?"

I knew she was right, but it didn't feel like the right dress and I needed it to be perfect.

"Fine, have it your way. But we've only got one more left and that's the one I'm least sure about. I still am not convinced you'll even like it."

Begrudgingly, she shooed me back into the changing room, helped unzip me out of the dress, and left me to put on the final one. I hoped this one fit.

There was something special about not having a mirror in the changing room. It made the reveal just as much a surprise to me as it did to Ruby.

Stepping out on tiptoes from behind the silk curtains, I did my best not to step on the back train, as I wasn't wearing heels.

Ruby turned around from where she was standing and talking on the phone.

"I have to go," she said to the person on the line.

Tentatively, she walked over and helped me step up onto the block in the center of the room in front of the mirrors.

Nervously, I opened my eyes and allowed myself to look at my reflection.

"Serena..."

Ruby's voice barely rose above a whisper.

The dress was stunning. It was a Marchesa embroidered illusion A-line gown, a fanciful embellished tulle gown with an illusion neckline, short sleeves, and scalloped cuffs.

The exquisite embroidered embellishments ran all along the bodice. The drop waist snipped me in, giving just enough illusion of my curves without my body looking very hourglass.

The back had a button closure at the top, but it was an open back. The stretch silk lining felt soft and buttery as my hands ran down it, leading to the small back train.

I'd never felt so beautiful.

I remembered going to my senior year prom, my date and I shared a limo with Ruby and Roman. I'd worn a dark navy dress and felt this would be a life-changing moment, thinking and feeling like I would never again feel so special in a dress.

How wrong had I been?

Gently turning around, I looked from mirror to mirror, wanting to see it from every angle. I knew it was corny, but this gown made me feel like a princess. I knew this was the one.

My stomach felt giddy with excitement, knowing I'd get to show off this masterpiece with Rhett at my side at such an important event.

"I love it."

I couldn't help the massive smile across my face.

"You know how you said you didn't want to wear the other dress because you were worried everyone would look at you?" Ruby asked. "Well, I can guarantee everyone will notice you in this dress. The women will be green with envy, and the men will wish they had you on their arm."

Ruby's words knocked me over and I felt a lump in my throat forming. Looking over at her, I saw her eyes were glistening.

"This is why I couldn't have had anyone else come shopping with me."

She walked over and gave me a massive hug.

"See? And you weren't even sure I would like it."

The dress was perfect, and I knew, despite its price tag, I wouldn't talk myself out of getting it.

After buying the gown, we took the elevator to the other floor, looking for shoes. With the dress being largely over budget, I was glad to find a gorgeous pair of nude Stuart Weizmann sandals for 30% off.

Ruby always teased me about how excited I was about getting a discount. Especially considering the irony of how much I had just spent on the dress.

We were in a little hole-in-the-wall pizzeria, and I was just finishing my last slice when Ruby steered the conversation from the workout class she was desperate to try out, to Julian.

"We had our first fight last week."

I knew how much she hated fighting, and given she had waited until now to tell me, I knew things couldn't have been good.

"What was it about it?"

"That's the thing, it wasn't even a big issue. He wanted to go out, and I didn't. But somehow, that escalated into something so much bigger than it needed to be. He did apologize, though, and put it down to his head being all over the place. Given everything that's going on with his dad and with Rhett's upcoming takeover of the company. It's just been a lot for him, I guess. And I realized how much he's struggling with dealing with it all."

I could see the worry and concern as she looked at me. But there was something else in her eyes that I couldn't quite place, but I could tell there was something else also bothering her.

"Is that all that worrying you?"

"Yes, of course. There's nothing else."

I knew that was a lie, but as she wasn't going to say any more, I didn't want to push her. I knew she would eventually tell me.

I just hoped that Julian didn't hurt her. I was really trying to give him the benefit of the doubt, but I just didn't trust the guy. He was an asshole.

Was that why she felt reluctant to open up about him because she knew I wasn't his biggest fan? I'd been keeping my opinions of him to myself, but maybe she could see something in my facial expressions every time she brought up his name.

She swiftly changed the subject and pressed me on all things regarding Rhett.

"I still can't believe he bought you a car. I can't wait to see what he gets you for your birthday," she jested with excitement.

I knew she was joking, but a part of me almost regretted accepting the car. I knew he'd done it as a sweet gesture, but I also knew what people would think. That was something I was struggling to shake off.

Not wanting to delve into those worries, I decided to change tactics and bring up the email we'd both been sent. It was an invitation to attend our school reunion.

It was late when I got back home, and I was beat. I changed into fluffy pajamas, wrapped my hair in my silk hair wrap, hung up the gown in my closet, and put away the rest of my purchases. I tried to catch up on some reading on my Kindle, but after only a handful of pages, I drifted into a deep, dreamless sleep.

Chapter 19

Serena

My intercom buzzed at precisely eight o'clock, with the doorman informing me that Rhett was downstairs.

I told him to let him know I'd be down in a second before returning to my room to grab my bag, then locking up and taking the elevator down to the lobby.

I took one last look in the mirror. Ruby and I had discussed the various ideas of how I should wear my hair. I wanted to wear it straight, she wanted me to leave it natural and curly.

So, I met her halfway. I decided on old Hollywood waves. I pinned one side up off my face and let the other cascade down my back. I kept my makeup basic, winging my eyes with black liner and adding a matte red lipstick.

My heels clicked along the tiled floor as I stepped out, alerting him to my presence.

He swiftly turned around, and I watched as his eyes traveled up my body.

"Wow."

I couldn't help but blush.

He looked at me like a hunter ready to devour its prey.

Taking my hand, he kissed the top of it. I did feel like a princess now.

He looked terrific in his black tuxedo, perfectly tailored around his strong, supple physique.

"You look breathtaking. I really want to kiss you, but I'm worried I will smudge your lipstick."

I wrapped my arms around his head, pulled him closer, and said, "Luckily for you, my lipstick is smudge-proof."

I crashed my lips into his. The wanton desire for him, that forever simmered beneath the surface, erupted in full force. His tongue felt like velvet as it played with mine.

He gently lifted me off my feet with his arms wrapped around me. I could feel his touch on my bare back, which sent waves of lust thrumming through me.

Setting me back on my feet, he looked me up and down again.

"I usually can't stand these benefits, but I have never been as excited as I am now going there with you. Especially formally introducing you to my parents as my girlfriend."

My heart was still racing as we walked to the car, and his driver opened the door for me to get in, followed by Rhett, before we merged into the flow of traffic, making our way.

The gala was held in the ballroom of the Plaza Hotel. Rhett held my hand for the entire car journey.

My stomach twisted into anxious knots. I was nervous about seeing his father again, and this time not in a work-related capacity, but mainly, I was scared about meeting his mother. Especially given the fact that she clearly wanted Rhett to be with Verity.

What had gotten me was that he called me his girlfriend. I was both thrilled and scared.

Were we moving too fast?

When we arrived, the flood of flashes from the awaiting paparazzi almost blinded me. I heard cheers and wolf whistles from the people gathered outside.

Photographers yelling at people to look this way than that. I heard rapid fire questions among the noise.

Mr. Chambers, who's your date? How long have you two been together? Does this mean the rumors of your engagement to Verity Lancaster are false?

It was that last comment that felt like a smack in the face. Rhett tightened his hold of my hand and quickly led us inside. Before entering the main ballroom, he looked down at me and kissed my lips tenderly.

"Ignore them. Let's enjoy ourselves. I can't wait to show you off."

I gave him a hesitant smile, rolled my shoulders back, and followed him.

Everyone who was anyone was there. It was the crème de la crème of high society. A mix of politicians, celebrities, socialites, and all the predominant forces of the medical, business, and legal worlds gathered there. It was a gossip columnist's dream.

After meeting various business associates of his and even one of my favorite recording artists, we finally had a few moments alone. Rhett handed me a glass of champagne and then laughed as I drank almost the whole glass in one gulp.

His smile made me relax. As I began to feel the knot in my stomach unwind, I followed his line of sight and saw his father walking towards us with a beautiful woman on his arm.

Rhett's mother.

Finishing off my drink, I handed the passing waiter my empty glass. Leaning down, he welcomed his mother with a kiss on the cheek and shook his father's hand.

"Mother, I want you to meet my girlfriend, Serena Parker. Serena, this is my mother, Alice."

I watched as she quickly scanned me from head to toe and hesitated before offering me her hand.

Shaking her hand, I gave her my sincerest smile.

"It's a pleasure to meet you, Mrs. Chambers."

"And you, dear."

Her smile didn't touch her eyes. I wasn't sure if it was just my nerves or if I was reading too much into it.

"And, of course, you have met my father before."

Rhett gestured to his father, who stood beside his mother.

"It's a pleasure to see you again, Mr. Chambers," I replied, doing my best to suppress my nerves.

"Please, call me Max."

His welcome was the complete opposite of his wife's as a warm smile spread across his face.

"I've been looking forward to seeing you again after Rhett told me that you two were now an item."

My face must have shown a frisson of apprehension as he quickly responded.

"I also want you to know I hope this doesn't change anything regarding you working with us. You and your firm are doing an amazing job for us, and Rhett speaks so highly of you. I'm glad he has finally found someone as successful and hard-working as you."

There was no way I could hide my feeling of embarrassment.

I looked over at Rhett, and he gave me a warm smile and wrapped his arm around my lower back.

I saw his mother watching us intently, a look of disapproval in her eyes. Now I knew I wasn't imagining it. What was her problem with me? I'd only just met her. Was it that she disapproved of me? Or that I wasn't Verity?

Rhett held my hand tightly as we walked by his parents' side, finding our seats.

~

Dinner had been excellent. The food was literally to die for. I genuinely thought my dress would burst at the seams with how much I ate.

Rhett had been excellent all night. Forever attentive, asking if I needed anything more to drink, engaging me in the conversation, and telling me how beautiful I looked. Occasionally, he'd squeeze my hand under the table, a reassuring reminder of his touch.

I'd been trying my utmost to converse with everyone at the table. His father and Mr. Carter Rutledge, who I learned is his father's lawyer, best friend, and Rhett's godfather, were both very endearing and asked me about my time at Columbia.

"Your family must be very proud of you. Not only did you finish top of your class but also go on to become a junior associate and now run your own firm. That indeed is an amazing accomplishment."

I couldn't help but blush but was also really grateful for the sincerity in Max's voice.

"Thank you, yes they are. I'm lucky I've always had such a great support system around me."

"There is no greater joy as a parent than seeing your children achieve great things. I know I am so proud of all the things my children have accomplished. As you know, Rhett has worked tremendously hard for Chambers Industries. The numbers speak for themselves. But even beyond that, his own investments have shown staggering success."

The way his father beamed with such pride made it clear how much they meant to one another.

Mrs. Chambers, on the other hand, was utterly unwelcoming. She made absolutely no effort in wanting to talk to me, and every time I tried to engage with her, she acted as if she couldn't hear me. It was becoming noticeably clear that this wasn't a mistake.

No, the woman didn't like me. For whatever reason, she didn't see me as important enough to give me her time or attention.

Once dinner was over, we all moved back to the other room as the band set up. Rhett and I had been talking to one of my former colleagues at Goldstein & Steiner. It felt odd as he'd been one of the senior associates and had barely uttered two words to me when I'd been working there. Now that I was there as Rhett's date, he seemed profusely interested.

I hated the feeling that I was only gaining this recognition and appreciation because of my association with Rhett.

Sensing something was up, Rhett excused us and walked me to an empty area where the caterers were clearing away items.

"Is everything okay? You've been quiet since dinner. Aren't you enjoying yourself? Shall we leave?"

"No, no, I'm fine."

I couldn't look him in the eye. I knew it would set me off.

"Serena."

His voice had a stern edge to it.

"I'm sorry. I just don't feel comfortable, I feel like everyone is watching me. Judging me."

"What do you mean? You look ravishing. You're beautiful, smart, charming, and you're what's keeping me here. Has something happened? Please tell me so I can fix it."

With one hand, he rubbed my arm in a soothing motion and, with the other, lifted my chin, forcing me to look him in the eye.

"It's your mother."

"What has she done?"

I expected him to sound annoyed or bitter, but he remained soothing and genuinely concerned.

"I think she doesn't like me."

I tentatively looked around, yet Rhett seemed to ignore the flurry of people around us.

"I'm not just being paranoid. From the moment she saw me, I could feel it. And it's not just a mother being concerned about who her son is with. There's something more to it. I'm sorry. I know this sounds horrible, and I know it's the last thing you want to hear, and I feel bad I'm telling you this. I'm sorry I've ruined your evening."

My whole body shook, it felt like I couldn't say the words fast enough. They simply came rushing out. I couldn't bring myself to look at him.

I had no idea what he was thinking. Was I overreacting? Would his opinion of me change depending on that of his mother?

I knew I held my dad's opinion in high regard, and there have been numerous times it had swayed my own. Would Rhett feel the same? Was this just another rerun of college? My mind was in utter overdrive.

"Serena, please look at me."

It took me a few seconds, but reluctantly, my eyes found his.

His kiss took me by surprise. Instantly, all my worries and frustrations were washed away. He kneaded my bare back with his firm, supple fingers. As he pulled my body flush against his, I felt his growing erection rub against my inner thigh through the fabric.

Our kiss evolved. It had started out as sensual and enthusiastic, especially on his behalf. As my desire grew, it became raw and intense.

For a few brief moments, I forgot where we were and just allowed myself to be taken away in the moment.

As our surroundings began to sink in, I knew I needed to bring us back to reality. I had to stop before I got too carried away. When Rhett and I gave in to our temptation, there was no going back. Besides, I was already dealing with his mother not giving me the time of day. I didn't need our little moment to become the talking point of tonight's benefit.

He rested his forehead against mine.

"I promise you I will speak to my mother. Please don't let her or anyone else ruin our evening."

I felt torn. Were these empty promises, and he was simply trying to appease me, or did he mean it then?

I knew this wasn't the time or the place for this conversation, and as I looked into his crystal blue eyes, I felt reassured by the sincerity I saw in them. I willed myself to forget what had happened so far and just let myself enjoy the rest of the evening.

I stayed true to my word for the next hour and had fun. We joined in on the charity raffle. I won a private afternoon trip for two to the zoo, full of a champagne picnic, feeding and petting the animals, plus the choice of adopting an animal of my choosing. Rhett won a week away to Nuremberg and a full day pass onto the infamous Nuremberg ring for himself and his guests.

The raffle was followed by dancing. He seamlessly spun me around the dance floor as one song rolled into the next. The band and the singer were phenomenal. They were currently playing a set that consisted of Rat Pack classics.

Mr. and Mrs. Chambers walked over, and my smile faded slightly.

"Son, may I interrupt and ask Ms Parker if I could have the next dance?"

"Please call me Serena, and I would be honored."

His father gave him a playful wink before we began to dance to another favorite of mine, Dean Martin's *Sway*.

I hadn't bothered to look at Mrs Chambers when they walked over, as I knew trying to engage with her was fruitless.

"So, are you enjoying yourself this evening?"

"Yes, it's been a lovely evening, and it's for such a worthy cause."

He tilted his head slightly as he looked at me, almost making me wonder if he knew what I said was a slight exaggeration.

"I'm glad to hear it. When I see Rhett at these events, he usually has a face like thunder from start to finish and never seems to enjoy himself. But tonight, he seems like a new man. Seeing him smile the way he does every time he looks at you makes me happy. And I have *you* to thank for that."

I wasn't sure what to say. It made me think of my father. I knew he'd probably be saying the same thing if he were there.

It was clear that Rhett had inherited his father's dancing skills. The band was halfway through the song as I looked at Max. It was then that I could see sweat forming across his brow and upper lip. He must have realized what I had noticed.

"I'm sorry, but I'm afraid this old man may have exhausted himself."

I suddenly felt terrible. I let myself be swept away and dance with a terminally ill man, encouraging him to spin me around and make circles around the dance floor. I was kicking myself inside.

"Why don't we go to the bar and get a drink? I know my feet could use a break."

"That sounds like a great idea."

He took my arm and led me to the bar.

By the time Rhett and his mother found us, Max seemed himself once again.

I was welcomed with a kiss from Rhett, and as I looked at him, I could see tension around his eyes. He held onto me, almost as if he were making some hidden statement.

As I leaned into him, about to ask him if everything was okay now, Max handed each of us a drink and made a toast. We all clinked glasses, and as I took my first sip, Mrs. Chambers spoke.

"Serena, I meant to say earlier, your dress is lovely. Is it a Jenny Packham?"

For a split second, I froze, then, not wanting to seem rude, I cleared my throat and answered.

"Thank you. No, it's by Marchesa."

"Well, nevertheless, it's a beautiful dress."

I was slightly bewildered. Was this her attempt at engaging in conversation? Being welcoming? I watched as she glared at Rhett as if they were having some unspoken conversation with one another.

For the rest of the evening, he stayed vigilantly at my side. I wanted to ask him what was wrong, but we got swept up in conversation with other couples, and the moment was lost. We danced some more and then decided to call it a night.

Once we got into the car, it was clear that he wanted me to stay at his place.

As soon as we stepped into his apartment, he was on me like an animal. He carried me into the kitchen before setting me on top of the marble island.

My pulse was racing like a hummingbird as I watched him get down on his knees, pushing my dress up to my waist. He started kissing his way up the inside of my leg before his eyes met mine.

"I hope you're not tired, as I plan on enjoying every single inch of your body."

Chapter 20

Serena

The next day, my body felt like I had completed a triathlon. Every limb was aching, and I could still feel him between my legs.

I had back-to-back meetings, followed by an hour-long teleconference call. Thankfully, my team had been on the ball all day.

So, by the time I finished the conference call at three, I decided they all deserved to finish early for the week and enjoy their weekend. I continued going through the paperwork for another hour before finishing up myself.

After work, I headed straight home, soaked in the tub for over an hour, ordered some Chinese take-out, curled up on the couch, and read a book.

Rhett messaged me earlier asking how I was, followed by the arrival of another beautiful bouquet. I called him back, offered thanks, and apologized for not calling sooner as I was swamped at work.

Naturally, being a busy man himself, he understood. However, I could tell he was a bit annoyed that I had to turn down his offer of dinner tomorrow as I had already planned with Ruby to see one of our friends in a play.

I informed him of my progress with getting five more signatures and properties for the company. I asked if he wanted to accompany me next week as I went to Queens to sort out the final paperwork.

To no surprise, he agreed and threw in that we should follow it with dinner to celebrate.

As I sat on the phone with my dad, I caught him up on all that had happened since I last spoke to him. I told him all about the gala.

"Yes, it looks like you enjoyed it. From the picture I saw, you looked beautiful," he said.

I still felt uneasy and super uncomfortable that one of the gossip pages had a photo of Rhett and me at the Gala and used it as one of their main features as they reported on the success of the evening. They had raised a staggering $4.7 million, a record to date.

I was plastered on every gossip website, which resulted in the media breaking down precisely who I was and everything I did.

Now people knew I was with Rhett, it apparently made me hot gossip. I didn't care too much and ignored the articles, as I knew it would be followed by the ever-present internet trolls criticizing every little detail about me.

Ruby sent me a link to a blog post. The title of which was ***The Butterfly among the Wasps***. Stupidly, that sent me on a deep dive, looking up everything.

Some people said I was a social climber. Others said Rhett was indulging in something tropical. Many hinted that I was using him and his family name to further my name and gain publicity. Even so far as misstating and misquoting statements I had made in past cases to fit their narrative.

There was so often a play on my name and micro-racist comments. I even found a link to a Reddit thread where someone was "investigating" if Rhett's family had any connection to the slave trade, and if they did, could my family have been owned by them?

I almost threw my laptop across the room when I got to the comment section. That's when I put a search engine block on both our names. I didn't want nor need to see any more of that shit.

"Just roll with it. You're a strong, successful lawyer. See this extra publicity as free press for your company."

I knew he was right. Yesterday, we'd been inundated with new clients wanting to hire us.

"I love you, Daddy. You always know the right thing to say."

We chatted through the rest of his lunch break when he asked how things were going with Rhett.

"Things are good. I'm just not used to being with someone everyone knows, wondering if every time we go out for dinner or an event, everyone will scrutinize my every move. It's bad enough I have that from his mother."

"What do you mean? Has she said something?"

I could hear the concern in my father's voice.

"Well, that's part of the problem. When I met her at the gala, she basically didn't speak to me. At first, I thought it was a misunderstanding. But as the evening went on, something about me clearly bothered her. And it's driving me freaking insane as I have no idea what it is."

"Is there anything you suspect that it could be?"

My mind was mulling things over, torn between the things I eventually read online and my own insecurities that had formed and mutated in college.

"You mean besides the obvious?" I grumbled.

"What's obvious, honey?"

"That I'm not white. That I don't come from blue-blooded pedigree."

"Do you think she has a problem with that?"

"Well, I don't know what else it could be. She knows I work. I'm sure someone has given her a breakdown and a thorough background check on me. And from what Ruby has told me of the women he's previously been associated with, I have more diplomas and qualifications than theirs all added together. So the only other thing I can think of is that I don't look like them. I didn't grow up going to the country club. I didn't grow up with staff catering to my beck and call. I'm not blonde. My physique isn't willowy, and my opinions aren't muted."

My eyes began to sting as I listed all the possible things I could think of. Each one felt like a direct hit. The sigh my father let out almost made me lose it.

"One of the things that makes me so proud about you is how you're always warm and welcoming to others you meet. The problem is, sadly, not everyone else is the same. Remember, these people live in a very small world. They attend the same parties with the same people they have known their whole lives. Despite their far reach of power, their circle is very small. I'm sure many of them even got into relationships by familial arrangements. And if someone doesn't fit or conform to it, they push them out. But don't for one minute think that doesn't make you worthy. You are worth so much more than that. Has Rhett ever shown this kind of behavior? Made you feel less than him?"

"No."

I didn't need to think twice. The answer fell fast and strong from me.

"From what you've told me, Rhett seems like a charming man and a hard worker. You've chosen to be with him, so he must be a good guy. Plus, like I said before, he's got good taste in cars."

I could hear the smile on his face through the phone.

I had to laugh.

"I'm sure that over time, things will be fine. Just remember the countless times we've had to deal with difficult customers at the shop. And I'll tell you what my dad once told me. *You can't change how people treat you or what they say about you. All you can do is change how you react to it.* And I know you, Serena, and you will be fine."

I always loved speaking to my dad. He really was the kindest and wisest man I knew.

It was always with a tinge of sadness when I said goodbye to him. But as I looked at my watch, I knew I had to make my way to Queens now, or I'd be late.

Rhett and I sat in Mrs. Cole's cafe, and I was filing away the last of the paperwork. I never realized how much I would appreciate being with someone who understood and respected how much I worked and just how nonstop it was.

There was something weirdly comforting, having my files and paperwork around me and Rhett close by.

We'd signed off on another handful of contracts. And even though Raya herself still wasn't willing to sell, she always welcomed us with open arms.

Once again, she brought a delicious medley of homemade cakes and cookies.

"Are you sure you're going to have room for dinner?"

I couldn't help but tease him as I watched him enjoy every morsel on his plate. I swore the man didn't have an inch of fat on him. And given how much he ate that truly was remarkable.

I could tell he was growing very fond of Mrs Cole's food.

"Surely you've worked out by now. I always have room for more. My appetite is never-ending."

His eyes were full of lust and I knew we were no longer talking about food. I scooted over closer to him in the booth.

He was too sexy to resist. As I kissed him, I could taste apple and cinnamon, which only made me want him more.

We have settled into a great new normal. Despite how busy our schedules were, we did our best to make time for each other. And despite everything that going on with Rhett's father and him becoming CEO, it hadn't made me feel second best.

It feels like every day, I was shedding another layer of worry and doubt away and slowly healing those wounds from the past.

The sensual strokes of his hand along my knee brought me back to the present.

"So, where would you like to go and celebrate? Do you want to go out? Or we could always stay in, and one of us cook or order in? It's your choice."

He ran his fingers past my knee, slowly making his way up my thigh, causing my skirt to inch higher ever so slightly.

"Hmm, why don't we go to your place, and we both cook? I might even get a chance at trying out that pool," I purred.

His featherlike touches were so soft and sensual that I could feel my panties growing wetter by the second and I knew it was time to level the playing field.

Now, it was my hands running up his thigh, making sure he understood my intentions for that evening. Rhett seemed to unleash something wanton within me, and my body was beginning to suffer withdrawal.

He answered with a slow and tender kiss.

Once again, it felt as if the world around us had disappeared before we both seemingly remembered where we were. I could feel his groan as I bit down on his lip, and the look of lust in his hooded eyes made me desperate to get out of there and devour him. It was as though he could read my thoughts when he bent down and whispered.

"Hold on to that thought," Rhett teased.

We were about to pay the bill and leave when his phone rang.

"Hello?" He paused, listening. "What? When? Where?"

His voice was full of panic, sending a cold shiver down my spine. All traces of lust were gone and replaced with panic and fear. As he listened to the person on the line, he straightened his body, and I let him have his space. Instantly, a cold shiver ran down my spine.

"I'll be right there."

As he looked down at me, his face was pale. The usual brightness of his cerulean eyes was dulled.

"I'm sorry, but I've got to go. That was my mother. My father has been rushed to hospital, and the doctors have recommended that she get all the family there as soon as possible."

He didn't have to say it. I knew what that meant. He knew what that meant. And instantly, my heart broke for him.

"I'm so sorry. Go... go. Let me know if there is anything I can do."

I didn't know what else to say.

He looked down at me and kissed me deeply. His whole body seemed tense, and I felt helpless. I couldn't even decipher if the trembles I felt were in his hands or my own.

A minute later, my eyes followed as he rushed out the door and got into his town car, waiting at the curb. As I watched the car speed off into the flow of traffic, I knew everything was about to change.

Chapter 21

Rhett

I hadn't realized my fists were still balled up until Kara sat beside me and tried to hold my hand.

We all arrived at the hospital and were tentatively sitting in his private room.

Father had been out for afternoon tea with Mother when he suddenly had a seizure. Once the medics got him to the hospital, they sedated him, and the doctors had been running tests nonstop for the past few hours.

I arrived first, followed by Julian, Heather, and then Kara. As soon as I arrived, I asked Mother what had happened, and it took a good five minutes to calm her down so she could talk.

She sat by my father's bed, holding his hand, staring. She turned down my offers of a drink, something to eat, or even some fresh air.

He had been there for over five hours, and the doctors still hadn't given us any sign of what was going on. I sat with Heather on the couch. Julian hadn't stopped pacing the corridor since his arrival. Kara sat on either side of Father's bed, holding his hand.

"Why have they still not told us anything?"

My temper was absolutely fraying, and the more time passed, the more I struggled to control myself.

"I'm sure they will tell us as soon as possible," Heather said faintly.

I needed to pull myself together. I needed to be strong. Strong for my father, mother, and the rest of my family. They were counting on me. I couldn't let my own emotions take over.

Looking over at him lying there, he looked so old, frail, and weak.

Every time a nurse or doctor came in, we thought we'd have more news, something to go on, but they just did more tests, letting us know that someone would come and speak to us soon.

The hours just seemed to blur together. Finally, Father's physician entered, and I could see from his expression the news wasn't good.

Father's condition has severely deteriorated, and he will be staying in the hospital under the palliative care team, as it's looking like he may only have a few days at the most.

He said he might come around once the sedation entirely wears off, but there was nothing more they could do besides making him as comfortable as possible.

The room was so silent I could have heard a pin drop.

Even Julian stopped his pacing. When I walked over to Kara to hug her, I was surprised that Julian followed suit and embraced Heather and my mother.

We'd never been a remarkably close family. Never close or affectionate. But right then, all that went out the window.

Julian's head was buried in our mother's arms. I was trying with all my might to keep my tears at bay, knowing someone had to stay strong. And right then, that duty fell upon me.

It had been several hours since the doctors told us the news. It was the middle of the night, and the room was practically silent. The only sound came from the machines attached to my father. My sisters and mother were in the visitor's room, trying to get some sleep. Julian slumped over the couch.

I was holding his hand in a chair by my father's bed. I felt my eyelids growing heavier by the minute. But I didn't want to give into sleep.

My body must have given in as the next thing I knew, I woke to the slightest movements in my hand.

Looking up, I saw my father's eyes open.

"You're okay. You're in the hospital. Mother, Kara, and Heather are asleep in the waiting room. Julian is over there asleep. We're all here."

It felt like everything was going in slow motion. Slowly, he reached up and pulled down on his oxygen mask.

"I.... want.... you... to tell... your mother... how... much... I... have... always... loved... her. She... will... forever... be... the love of my life."

He replaced his mask, took a few deep breaths, and removed it.

"Tell Julian... he... needs... to... believe... in... himself... and... that... I... love... him."

Once again, he took another inhalation from his mask.

Every time he spoke, my heart shattered into smaller and smaller pieces.

"Heather... is... such... a.... dedicated... beautiful... woman... with... the... biggest... heart. She... should... never... change. I've... loved... her... since... the... day... she... was... born."

I knew I should wake Julian and call everyone in. But I didn't want to miss anything he was trying to say.

"Kara... is... bright... beautiful... and... such... an... amazing... mother. If... she... ever.... feels... sad... she... should... look... at... Kai... as... I... will... forever... be... watching... over... him."

The lump in my throat was beginning to make me feel like I couldn't breathe.

"And you, my son... I... am... prouder... of... you... than... you... ever...will... know. You... have... and... will... continue... to... achieve... greatness... but... remember... to... listen... to... your... heart. Never... forget... that. I have left... a... folder... for... you... with Carter."

He took another deep breath through the mask.

"I love you."

My voice was barely above a whisper.

"I love... you too... son."

A single tear fell down his cheek, and his hand slipped by his side.

The machine monitoring his heart began to flatline. In the next few moments, the nurses and doctor ran in. They checked his vitals. But I already knew he was gone.

The commotion of their entrance woke Julian up. I watched as he raked his hands through his hair, falling to his knees.

Then I heard a scream. Following the sound, I saw my mother with Kara and Heather on either side.

They were trying to hold her up, but as the realization hit them, they all fell to the floor.

My ears blocked all the sound out. Nurses and doctors left the room, allowing us to have some privacy.

I walked back to my father's lifeless body and kissed his forehead, and my own tears fell upon his face.

We stayed at the hospital for a few more hours. Everyone wanted to say goodbye in their own way.

The ride back to my parents' house was in absolute silence. My father's physician gave my mother and both my sisters a light sedative to help them through the next few hours.

As soon as we arrived, Julian went to the bar and drank. For once, I wasn't mad at him. Instead, I joined him.

My mother and sisters went to bed. The staff rallied around, trying to be helpful while simultaneously dealing with their own grief. Julian retreated to the pool house, taking a bottle of bourbon with him.

I found myself sitting in my father's office.

I spent the next hour on the phone with different family and friends. I was informing them of my father's passing. I needed this. I needed to keep myself busy.

When I spoke to Carter, I told him what my father had said. I was surprised as he broke down. Once he got himself together, he told me there was a copy of the folder my father spoke about in the top drawer of his desk before giving his condolences, and we ended the call.

My hand lay resting on the drawer handle for God knew how long. My mind was in turmoil about whether I should open it.

Finally, I did.

In the folder was Father's will. He outlined the various assets he divided between my mother, me, and my siblings.

A contract had been drawn up, which defined that my siblings were to have multiple properties divided between them, and others would be given to my mother. It also stipulated that all my father's money would be split between my mother, brother, and two sisters, but not me.

That didn't surprise me. I'd been lucky enough to amass a large fortune and didn't need it.

What did surprise me were the final pages of the contract. It stated that I was to inherit the company in full. And that a minimum of twenty-five percent of its future profits would be split between the family. I was to take over as owner immediately after his death. I read the various other legalities and documents in the folder. Then I found an envelope that had been addressed to me.

My hands shook as I opened it.

My Dearest Rhett,

The fact that you're reading this means my time has ended.

I hope you have read all the documents in the folder. If you have, it also means you understand that I have left the company to you.

I've spent long and hard thinking about this, and I hope it is met with understanding on everyone's part.

As you know, our company has been in the family for generations and passed on from father to son for decades. I don't want you to think I have decided to leave it to you simply because it's tradition. I have done it because there is not one person I would trust more in the world.

You have grown up to be such a dedicated and hardworking man. It has been an honor to call you my son, to work with you for the past few years, and watch you succeed beyond anyone's expectations.

You are enthusiastic, caring, considerate, forgiving, and loyal. I am so proud of you son. I wish I were around to continue watching you succeed. I remember the day you were born like it was yesterday. I had never felt so nervous as the doctor handed you to me.

But as I looked into your eyes, I felt my heart be filled in ways I never thought imaginable.

You have been an amazing older brother to your siblings, a phenomenal colleague, and an outstanding son.

These next few months will be difficult for everyone. Please always remind your mother she was the love of my life. And look out for Kara and especially Heather. Kara has Austin and Kai to help her, but Heather is sensitive. Please keep a watchful eye out over her. As for Julian, I know you two bicker as brothers often do, but please find it within your heart to at least get onto common ground with him. He is brash, and his judgments and choices are often questionable, but he will forever be your brother. Try to support him and be there for him. At least as much as he lets you.

And you, Rhett, I feel least worried about. I see so much of myself in you. It has been a privilege to call you my son. You have inherited my drive and passion for work, but please promise me you'll also find time for love. Because leading your life without somebody to love and share it with, well, that isn't a life worth leading at all. Follow your heart and never let anyone deter you from it.

I will always be grateful for having the chance to watch my children grow, meet my first grandchild, and be surrounded by family and friends that I love.

Forever in my heart.

I love you.

My fists slammed on the desk as everything began to sink in.

My father was never coming back.

He'd always been my idol. Since I was a kid, I always looked up to him. I have always wanted to be like him.

Now, he was gone—the realization and magnitude of how everything was now upon me. The company, stepping up and becoming the head of the family, all responsibilities now fell upon my shoulders.

While simultaneously all hope of breaking free from these expectations, feeling like a prisoner within my own life, having a chance to speak to my father and open up about what I truly wanted to do, the things I wanted to change—the life I wanted to set up for myself. It was all too late now.

I made it over to the drink cabinet in the corner. My legs felt like lead. I poured myself a large drink and finished it off in one gulp.

The burn of the liquor didn't come close to relieving the pain in my heart.

Finally, I let my body give in. I fell to the floor, and I was undone—a broken man.

Chapter 22

Rhett

I left my mother's house at around two in the morning, calling Russell to come and pick me up.

At first, I asked him to drive me home. Then, the thought of being alone made my stomach turn. Changing my mind, I told him to head to Serena's house.

As we arrived, I sat in the car, unable to move. Suddenly, I wasn't sure if it was best for me to see her. What should I say? Did I want her to see me like this?

We were pulled up on the sidewalk for almost half an hour before I told him to take me to the office and, ignoring the confused look in his eyes through the rear-view mirror.

It was almost as puzzling to me. But it felt like the right place for me to be. As he dropped me off, I sent him on his way, telling him to go home and sleep. If I ended up going anywhere else, I'd call a cab.

He was hesitant to leave.

"I'll be fine. Just go."

I didn't mean to snap. I just wanted to be left alone.

Word must have gotten around quickly, as even the evening

security staff gave me a sympathetic look. As I entered my office, the clock read 3:00. I was about to make another drink, but something within me said coffee would be better.

Sitting at my desk, I watched the swirls of steam rise from my cup, not believing all that had happened in the last forty-eight hours—yesterday seemed like a blur.

Even though we were all aware of my father's condition, it still came as a shock. I had still been getting my head around the fact that my father was dying. But I thought I still had weeks to deal with things and spend time with him.

But it was all too late. He was gone. I would never hear his voice again. He'd never make fun of me after showing me a stupid splash piece article he'd read about me in the gossip column. Never see me get married. He would never get the opportunity to meet my children.

My stomach began to heave, and I just managed to make it to the toilet in time as I threw up.

After washing my face in the sink, I downed a bottle of water from the fridge.

I had to pull myself together. I needed to work. I needed to step up. Do what was expected of me. Make this my priority. Everything else must come second. I owed it to my father's legacy. How could I turn my back on what my father spent his whole life working on and building up? I knew the only way for me to function right now was to power through with work.

My emotions and energy were too restless. I couldn't be who Serena needed, who she deserved, who she wanted me to be. I couldn't show her how much I was struggling.

In order to get through everything, I needed to clear all my thoughts of her aside. There was now a company for me to run. It was what was expected. It was all I'd known. All I was good for.

Hours later, I still hadn't moved from my desk. It was ten o'clock by the time someone walked through my office door. I was surprised that no one had come in sooner. Then, I was even more shocked when I saw it was Dough, my father's right-hand man, instead of Charlotte.

"What are you doing here? I didn't think you would come in today."

Looking up, I watched as he approached me slowly, tentatively—as though I was a wounded animal. His brows creased, and even I could see the sorrow in his eyes.

"I'm so sorry for your loss."

My body ran on pure caffeine. I'd had six cups of coffee since I arrived and was in no mood to slow down.

"I'm here because I need to be. Where is everyone else?"

"Everyone else is working, in their office or a meeting. We called Charlotte last night and told her not to come in, as we didn't think you would be. Would you like me to call her and get her to come in?"

"No, it's fine. She deserves a day off." I took a deep breath. "Can you get the guys from finance to come in as soon as possible? I need to clarify a few questions about the overhead expenses, including the accounting fees, advertising, insurance, repairs, supplies, taxes, travel expenditures, and utilities we are covering this month."

I expected him to listen to my orders and be on his way. But instead, he just stood there, staring. And it was making me angry.

"Is there something I can help you with, Dough?"

The angry tone in my voice registered with him as he once again gave his condolences and then left.

I hit the ground running. I knew I couldn't stop because I knew my body would give in as soon as I did.

I'd been up for almost two days with no sleep. I was having meeting after meeting. I called people in, asking them to give me up-to-date reports on their departments. In more than one meeting, I lost my temper.

By the end of the day, everyone was walking on eggshells around me. Earlier, I'd gotten calls from my mother and sisters asking if I was okay. I reassured them I was fine, stating I needed to return to work. They tried to persuade me to leave. Each one took turns trying to convince me to go home and grieve.

I let them know I'd leave the office as soon as possible. And that they should rest, and my sisters should focus on our mother.

Serena tried to call me a few times, but I couldn't bring myself to answer her calls. I still didn't know what to say. Or how I would feel or act around her. She was always so strong. She was sure of who she was, what she wanted in life, and what she wanted to achieve.

I felt the polar opposite and that was a side I didn't want her to witness. For now, I needed to keep her at arm's length.

I finally called Russell to pick me up at four. I could feel both my mind and body shutting down. Sitting in the back of the car, I heard my phone go off and retrieved it from my jacket pocket.

> I am so sorry for your loss. Ruby told me what happened. I am truly deeply sorry. If you need your space, I understand. I will always be here if you need me. X

I read and re-read her message countless times by the time I got back to my apartment. I felt a sense of guilt that I hadn't spoken to her. Even just to tell her what happened.

It couldn't have been nice for her to find out from her best friend.

Fuck!

Everything was so goddamn messed up.

I slept through from Friday to Saturday evening. When I woke, I called my mom to see how she was coping.

She and Carter had already arranged most of the funeral. As it turned out, my father already paid and planned for almost everything. It wasn't surprising how organized he was.

Was.

It felt weird thinking about him in the past tense.

The funeral was going to be on Tuesday at St Andrew's church, followed by a wake at mother's house. I let her know I was there for her should she need me.

I ordered takeout and washed that down with a whole bottle of whiskey. I passed out on my couch and only woke up again Sunday afternoon.

I worked in my home office for a few hours, took a shower, ordered more takeout, followed it with some beers, and then was in bed by nine.

Going to bed so early felt weird, as I usually only needed four to five hours of sleep a night. But things were different now.

It was as if my body couldn't manage me being up for more than a few hours before I needed to rest again.

Monday morning hit me like a freight train. It felt like I

endured the worst hangover known to man. Everything felt painful. Walking, talking, even breathing.

Charlotte had been overly attentive all morning. It was beginning to drive me insane. I hated the way everyone looked at me, always watching. Like they were waiting to see if I would cry, break down, or bite their head off.

Everyone was making me angry.

I called every department one by one. It was vital for me to be in control and work was the one thing I could control.

Some of my staff seem surprised by my sudden interest in every department. Now that I owned the building. The company. I was now fully responsible.

Everything rested upon my shoulders.

One thing I knew when I found out my father had left it to me was that I would be running a very tight ship. I wanted to know where my company stood in every division and sector.

This was my father's legacy, his father's, and his before him. Each generation turned it into something bigger and better than they had inherited.

Now, it was my turn to show my father he'd been right to trust me. I needed to make him proud.

At around three in the afternoon, Charlotte came running into my office.

"Is everything okay?"

"Yes, Mr. Chambers. I'm sorry. I wanted to know whether to call security. I... um. It's your brother. I think he's drunk. He stumbled out of the elevator, and I tried to help him to his feet... but I think he got the wrong idea."

I suddenly saw that she was holding her shirt closed and that her skirt had a tear down it. My blood boiled as my fists were tightly clenched.

"Did he hurt you?" I growled.

"I think he got the wrong idea. He tried to pull me into

him, holding onto my blouse and skirt. I tried to brush him off, but he wouldn't let go and kept a hold of them. As I pulled away, my clothes tore. He's currently sitting on my desk. He also has a bottle of something in his hand. I'm sorry, Mr. Chambers."

I walked over to a cabinet and grabbed one of my spare shirts for her.

"Charlotte, you have nothing to apologize for, he is the fucking asshole. Call security. Also, call the police if you wish to press charges. I will fully back you. He cannot get away with this."

"I'll call security, but no police. I'm sure he didn't mean to. I know it's a tough time for you all now."

She started to say more, but I needed to get my scumbag brother out of there.

Storming out of my office, I saw the pathetic excuse of the man with his feet up on Charlotte's desk, reclining back in her chair.

I must have blacked out as the next thing I knew, I was running at him and landed a punch straight to his jaw, sending him flying off the chair.

Slowly, he staggered back to his feet.

"What the fuck was that for?" he slurred, drunk.

"First, you assaulted Charlotte. I've told her to call the police, but luckily for you, she won't. I can assure you if you ever come within one meter of her again, I will destroy you. Second, I never want to see you in this building again. You pathetic piece of shit."

Julian then ran at me, trying to tackle me to the ground and take us both down.

I got him into a headlock to gain back control. He landed a few body shots, but his strength waned with the growing pressure I applied to his neck.

After a few more cheap swings, he finally gave up just as security burst through the doors and hauled him to his feet.

His mouth was bleeding, and I could see his jaw starting to bruise.

"Of course, Mr. Perfect gets everything he wants. Father's love, now his company. You don't deserve it."

"And you think you do? Have you seen the state of yourself? All you ever care about is yourself. You have a drinking and inferiority problem. Are you telling me father would be proud of you if he could see you right now? Sober up. Not just for the funeral tomorrow. Please do it for good. Become the man father always thought you could be."

I took a step closer, hoping to make him understand. Instead, he spat in my face.

I used my shirt to wipe my face clean and then directed my attention to the security guards holding Julian.

"Please escort him out of the building, take any keys and passes he has, and inform all staff that he is not allowed entry unless authorized by me. And should he try to gain access when I am not here or cause a scene, you are to restrain him and call the police. Are those instructions clear?"

"Yes, sir."

Walking back to my office, I found Charlotte standing by the door.

"Please, take a seat. Which of the other PAs are you closest to?"

"I'm not sure I understand what you mean?"

"I'd like you to call who you are closest to and send them out to grab you some new clothes. And if you'd like, you can take the rest of the week off."

"That is very kind of you, but I always have a spare outfit just in case I need to change into that. Also, it isn't as bad as it looks. I can assure you that I'll be fine."

"Are you one hundred percent sure? It's fine if you want to have a few days rest. Also, if you change your mind about calling the police, I fully understand and will help and support you."

"Thank you, sir, but I'd prefer to move on from this. Would it be okay for me to change in your private bathroom instead of the ones by the break room? It would save me the risk of someone seeing me like this?"

"Of course."

I picked up my phone and called for Russell to bring the car around.

"I'm going to be heading out. I also want to make sure Julian has left the building. It's the funeral tomorrow, so I'm unsure if I will be in later. I'll let you know if I do. Thank you, Charlotte."

"Thank you, sir. And I'll be thinking of you and your family tomorrow."

With that, she grabbed her bag and headed into my bathroom. Picking up my jacket and briefcase, I made my way downstairs.

After being reassured by the security that Julian had been escorted off the premises and all his entry cards and passes had been confiscated, I got into the car and asked Russell to drive.

I had no idea where I wanted to go or what to do. All I knew was that I needed to get away.

We drove down Broadway when Serena popped into my mind.

"Russell, please take me to Serena's office."

"Yes, sir."

He spun the car around, and we set off.

Once we were parked outside her building, I, yet again, couldn't bring myself to get out. Russell cleared his throat a few times in an attempt for me to realize we were there.

I was already aware we had been sitting here for ten minutes, but all I could do was stare at her building. My mind bounced all over the place. I wanted her, needed her, but I was so damn angry.

Angry because my father was gone. Angry at what Julian had done. I was angry that this all was happening to me.

An hour passed. I kept prepping myself to get out but couldn't muster the courage to do so. I was looking out the window when suddenly I saw her exit the main doors.

"Follow her!"

I knew it was rash, but I needed to see her, and this was as close as I could be to her, at least for now.

Despite being in midtown traffic, Russell had somehow managed to drive at a steady pace. Stopping every time, she stopped and looked in a store window. She walked past a couple that were in a deep embrace. I watched as she studied them, her face suddenly marred with sorrow. Then, she retrieved her phone from her bag.

Moments later, my phone alerted me to a message.

> I'm sure things are difficult now, but I mean it when I say I am here for you whether you want to talk or even have some company. My door is always open. X

It was surreal that I was only a few feet away from her, following her, but I couldn't find the courage to get out.

Yet there she was, offering to be there for me. What was I doing? Was I so used to being alone that I couldn't behave like an average human?

I was so used to being told what to do—something I was beginning to realize I had heavily relied on, yet, I was utterly clueless, and I wished someone would tell me how to handle everything. What to do.

I typed over a dozen replies but kept deleting them instead of pressing the send. I kept doubting myself. And that was something I never did.

We followed her for another few blocks until she disappeared into a building. After googling it, I found out it housed a gym. I got Russell to pull up and wait.

The look he gave me made it clear he thought I had gone mad.

She finally reemerged after what felt like the longest hour and a half. She was still in her gym clothes, so I presumed she was heading home. I watched as she hailed a cab. This time, without instruction, Russell followed the car.

Just as I had expected, she arrived at her apartment. I could see every inch and curve of her. Her ass looked amazing in her tight yoga pants and I was getting harder by the minute.

Once she disappeared into her building, I waited until the lights in her apartment came on. I was finally deciding to get out of the car, I told Russell he was done for the day.

Yet again, my legs turned to stone. I tried crossing the road but froze. Looking around me, I noticed a bar a few doors down and decided to go and have a drink.

The bar was nothing special. It was just an average place where people would stop by after work.

Sitting at the bar, I nursed either my third or fourth drink. I couldn't remember.

At some point, a woman sat beside me and tried to chat me up. There was no way in hell I was interested, although she seemed surprised by my brush-off. I guessed she wasn't used to the word no.

As I made my way over to the restroom, I realized I was

drunk. The ground beneath me felt like it was moving, and my vision became blurrier by the second.

Rushing to the cubicle, I thought I was going to be sick, but instead, I dry heaved.

Splashing some water over my face, I tried to sober up.

Having left the bar, I found myself standing outside her building. The doorman greeted me by name and let me go straight up. I knocked on the door and waited.

Opening the door only in her towel, I could watch the shock register on her face. Her hair began to curl as it lay damp across her shoulders and chest, and little droplets of water ran down her golden-brown skin, disappearing into the towel.

"What are you doing here?" she said breathlessly.

"I needed to see you."

She looked at me, and I saw some hesitation marring her face. Finally, she stepped aside and let me in. She must have smelt the alcohol on me.

"Would you like tea or coffee?"

"A coffee would be lovely, thank you."

She walked over to her kitchen and began to prepare two cups. I took my jacket off and felt out of place as I walked around her lounge.

What was I doing there? It felt like she didn't want me there. Having prepared our drinks, she went over to the couch and lifted her chin, indicating for me to sit.

"I'm so sorry for your loss. How are you?" she asked me, eyes brimming with concern.

I ignored the question and took a sip of coffee, trying to gather my thoughts.

"I'm sorry I haven't called you back, my head's been all over the place. I guess I don't know what to say."

I watched as she listened.

Once again, we fell silent and I knew she was willing me to continue.

I wanted to tell her how I was feeling, wanted to let her know that I have been thinking about her.

Fuck, she was the only thing keeping me sane. I needed to get closer to her once again. Bridge the gap that I created between us.

Slowly, I placed my cup on the coffee table. She watched my every move. I edged closer to her until our faces were only inches apart. I ran the pad of my thumb across her lips. Every fiber of me was drawn in. As I moved in to kiss her, I waited.

I needed her permission. I needed her to want this as much as I did.

With just the slightest movement, she tilted her head up, and that was all the confirmation I needed. Skimming my tongue against her trembling lips, I tasted the hot flavor of desire that ignited my deep-rooted hunger for her.

My mouth crashed into hers. Seconds later, I had her flat on her back. One hand ran through her damp curls, the other tugged her towel open. I pulled my mouth away to see her glorious body. Her skin smelled of coconut, it was as soft as velvet.

There was no slow build-up. I yanked at my belt, racing to be inside her. Lifting her upright, I began kissing her neck, then worked my way to one breast and then the other. She let out a cry as I bit down on each nipple.

The sound made my cock painfully hard. She was my drug. And I was a junkie in desperate need of a fix.

Laying her down, then grasping her knees and easing them apart. I ran my hand down her thighs, kneading and rubbing her. Once I reached her soft, wet center, I knew I couldn't wait any longer.

Spinning her around, I bent her over the couch, gazing in

wonder at her nakedness. My palm smacked down on her juicy ass. Kicking my shoes off, I pushed my slacks and briefs down and then thrust deep inside her. The noises escaping her throat geared me on further, each thrust got harder and harder.

This was as raw and intense as we ever had been with one another.

One hand on her hips, controlling her body, riding her to the tempo I had set, the other reached around, pinching and tugging on her nipples. I could feel she began to tighten and clench on my cock, and I knew she was getting close. So was I.

There was no time to be gentle. I needed my release, and she was the only person I wanted to give it to me. The sounds of me pumping into her echoed across the room.

We both cried out as we came, and I continued slamming into her, riding out every drop.

Finally, my body slowed to a stop, and she winced as I pulled out of her. Sitting back on the couch, I tried to catch my breath. Serena turned and wrapped the towel around herself once again. She gave me a shy smile, and how she looked at me stopped my heart.

"Serena, I think I have fallen in love with you."

The smile on her face instantly faded. Her body became rigid, and I wondered if she heard me correctly.

"No."

"What do you mean, no?" I lamented.

"I mean, you have a lot going on now. As you said, your emotions are all over the place. There's a difference between loving someone and lusting someone."

"Are you fucking kidding me?" I cried.

Suddenly, she looked like a frightened child. It pained me to look at her. Setting myself to rights, I began to put my shoes on.

"Rhett, wait. We need to talk."

"I think I'm done talking. It doesn't do much for a man's ego when he tells his girlfriend he loves her and she rejects him. I'm not sure what kind of relationships you're used to having, but I don't deal with this kind of shit!"

She grabbed my arm, but I pulled away. I couldn't let her touch me. I needed space.

"Please, Rhett, listen to me."

I couldn't look at her and began collecting my things.

"Stop!" she shouted.

I froze at the sound of her voice.

"I'm not dismissing you, but what you said.. you don't know what you're saying. Your father has just died and I know how much he means to you. We've only been together for a couple of months. I think you're pushing for one emotion... and trying to replace it with another."

I couldn't listen to this anymore, but I needed to know. Did she truly not feel the same?

I stood squarely in front of her.

"Do you love me?"

"Rhett, it's not as simple as that."

"Yes. It. Is. Do you love me or not?"

"Rhett."

She couldn't finish the sentence. Instead, she looked down at the floor. That was enough of an answer for me so I grabbed my coat and left.

Part of me hoped she would come after me. But as I stood on the sidewalk trying to hail a cab, I knew she wouldn't.

How could I have been so stupid? How could I have thought I meant as much to her as she did me?

Chapter 23

Rhett

My father's funeral was one of the hardest things I ever had to endure in my life.

The service went just as he had planned. At the church, it had been an intimate one.

Julian, Austin, and I were pallbearers alongside my father's two closest friends, Carter, Riley, and my Uncle Benjamin.

Seeing my uncle was weird, as he had cut himself off from my family many years ago.

My father once told me that Ben had a falling out with my grandfather when he was around eighteen years old, as he'd had no interest in wanting to be involved with the family business. It had escalated into a massive fight as Ben had wanted to dedicate himself to charity work worldwide. So, my grandfather cut him off, and Ben traveled the world, helping build schools and villages and living life as a voluntary community worker.

My father was the only family member that stayed in contact with him.

I remember getting postcards from Peru, Guatemala,

Kenya, Cambodia, and other places. Father had often held various charity functions honoring his brother's work.

As we walked into the church, carrying my father's coffin, the musicians were playing Adagio for Strings by Samuel Barber.

I looked over at my uncle and could see the tears slowly fall down his cheek. Carrying my father's coffin felt like one of the most challenging yet honorable things I could do for him.

Various people read several poems and stories my father had picked out. The music and hymns were a mix of some of my father's favorite pieces.

Throughout most of it, I focused my attention on the coffin. I could hear the gentle cries and sobs from my mother on one side of me and my sisters on the other.

Once the service ended, we went to the family burial chamber. His ashes were to be put alongside my grandfather and grandmother.

His name was already engraved on the headstone. It felt so surreal as I read the text repeatedly.

Maxwell Henry Chambers

18.01. 1949 – 26.09.2016
Beloved Husband, Father, and Grandfather
What we have once enjoyed, we can never lose. All that we love deeply becomes a part of us.

Serena had been at the back of my mind the entire day. One minute, I wished she could have been there with me. The next thing all I felt was heartache and anger.

My mind kept flashing back to her apartment and seeing if I could make sense of what had happened. How could she so easily dismiss how I felt about her? Did she do it to mask her lack of feelings for me? Did she have any? Was I the only one believing we had a future together?

Nothing made sense to me.

I sat in my father's study, needing to escape from the other guests at the wake.

Even though we'd had a private and intimate service with only family and close friends, my father had stipulated that my mother could do the wake as she saw fit, which meant it was a complete circus. Over two hundred friends, colleagues, and acquaintances had come to pay their respects.

Ruby had arrived, as per Julian's request, I imagined, and came over to give her sympathies. I could see in her eyes that she knew what had happened between Serena and me. I wasn't sure what else to say besides thank you.

I knew she, like many others, would have expected her to be here today. But I was not surprised after what happened last night. Hell, I'd been pushing her away since the moment my father died. Why would anyone want to deal with me?

The next hour was spent listening to people speak of their fondest memories of Father. Hearing them felt bittersweet. Although it was nice listening to some, it still didn't help ease the dull feeling within.

Julian hadn't stopped drinking since we got back from the church. I thought he might ease up after Ruby's arrival, but instead, he used her as his verbal punching bag. On any other day, I'd have called him out, but today, I didn't care anymore. Besides, she was now with him. It was her choice, maybe one of these days she'd open her goddamn eyes and realize the asshole he was.

I was just about to fix a drink when Benjamin walked in.

"I knew I'd find you in here."

"Hmm," I grunted as I poured myself a scotch.

"You want one?" I asked Ben.

"Yeah, sure."

I could see that even he wasn't sure how to approach me.

"How are you holding up?"

I paused to think of how to answer the question.

"If I said I was fine, I'd be lying. If I said I was distraught, that would also be a lie. How about we settle on fucked up?"

Handing him his glass, we drank to my father.

"I must say, I expected Serena to be here today."

I hadn't meant to slam my glass on the desk, but the simple mention of her name seemed to tip me over the edge.

"I thought things were going well between the two of you?"

"They were. Until last night." I watched my uncle walk around the coffee table and sit in the chair next to me.

"So, what happened last night?"

Raking my hands through my hair, I suddenly became desperate to talk to someone about it.

"My head has been all over the place...work is the one thing that I seem to be able to handle. Serena had been trying to get in touch, asking if I was doing okay, letting me know she was there for me."

"And I'm guessing you ignored her?"

"I did for a while, I didn't know what to say. I didn't want her to see me in the state I was in. I finally gave in and followed her back to her place. We talked for a bit, then had sex. Then it all went wrong."

"What happened?"

"I told her I was falling in love with her."

Ben's hand stopped in midair.

"And guess what? She didn't say it back. She said I was wrong and didn't mean it, that my emotions were all over the place because of Father's death. How I was confusing my feelings with everything that was going on."

"That can't have been easy to hear. I don't think I've ever known you to tell a girl you love her—at least not this quick. Now, don't bite my head off, but is there even the slightest chance she could partially be right?"

"No!" I shouted, simultaneously trying to suppress that niggling thread of doubt that began to worm its way into my head. "You don't understand, I've never felt the way I do about her with anyone else. Ever. When I'm with her, I forget everything. I don't think about work or my family. For a brief time, she even made me forget the pain."

I fixed myself another drink. Ben declined the offer.

"So, what then happened?"

"I left."

"You just upped and left? No talking to her? Try to convince her that you meant every word?"

Unable to look him in the eyes, I ran my hands through my hair before leaning my elbows on my knees. My eyes followed the intricate engraving on the wooden mantel above the fireplace.

"No. I couldn't be around her, I couldn't face even looking at her. She doesn't feel for me what I feel for her. I needed to get out of there."

"Have you spoken to her since?"

I looked over, and at that moment, all I could see were the similarities my uncle's face had to my father's.

I'd never previously noticed they had such a strong resemblance, but right that second, it felt uncanny. The sympathy, sorrow, and empathy seemed to seep from his eyes.

For the first time in god knew how long, I felt close, or at least closer to someone in my family and safe enough to let my guard down. At least a little bit.

I shook my head.

There was a long stretch of silence, but it seemed comfortable for both of us as we each sat back and relaxed further into our seats.

Eventually, Ben broke the silence. "What now?"

"Now? Well, I've got to get through this damn wake first."

"And then?"

"Then, I honestly don't know. Maybe go away for a couple of days? Give us both some space? I don't know."

Taking a deep breath, I ran my hands over my face, trying to hide the fears and uncertainty that began to rise to the surface.

"I feel like I'm at a crossroads. It is like my life is being split into two polar opposite directions, and if I pick one, I lose the other."

"Tell me, explain both. Why do you believe you can't have both? Why can't it happen?"

"I don't know how to explain it."

"Just try. There is no right or wrong answer."

Leaning forward, I rested my elbows on my knees. Finally, I let it all out.

"I have never been able to choose anything in my life for myself. I'm torn between the expectation that has been drummed into me since infancy and what I truly want to do and achieve with my life. I can't show weakness. I can't show vulnerability. Family and love were never something I aspired to, nor was it ever hinted at as something I should actively seek. That's the freedom and prerogative my siblings have. All that's ever been set out for me was the business—continuing the legacy. All I know is that I only function by structure and order and by following the guides and precedence set before me. How do I go against all that I've ever known? All I've ever been taught? What I was born for. Molded into. But then Serena came along."

My eyes drifted over to Ben's, and he gently nodded, encouraging me to continue.

"She's like a mermaid, unreal, alluring, with an essence of unattainability to her. She isn't something I can grasp in my hands and haul off into the sunset with. That's not my path. That's not what is expected of me or what I can allow myself to want or even to believe. She's an enigma. At the same time, she makes me feel free. Free to change my life. Free to think beyond the lines and boxes that have always been around me. When I'm around her, I feel comfortable opening up. Not hide behind the mask. She pushes me to question things I had never thought of before. She has so much passion and drive and wants to fight for those who can't. She wants to make a difference in the world, and it's not attached to dollar amounts. It's about making a better life for those who enter her orbit. But in that same breath, it makes me doubt her opinion of me. Is she just like everyone else—trying to turn me into something I'm not? Is she simply writing a new script I'm now expected to follow? Just like everyone else always has."

My mind felt like it was spinning in circles, never reaching an answer. Unable to look at him, I bowed my head between my legs, pulling the strands of my hair in frustration as my voice was so low, just above a whisper.

"I'm scared I can't be who she wants me to be. There's too much at risk. Going against what I've been taught my whole life means tarnishing my father's memory, it's not inventive or progressive. It will be seen as rebellious and I can't do that."

Once again, we sat silently, the words ricocheting relentlessly around my head. After several minutes had passed, Ben took a deep breath, unbuttoned his jacket, and faced me head-on.

"I know it would be easy for me to give you an answer or a plan that you could decide if you want to follow, but that's not for me to do. This is your life. Yours. Nobody else's. I will say though, I have always resented the pressure thrust upon you. I never understood it. It's also one of the reasons why I separated myself from this family. I didn't want to sit back and watch a repeat of what my brother—your father, had gone through be drilled into you. I've never understood it, it's always been rather archaic to me. I've always loved my brother, and now that he's gone, I truly regret not having had the chance to fix things between us. But I do know he wouldn't want this turmoil for you. He'd want you to be happy."

We continued talking briefly, but I diverted the conversation to Ben's life. I needed to get off the subject of Serena. Today, out of all days, I just couldn't.

Finally, I decided to show my face again and do my best to mingle with the other guests. I was just about to go and find Heather when Verity walked straight up to me and tried embracing me in front of everyone. I instantly pushed her away.

"What the fuck do you think you're doing?"

"I'm sorry. I just thought..."

"You didn't think. You never do. What is wrong with you?"

"Your mother invited me and my parents. Your father was like family. I came to pay my respects and to make sure you're okay. I want you to know I'm here if you need me."

I couldn't take this anymore.

"I've told you countless times I am not interested. I am with someone."

"I've heard. That brown girl? The mechanic? Oh, Rhett, come on, we both know you're just going through a phase with her."

I never condoned any man raising their hand to a woman, but she made me almost wish I felt different.

"Verity, go fuck yourself!"

I didn't shout, but my voice was raised enough for several guests, including my mother, to hear.

"Rhett!"

My mother turned and walked towards one of the studies. Swearing under my breath, I watched her hasty retreat.

Before entering, she looked back at me, and I could see the tears streaming down her face. Frantically, I ran after her, closed the door, and found her sitting on the couch, crying her eyes out.

"I'm sorry, I didn't mean to cause a scene."

"Why are you making today even more difficult for me than it already is?"

"I'm sorry. Today's been horrible for me too. God dammit. Every day has been hard. I've been trying to stay strong for you, for everyone. Then, when Verity confronted me, I just snapped."

"All she was trying to do was give her condolences. What did that poor girl ever do to you for you to talk to her in such a horrible way? This isn't like you. I know things are difficult for all of us now. That's why we must stay strong. Be there for one another. Not lash out at every person who is trying to be kind."

"Verity has continuously lied. She has manipulated and twisted so much, and to top it off, she said some unpleasant things about Serena I won't stand for."

"Oh? And where is Serena? I thought you'd have her here, making a show of being with her as you seem to be doing it nonstop," she spat with pure venom.

I took a few deep breaths, knowing I couldn't lose it with my mother today.

"I'm not sure what your issue is with her. She makes me happy. She isn't here as I didn't think it was the right time."

There was no way I would tell her what had happened last

night. I was beginning to wonder how deep-rooted my mother's hatred for Serena was.

"The right time for what?"

"For her to meet everyone. Not here. Not like this."

She huffed and then retrieved a handkerchief from her pocket. My patience with this entire day was beginning to wear very thin.

"Well, at least you'll be able to focus now on stopping Julian from drinking his body weight. I'm barely getting by today. Please promise me you won't make things any worse?"

She went silent and walked over to a picture of her and my father. It had been taken while she was pregnant with me.

Father had surprised her with a trip to Miami. Walking over, I look at the picture. I couldn't help but smile. The way they looked into one another's eyes, they were clearly madly in love.

"I miss him so much. I go to bed, and it feels so empty. Every night, I wake up in the middle of the night and forget for a few brief seconds. The pain goes away for those brief moments. Then, it all comes back to me. Every time."

"I miss him too."

She turned and hugged me. After a few moments, she walked over to the mirror, wiped away the faint streaks of her mascara, and both made our way back outside.

I stayed for a couple more hours. Trying my best to help stop Julian from making a drunken fool of himself. But it was to no avail. Finally, I knew I had to go.

Once home, I changed into something more comfortable, made myself a drink, and went and sat on the balcony.

I wasn't sure how long I had been out there when I heard a noise from inside.

As I made my way in, I found Verity standing in the middle of the room. The door to my apartment was wide open behind her, and she stood there, looking as if it was both expected and okay for her to be there.

"What are you doing here? How did you get upstairs?"

"The doorman was on his cigarette break and talking to someone outside. Your mother was worried when you left. I overheard her asking your sister to check in on you. So, I pulled Heather aside and offered to do it myself as I had to pass by your apartment to return to mine. And given how tired and emotional everyone was, it was the least I could do, she was grateful for my offering to help and gave me your spare key."

Verity was the last person I wanted to see or speak to right now, but I was so drained that I didn't even have the energy to fight back.

Walking over to the kitchen, I started looking for something to eat. I heard her follow me. As I turned around, I saw she took a seat on one of the bar stools.

"I won't stay long. Unless you want me to?"

Her attempt at flirtation was an absolute waste on me.

"I'm tired. I want this day to be over already, and you are pretty much the last person I want to see. You've clearly come here to get something off your chest, so can you either get on with it or get out."

In the fridge, I grabbed a beer and a leftover pasta salad from the deli.

"I need to talk to you about Serena," Verity said her name as if it pained her.

"What about her?"

My hackles went up once again.

"She's not right for you. She never will be. I'm not the only one who thinks so. I've tried to explain to your mother that you're only going through a phase, and it'll all be out of your system soon. But she's worried, and the way you snapped at me earlier, I'm starting to get worried, too."

My body froze. I couldn't quite believe what I was hearing.

"Your mother has really turned to me recently. I've been her shoulder to cry on. We both don't want to see you make a fool of yourself. Especially now that you're the owner of Chambers Industries, it's time you think about settling down. And we both know you'll never be able to do that with her."

"And what makes you so sure of that?"

I looked down at the counter, my fists clenched so tightly my knuckles turned white.

"You know what we're talking about. She doesn't fit in. She never will. Besides what she looks like, she is of lower class to us, and she'll never understand how things should be done. Gosh, can't you see it? Suppose you invited her to a family luncheon. In that case, she'd expect fried chicken and talk about her family, who are probably felons, or hammer on about BLM and make others feel uncomfortable. Surely, you're not too blind to see she's only after you for your money? Have you ever done a proper background check on her? For all you know, her credentials could be faked, and it's all a big trap to get herself pregnant and entrap you. Rhett, you must understand, I'm telling you all this because I care. Because I love you. We all love you. We don't want to see your name get dragged through the mud, you've worked so hard. The last thing we would want to happen is for this gold-digging whore to tear you down, and rip apart all the arduous work you and your family have done in building up the Chambers name. If your father were here, you know he would want the best for you."

I threw my bottle of beer against the wall. The sounds of

the smash made her jump. I had never been so angry in my entire life.

I heard a gasp and a sob. The hairs on the back of my neck stood up. Instinctively, I spun around and saw Serena walk around the corner. She had tears streaming down her face. How long had she been standing there? She must have heard everything.

"Serena." I cried out, running over to her.

As I tried to embrace her, I could feel her whole body shaking.

"Serena, Serena."

I tried to calm her, but it was of no use. What Verity had said was beyond despicable. I wrapped my arms around her to keep a hold on her, as I wasn't sure she had the strength to stand. Turning only my head, I looked straight into Verity's eyes.

"You are a jealous, vindictive, psychopathic racist. Serena is worth more than a million of you. You're not even worthy of saying her name. I have never met someone as disturbed and pathetic as you. I would pick a lifetime of Serena hating me, over spending just an hour alone with you any day. You have used my mother's fragile, mourning state to push your own agenda. Do you think I would ever lower myself to such an extent and be with you? You make me physically sick. It disgusts me that you try to class yourself in the same circles as me. You are a conniving, intolerant, narrow-minded, opinionated, prejudiced bitch and I want you to leave now. If you ever come near me or try to repeat a bad word about Serena, I promise I will make you and your family's lives a living hell. I've had people investigate you, I know every hidden skeleton and dirty scandal. Your name will become a joke told at parties. Your friends will disown you. Society will shut you out, and you'll just have your washed-up self to keep you company. Now get out of here!"

I could see the shock on Verity's face. I watched as she quickly made her way out of the apartment.

I sat Serena on the couch and then closed the front door, locking it and sliding the chain into place.

Sitting beside her, I held her hand and tried to help her calm down. Her breathing began to slow down. As her body stopped shaking, I could still feel mine vibrating with anger.

"I'm so sorry you had to hear that. I promise she will never speak of or to you again."

She stared out into the distance. I needed her to know that not a single part of me felt there was any substance to Verity's attack. As that was what it was.

"You must know, that's not what I believe. She doesn't speak for me or my family. I don't agree with anything she said." I paused, hoping my words would register. "Please speak to me. This is killing me."

Looking into her eyes, I waited. After what felt like an eternity, she turned, and all I could see in her eyes was pain.

"I shouldn't have come here."

"No, please. Wait. Talk to me. What made you come here?"

"I wanted to see you. I hated what happened last night. Especially as it was the eve of the funeral. I wanted to make sure you were okay. I knew today was going to be difficult. And with what happened last night, it was probably worse. But I had to come and see you, even if you didn't want to see me."

"I always want to see you. Especially after today. I wish you didn't have to hear the disgusting shit that came out of her twisted mouth."

I wiped away a tear that fell down her cheek.

"All of today, I couldn't stop thinking about you and your family. I kept wishing there was something I could do or say that would have made things better. But I knew there wasn't. I couldn't concentrate at work. Once I got home, I was restless. I got changed and came straight here. As I got to your building, the doorman was outside having a cigarette. He called me over, and we began talking. He used to work part-time at the door of my building a year or so ago. We made small talk, and I explained that today was your father's funeral, and I was coming to check that you were okay. He said it was fine for me to go straight up, so I did."

She stopped and took a deep breath. Then it suddenly hit me, I remember Verity saying she'd seen the doorman talking to someone outside. She must have realized it was Serena. She was probably expecting her to come up and that's why the door was still open behind her when I first found her. How twisted was she?

"As I took the elevator up, I had a million things running through my head. I wasn't sure how you'd be or if you'd even want to see me. Your door was open, so I let myself in. I heard two voices and froze. Suddenly, I thought, what the fuck have I done? I shouldn't be here. Then I heard my name. I froze. I couldn't move. I knew I shouldn't be here, listening, but I couldn't leave. I wish I had."

She hung her head in her hands. I needed her to know how I felt.

"Please tell me you understand I don't agree with a word she said?" I begged.

"I know."

Relief flooded through me.

"But... I know other people do."

"What do you mean?"

"I've been dealing with people like her my whole life. Some are open and unapologetic with their opinions. Others hide them but let them slip with crude jokes or stereotypical remarks that they think aren't bad. My dad always told me I had to work twice as hard to get half as far. One, because I'm a woman, and two, because I'm not white. It's not something new to me. I've dealt with it for far longer than you could ever imagine"

"But I don't see race or creed or background. I just see the most beautiful woman I have ever met."

"Saying you don't see my race is just as precarious. I know you don't mean it in a bad way, but saying you don't see it means saying you don't see a part of who I am. People like Verity and your mother will always see me as less. It's one of the reasons why I came here tonight."

My brain couldn't keep up with what was going on.

"I care about you so much. You make me happier than I ever could have expected. But what happened tonight is just another example that it isn't enough. We shouldn't continue with this relationship. One thing Verity said that is correct is that we do come from different worlds. That's just a fact. Your world, your family, and the people around you don't believe I fit in it. And I don't have the strength to fight. I don't want to fight for people to give me a chance. Get to know me. See who I really am. I'm sorry. I really am, especially today of all days."

This couldn't be happening. It felt as if my body wasn't my own. In shock, I watched her stand. She kissed me, and I felt her tears against my cheek. Then I watched as she walked out the door and closed it behind her, the sound echoing right to my soul.

Chapter 24

Serena

"Do you want tea, coffee, or something stronger?"

Ruby did her best to gauge how to act around me. I knew she was utterly surprised when she opened the door at 11 p.m. to find me standing there, eyes red and my heart split in half. I didn't know where else to go.

After leaving Rhett's apartment, I was a complete mess. Knowing I couldn't face going back to my apartment alone, I jumped into a cab and came straight there.

She hadn't been back long, as she'd spent the last few hours trying to get Julian to sober up enough for her to leave him at his apartment.

"I'm sorry. I should have called before."

"Don't be silly. You know you're always welcome, and I'm always here for you."

I settled on a brandy, needing something soothing. I shivered as Ruby made our drinks and handed me a blanket. I wrapped it around me, but I knew there was no point. The cold was coming from within.

Handing me a glass, she sat down next to me.

"So, I'm guessing you went and saw Rhett?"

"I did."

"And what happened?"

I took a big sip, and then I told her what happened.

"Are you kidding me? Who does she think she is? Is she a damn psycho?"

Drinking more of my drink, I told her about Rhett being angry with her but how her words had a more significant effect on me than I wanted them to have.

"As awful as it sounds, it felt like something shifted. Suddenly I saw things in a different light, and I couldn't unsee it. That's when I told him we couldn't be together anymore."

"You did what?"

"The words just came out. I feel that through doing this, doing it now, I'll be saving both of us so much. I thought it was the right thing to do."

"And how did he take it? I don't mean to rub salt into the wounds, but the poor guy has probably just had one of the worst days of his life, and this is how it ends?"

"Don't. I feel terrible. He just sat there and looked at me, his eyes looked broken. So, I just left."

"Oh, Serena."

She came over and wrapped her arm around me.

Finally, the dam broke and tears flooded out of me. My chest heaved, my body trembling.

I didn't remember ever feeling like this. Even after my mother left us, I never felt this shredded.

"It's okay. It's okay."

Her words were soothing but they couldn't change things.

Once I managed to calm down, I grabbed my glass and finished my drink.

"The problem is I've just pushed away the man I may have

wanted to spend the rest of my life with. I... I... think I'm in love with him."

"Oh, honey."

I looked up and could see even she had tears in her eyes.

"What have I done?"

"When did you realize? Was it what happened tonight?"

"Yes... no... I'm not sure. You know after I told you what happened last night when Rhett came around and told me how he felt?"

"Yes, but I thought you'd said you didn't feel the same as he did?"

"I didn't. Well, I didn't think I did. What he said came as a shock, never in a million years was I expecting him to tell me he loved me. It just really took me off guard. But then, after he left, and after I spoke to you, I went to bed and couldn't sleep. I kept thinking back on the amazing times we had together. All the unexpected, surprising things he'd said and done. The way he looked at me, but most importantly, the way he made me feel. And the more I was thinking, the bigger the smile got on my face when I pictured his face. That was when I realized. I know it's too soon, and I don't usually let people in this quickly, this hard. But with him, everything is different. Most of the time, it doesn't make sense. But that's also what somehow makes it all feel right."

"So why didn't you just tell him?"

"I wanted to. And if it hadn't been his father's funeral, I would have. I'd have gone straight to him. But I knew it wasn't the right time. Especially with how things had ended the last time I saw him. Then, when I went over to his tonight, I was going to tell him. I finally thought I'd have the strength to let it all out. But after what Verity said, I just couldn't. Everything became messed up. I was suddenly panicking. She said she had discussed her feelings with his mother and agreed with her. And like I said, I'm sure she wouldn't be the only one. How was I meant to tell him I loved him, too? What kind of position would that have put him in? I wouldn't be able to live with myself, knowing that my declaration could affect his relationship with his family. I'd be pushing him into a corner. I'd never want him to choose between a relationship with me or one with them. I'd never be able to forgive myself. So, I did the only thing I could. I told him we weren't right for one another. I knew if I told him that, I wouldn't be ruining his family."

"But can't you see? He told you that he loves you. You love him. He's a grown man. You haven't met his sisters yet, but they are so lovely. And I know that if they had the opportunity to meet you, they'd love you, too, especially as you love Rhett. And in regard to his mother, well, I honestly don't think she'd want to see her son unhappy. Yes, she's arrogant and stuck up, but she does love her children. And I'm sure Verity has been twisting and manipulating everything."

"But his mother was off with me when I met her before. I know she was." I said, not hiding the agony.

"She might have been, but you must remember that's Rhett's burden. Not yours. And it's not that you're pushing him into a corner. It's you choosing love."

I didn't know what to do, so I sat and cried until I fell asleep.

I woke to the smell of coffee and food. My head felt fuzzy, and it took me a minute to realize I must have passed out on Ruby's couch.

"Morning. How are you feeling?" Ruby asked tenderly.

"I'm not sure. What time is it?"

"It's 9:30."

Shit. I was late for work.

"Don't worry. I called Sarah earlier and told her you had an impromptu meeting this morning and wouldn't be in before lunch."

I knew Sarah would be intrigued, especially as I was always on time. Nor did I ever have unexpected meetings first thing in the morning.

"Aren't you working today?" I asked.

"Nope. I had boot camp Pilates at seven this morning and when I got back, you were still asleep. I knew you must have needed it. So, I called your office and decided to let you sleep in and make you breakfast. You can either borrow something of mine or grab something from yours on your way in."

She plated up poached eggs with smoked salmon. To my surprise, my tummy was awake and grumbling. We sat and ate as she told me about the wake and how there'd already been a scene between Rhett and Verity. And how Julian was a mess.

"I'm sorry I've been such a shitty friend. How are things between you two?"

This time, she was the one looking lost.

"Things are so hot and cold. When times are good, they are amazing. But when they're bad, it's horrible. And it usually coincides with when he's drinking a lot."

"Do you think he has a drinking problem?"

"Yes. At first, I just put it down to him being outgoing and a bit of a party animal. But once we began spending most days and nights together, I realized he was justifying getting drunk on almost any occasion."

I still didn't understand what she saw in him. She could do some much better.

"I know you don't like him, but you don't see the times when things are good."

Her smile didn't touch her eyes and I think she was saying it more for herself than me.

"I mentioned maybe both of us doing a detox or cleanse or

something to help with his drinking subtly, and things were starting to look up. Or so I thought. Then, when Max told everyone his diagnosis, Julian started up again. When he died, it became apocalyptic. In the past few days, it's been easier to count the hours he's sober than the ones he's drunk."

"Do you love him?"

"Yes. We told each other a few weeks back. But now I'm wondering if I'm his girlfriend or his shrink or just the woman he fucks and helps sober him up. Plus, now he's not working anymore, I don't know what will happen."

"What do you mean he's not working anymore? Did he quit?"

"No. I'm guessing Rhett didn't tell you?"

"No, what happened?"

"Apparently, they got into a fight at the office. Julian hasn't said this, but I'm sure he was drunk. Anyway, now that Rhett's in charge, and with the loss of their father, he couldn't deal with him there anymore, so he kicked him out. He took his passes and everything. Even told security not to let him back in."

My hand went straight to my mouth.

Was that why he seemed so tense and stressed when he came over to see me?

"How is Julian dealing with that?"

"He says he doesn't care, especially with the large amount of money his dad had left him. He says now he can retire and enjoy life."

She turned her back and busied herself with loading up the dishwasher. I could hear in her voice she was holding back tears.

"So where does that leave things with you two now?"

"I don't know. I love him. And I know he has a strange way of showing it, but I know he loves me, too. So, the only thing I can do is let the dust settle, let him grieve, and then tell him he needs to get help."

"And if he doesn't?"

I felt awful asking it, but I had to know.

"If he doesn't, then I'll walk away. I can't stand by and watch him self-destruct. Under all the arrogance and cockiness, he is a great guy. I wish he'd let that side out more. It's like he's fighting some battle, rebelling against something. I just don't know what it is."

"Could it be something that happened when he was younger?"

"I'm not sure. I've tried talking to him about it, but he shrugs it off and usually then diverts the conversation by initiating sex."

I'm not a shrink, but I am good at reading people. Something's going on, something he isn't dealing with, and this is his way of masking it.

Was it a painful memory? Was it abuse? Jealousy?

I'm not sure, but I know he's got to sort his shit out, or he'll lose Ruby for good.

One thing I learned from her relationship with Roman is that once he stopped making an effort to be in the relationship with her, she stopped trying, too.

And I understood that.

Chapter 25

Serena

I'd left Ruby's just after eleven. Grabbing a cab to my place, I quickly showered, changed, and made my way to work.

By the time I'd gotten a feel for what still needed to get done for the day, it was lunch. I worked through and stayed till eight in the evening.

On Thursday and Friday, I came in early and focused on work. Each night, being the last one to leave. I'd gone to call Rhett hundreds of times, but each time, I couldn't go through with it. So, I just buried myself in work to numb the pain. Endlessly, my mind kept replaying all the ways in which things could have gone differently.

Was I too rash with my assumptions? Especially given the utter grief I could only imagine Rhett must be feeling. Should I have given him the chance to fully process everything that was going on in his life, the loss, the company takeover, his feelings —all of it, before breaking up with him? Should there have been a couple of days or weeks for both of us to cool down before leading down this road?

Work has always been my passion—at times, my escape from my life—my feelings and emotions. But now, everything felt boring, empty, and dull. Now that I no longer had him, I realized how much happiness, hope, and excitement he brought every day, whether by phone calls, messages, surprise visits to my office, or stunning dates we would go on.

For the first time ever, I really opened myself up. I allowed there to be a chance to love and be loved unconditionally in return. Yet it wasn't enough. I felt I wasn't enough. I wasn't enough to keep my mother around. I wasn't the right fit for Rhett. Everything was just too much.

I decided to spend the weekend at Dad's, mainly because the monotony of work and my continuously fraying emotions were becoming too overwhelming. I couldn't stand another night sitting alone in my apartment, crying, wallowing, and just feeling super lonely.

I'd spent the last couple of hours catching him up on everything that had happened. He listened, passed me tissues when I cried, hugged me when I needed one, and was just there, just like he always was.

"I know you're my baby girl, and I will always do and say everything I can to make you happy. But I must admit, I agree with Ruby on this one." He ignored the pouty glare I shot him. "You should've told him how you feel already. Life's too precious. Look at what happened to his father, no one was expecting it. No one thought his life would be taken so suddenly from him. But it was."

I knew he was right but it still didn't make things any easier now. Still didn't change what had happened and still couldn't change the past.

"And about that Verity girl, most of what she said was just sad and showed the terrible job her parents did in raising her. But again, as you said, she was right on one thing. You two do come from different worlds. The thing is, sweetie, that isn't a bad thing."

Dad shifted in his seat, and his arms encased me in a big bear hug before he lifted my head and looked straight into my eyes.

The feel of his callused hands as they gently stroked my cheek sparked a sense of déjà vu from when I was a little girl.

"In life, we come across all different kinds of people. But it's what we learn from then, how we as individuals evolve, that's what defines who we are."

"I know you're right."

"And in a way, you should feel sorry for her. She's been desperate to marry into that family, going to extra lengths to do so. And she never will be. I know you said Rhett threatened her with what she values most, her appearance to society, but for her sake, let's hope she never comes across Olivia. When you tell her, and should the two ever meet, then she'll know what it means when somebody upsets you."

Affection for my sister ran through me and I knew Dad was right. Despite our differences, my sister was fiercely protective of me. Dad yawned loudly before rising off the couch.

"You planning on staying up?" he asked.

"No, I'm gonna head to bed as well."

I helped him switch everything off before saying goodnight. I knew I should have a shower, but my body felt too tired to stand up, let alone wash my hair. That could wait until tomorrow.

As I lay in my old bedroom, tossing and turning in bed, I ran through my conversation with Dad, which in turn made me think of someone I hadn't let into my mind in a very long time.

My mother.

Growing up, having my mother abandon us, well, it took its toll. I didn't realize its effect on me until I was older and more mature. Dad had to play the role of both parents, and he worked his ass off to give us the best education and as many opportunities in life, whether it was taking my brother to football practice or my sister and me to dance recitals, concerts, or any club or camp.

Yet, he still always made the time and effort to listen, make us laugh, or be a shoulder to cry on, just like he did tonight.

I often wondered how our lives would have turned out had my mother stuck around. But there were never feelings of longing or loss.

What kind of woman left her husband and three children for another man and a carefree life?

As much as my mother wanted to portray to everyone that she was happy being a wife and a mother, it wasn't enough for her, as two weeks before my fifth birthday, we came home to find all her stuff gone and a letter on the kitchen counter.

> *I'm sorry, I can't do this anymore. I want you to know I love you all, but it's time for me to be happy. I have paid my dues, and it's time I focus on myself. Goodbye.*
>
> *Mom*
>
> *X*

It wasn't as if she was a great, caring mother or wife in the first place.

Especially as we later found out she'd left with the guy she was having an affair with to start a new life. And as much as my dad wouldn't admit it then, I know he knew about all the affairs she used to have and just put up a happy front for us.

My sister took it the worst, as she was thirteen at the time and had always tried to be mommy's little girl. My brother and I, who were only eight and nine years old, were always closer to Dad.

That's why I admired him so much. His wife left him for another man, but he never let that stop him from living his life.

I knew we were all better off without her. It made me more grateful for the family I had but those feelings put a bittersweet taste in my mouth.

I couldn't imagine losing my dad. He meant the world to me. I knew that despite the pressure and expectations Rhett's father had on him, I knew they loved one another. Once again, my heart broke for him. Was there any going back for us?

The thought left me with a pit in my stomach.

And as I finally fell asleep, it was with the fear that there was no longer any hope.

It had rained last night, yet today, the sky was cloudless, and the air was fresh. There was something so soothing about that.

Here, neighbors would help one another. I remember, especially after Mom left, it felt like people were always around, offering to help my dad babysit or inviting us over for play dates or dinner. When I was younger, I didn't quite understand it.

I just shrugged it off and thought we had become so cool that everyone just wanted to be our friends. Now, I could see and appreciate everyone who tried to help. They were supportive and caring.

The fact that we had a lot of family living there as well, as my father's business was the most prosperous one in town, might have had some influence.

But honestly, I thought people had time for one another there. And the longer I was away from there and just in the city, the more I'd learned to appreciate that.

I decided to take a walk, hoping the exercise and clean air would help shift the ever-present dark cloud that seemed to be looming over me.

I'd been walking for about twenty minutes, not really paying attention to where my legs were taking me when I realized I was heading in the direction of the lookout.

The place I had taken Rhett to - it felt like a lifetime ago now. Knowing I couldn't face the place that once gave me peace and refuge, was now filled with bittersweet, heart-breaking memories. I took one of the other rockier trails that required some light rock climbing, but I knew it'd be worth it as this one led toward the lake.

Sweat began to bead at my temples, and my thighs were beginning to burn, so I grabbed a bottle of water and a coffee from the little refreshment stand nestled between the lake and the trees.

I sat by the lake, lost in my thoughts.

How could any of this be fixed?

Chapter 26

Serena

I must have been daydreaming as I hadn't realized someone had come and joined me at my table.

Looking over, I recognized him instantly. Danny Gleeson.

I'd had the biggest crush on him throughout my whole senior year. He wasn't into sports, so he didn't hang around Roman or his friends, nor was he into any of the leading social groups you have in most high schools.

I remember he generally kept himself to himself. We went to lots of extra credit clubs together, we were on the debate team and took Spanish, Italian, and German classes.

And if I remember correctly, he was also involved in the Giving Projects the school used to run. They were involved in the school with various events and activities in the community.

I remember finding him so intriguing. He had this mysterious air about him. I cringe when I remember how I wrote about him in my diary for weeks, even to the point where I used to get depressed, wondering if he even knew I existed.

"Serena Parker."

I almost choked on my coffee. My inner teenage self was jumping up with joy just because he knew who I was.

God, was I pathetic.

"Danny. Wow, I can't believe you know my name."

"Of course I do. You were the hottest girl in school, I had the biggest crush on you."

"Wait, hold on, are you being serious? You have got to be kidding me?"

"No, I'm being serious. Why?"

He chuckled slightly. Seemingly genuine.

"This must be some sort of joke, I had the biggest crush on you throughout the whole of senior year. I always thought you never noticed me."

"Oh, now you're the one that must be kidding. I remember once we were in debate class, getting ready for an upcoming competition, and Mr. Edwards had us on opposing teams. You had gone first, then it was my turn for a rebuttal, and I thought I would vomit. I was convinced I would freeze right there in front of you. How could you not tell that I was a nervous wreck?"

I knew the exact time he was talking about.

"I thought you didn't care. I remember watching you, hoping you'd look at me, and instead, you just kept your focus straight ahead!"

We both sat there and laughed.

"So, what have you been up to?" he asked.

I told him how I went on to study law, passed the bar, managed to get work straight out of college at a prestigious law firm, and was now running my own.

"I can't say I'm surprised. You were always such a strong and determined woman, even back then. I remember you were always our biggest asset on the debate team, you would make our opponents quiver. I can only imagine what it must be like coming up against you in a courtroom or a meeting."

"Thank you. But I wasn't that bad, was I?"

High school felt like a lifetime ago.

"Yes and no. You only ever fought for the right things."

We both took a sip of our drinks.

"So, are you married?"

I was slightly taken aback by his question. I was beginning to feel like I was on some timer, as if everyone was expecting me to be married, have kids, and live in a house with a white picket fence.

"No, I'm not married and don't have kids."

"Are you seeing anyone?"

I couldn't tell if he was flirting or asking out of general interest.

"It's complicated. I was seeing someone, but he recently lost his father. Then everything changed. There were issues before, but I never spoke about them. Everything came out, and now I don't know where things stand. He told me he loved me, and I didn't say it back."

"Do you love him?"

"Yes."

It feels so easy saying it. That's what was even more frustrating.

"Then it's never too late."

I knew I needed to explain the various things that happened in more detail, wanting him to understand that it was more complex than he may have thought.

"I'm not so sure about that," I murmured.

"Okay, enlighten me."

"I met this guy. His name is Rhett Chambers. I'm not sure if you've heard of him?"

Looking up, I saw Danny's eyes widen, and he rolled his

lips inward, I'm guessing to suppress his smile, but he nodded and waved his hand for me to continue.

"It was actually by fluke during one of my visits here, and I was helping Dad at the garage. There was an instant spark, but I left before giving him my name. Anyway, after that, I was at work - meeting a new client, and low and behold, it was the guy from the garage. Well, his father's company was the new client, and he works for the family business and will take it over. Initially, there was a lot of back and forth, but eventually, I gave him a chance. Then his crazy ex tried worming her way in—trying to end things before they'd even really started between us. He found out his father was diagnosed with terminal cancer, and Rhett understandably took it hard. We worked through it, and things were looking up. He met my family, and they all loved him, but then I met his mother, and let's just say it didn't go well. Plus, given his name, when we went to a gala together, the press and a hell of a lot of internet trolls tore into me. I'm used to it in a work capacity, but I'd never experienced it on that scale. One of the biggest issues was how I didn't fit."

"How do you mean you didn't fit?"

"Because I'm not white."

"He said that to you?"

His hands clenched, and I could see the anger rolling off him.

"No, no, of course not. Rhett isn't like that. But those around him, his mother, the ex, hell, even the tabloids, made it crystal clear. At first, I didn't let it bother me too much, but it was always in the back of my mind. Then his father passed, and Rhett shut himself off, and things just got worse from there. I couldn't fight anymore. I didn't want to fight for people to accept me. But when he started pulling away and distancing himself, it just became too much. I don't know if you remember, but my mom left us when we were kids, and abandonment is something I've always struggled with. To the point that I hardly ever let anyone in. So, to finally let someone in and then feel like they are walking away I couldn't take it. So, I ended it."

I quickly wiped away the tears that rolled down my cheeks. We sat silently for a minute as he gave me a moment to compose myself.

"Trust me when I say this. If you love him, and he loves you, nothing will get in between that."

My pulse began to race as those words planted a seed of hope within my chest.

"Enough about me. What about yourself? Married? Kids?"

He looked away and took a long swig of his coffee. I was about to change the subject as the silence began to feel uncomfortable.

"I was. Seven years ago, I married the love of my life. We traveled around Europe and Asia for almost two years. It was amazing. If you haven't gone traveling yet, I'd recommend it. A few months after we returned, Lucy found out we were pregnant. I was so excited. I'd never pegged myself for the father type, but everything felt right when I saw our baby on the screen at the first scan. The first two trimesters were fine. Then, in the third, we found out she had pre-eclampsia. She went into labor five weeks early and I lost both my wife and the baby."

Tears were rolling down my cheeks. How devastating. What an awful thing to happen, to anyone.

I must have sounded like such a jerk going on about my problems. Everything I spoke about was inconsequential in comparison to the horrific ordeal he'd gone through.

"I'm so sorry."

I didn't know what else to say. Nothing else seemed right to say.

I wiped my tears away and finished off my drink.

"I now work closely with various charities, raising awareness of the importance of regular testing for it. While she was pregnant, we decided to name the child Matilda if it was a girl and Matthew if it was a boy. It was a girl. So, I set up the Lucy & Matilda Foundation. I now go around the country giving talks in hospitals and pre-natal clinics and classes. I want to help prevent there from being another tragedy like mine."

"Danny, you truly are amazing. The strength you have and what you are doing is truly remarkable. I can't imagine what you have gone through. My dad used to say some people are stars - they're too bright for this earth, so they go and brighten up our skies."

"I love that, I might use that for our next campaign if that's okay?"

"Of course. Also, please let me know if there is anything else I can do to help. Whether it's donating, fundraising, or even offering my legal services."

I grabbed a napkin and wrote down my number and email address.

"Thank you. I'll definitely be in touch."

He stood and kissed my cheek.

He began walking away towards one of the trails, but then stopped and turned.

"I meant what I said about love. If you do love this guy, then please don't let anything get in the way. Trust me, life is too short. You must live each day to the fullest. There's no time for regret."

Giving me a nod, I watched as he threw his empty cup in the trash before walking back down the path to the car park.

My head felt like it was going to combust. It was unbeliev- able how one conversation can change my perspective so much. I really couldn't imagine what it must feel like to go through such a thing as that—losing both your partner and your child. There really can't be anything worse in the world.

My mind began racing through every memory and experience with Rhett—the exciting and challenging times. Even though we had only been together a few months, there was no way I could deny that we had something special between us.

Was it worth me risking a potential future with the man solely on the dislike and opinions of his vile ex-girlfriend and his old-fashioned mother? Didn't we deserve the chance to give this relationship all we had?

The more I think about it, the more I know Danny's words are utterly correct. Time was something none of us could control, nor is it something we should gamble with. And the longer I let it go by, the more I was just risking it all.

My hands began to shake as I reached into my purse to grab my phone. I scrolled down to Rhett's number, I knew what I must do. Pressing the call button, I put the handset to my ear.

I listened as it rang three times, then suddenly went to the answering machine. I didn't know if he cut my call or if I miscounted the rings. Scrambling, I tried to find the right words to say. Taking a deep breath, I left him a message.

"Rhett, it's me. I'd ask how you're doing, but that's a stupid question. I'm visiting my dad and bumped into an old friend from high school. We were catching up and talking about our lives and plans for the future, which made me think about my own. I know I'm babbling on, but I just wanted to talk to you. There's something I need to tell you. I understand you probably don't want to talk to me right now, but I'd appreciate it if you'd give me a chance and hear me out. Thanks."

I cut the call and began kicking myself at how stupid I sounded. I was a goddamn lawyer, and talking was one of my strong suits. Obviously, not at times when it mattered.

Suddenly, panic rose in my throat. What if I was right that he had cut my call? What if he wanted nothing more to do with me? What if he'd already moved on? Hitting his number again,

I call him back. I knew it seemed irrational, but part of me needed to know.

It went straight to his voicemail.

He was done.

He didn't want to speak to me.

Maybe, in this case, love wasn't enough. Perhaps it wasn't really love. Tears began to fall down my face once more. I sat there in utter silence for what seemed like an eternity.

Once the tears had finally stopped, I started thinking that maybe I needed to get away. Not just like this weekend.

I never took a gap year between studies. Maybe I should take Danny's advice and go traveling? I'd always wanted to go and visit the vineyards in Italy, see the Eiffel Tower, and swim in the Red Sea. I could even try out a beach Christmas in Australia.

If Rhett didn't want to speak to me now, how was time going to make things any better?

Maybe now was the time to fully accept everything and move on. Move on with my life—a life without him.

Focus on what was good in my life—not thinking about what I was missing, not let others dictate and influence who I am and what I am worth.

Chapter 27

Rhett

It's only 10:34 a.m. on Monday, and the day already felt like it would never end. I basically drank myself into oblivion for most of the weekend.

Dominic turned up at my place on Saturday night in a vain attempt at cheering me up. In a way, he did, as he brought over some beers, and we watched the fight. I suggested going out after and was the one who ordered the bottle of vodka. That wasn't such a clever idea.

Of course, being two guys spending lots of money, we weren't short of female attention. Dom was lapping it up.

But despite the attempts of the Victoria's Secret model who'd whispered the dirtiest shit into my ear a man could imagine, all I could think about and want was Serena.

I slept off most of Sunday, and when I finally woke up, I went swimming. The water gave me the first bit of calm and solace I had felt in days. My lungs were heaving for air, and my arms and legs were burning. I could tell I had been slacking as I hadn't swum in over a week, and my body felt it.

After about an hour, I gave in. My body was screaming. So,

I showered, ordered from my favorite Italian restaurant, and passed out again.

Now, I was at my desk in the otherwise deserted office, trying to make a dent in the massive backlog of work I had not done in the past week. The office was officially closed for a day of respect and to allow those who worked for and were close to my father to have some time off to mourn.

Although some lower-level employees were there, working away, possibly trying to ease up on work for the upcoming week. That or they have no life besides work.

My head throbbed as it turned to midday, and my stomach rumbled. I'd sorted through twelve accounts, completing them, signing them off, and sending them to the legal department to finalize the paperwork. I had also spoken to our London and Hong Kong offices, getting complete updates on our current projects.

As I went to buzz for Charlotte to order me some food, I realized she wasn't in. I went to her desk to retrieve her index to look for the number for the deli.

As I'm flicking through her Rolodex, the phone rings. It feels weird answering her phone, especially as it is more than likely a phone call for me.

"Rhett Chambers speaking,"

"Oh. Hello, Mr. Chambers. It's Raya Cole. I wasn't expecting you to be in your office today."

My mind was scattered, trying to work out where I knew that name and voice from. Then it hit me. Raya owned the cafe we were negotiating.

The last time I saw her was when I got the phone call about my father. I remember running out of there, knowing nothing would ever be the same after that moment.

"Yes, well, there's work that needs to be done. So, Mrs. Cole, how can I help you?"

"I was simply calling to send my condolences and to leave you a message. I am sorry for your loss. I also wanted to see how you were coping with everything."

"Thank you, I'm fine. I really am."

"Do you have any plans for lunch?"

"No, I was just about to order a sandwich from the deli. Why?"

"Well, today's special is chicken pot pie, and I've just finished icing my homemade spiced carrot cake. I know a man like you needs a proper meal, not a sandwich."

I knew what she was doing but I didn't care. I was starving, and I'd been lucky enough to try her cooking on more than one occasion, and there was no chance I would turn down that invitation.

Plus, I could talk to her some more and have some luck trying to persuade her to sell.

"How can I refuse an offer like that? I'll be over shortly."

Hanging up the phone, it was as if my stomach had heard every word of that conversation and began rumbling like mad.

Upon arrival, Raya greeted me as if I were family, grabbing my arm and pulling me into a big hug, which, by the look on Russell's face from outside the window, must have been amusing, as the woman was half my size.

She then led me to the bar stool where she'd served a massive plate full of pie, veg, and creamy buttery mash. The smell of the food was so inviting, there was no chance of me standing on ceremony.

"Would you like a drink?"

"Yes, a beer, please."

She walked over to the fridge and grabbed me a bottle of homemade peach iced tea. I couldn't help but laugh at her gesture.

I wasn't sure if she did it because she didn't approve of midday drinking or if she suspected me of having already consumed a lot of alcohol recently.

Either way, I couldn't fault her.

The food was delicious. As I ate, she told me about an incident on the weekend, with one of her customers proposing to his girlfriend in the cafe.

With the help of Raya, he had hired out the whole restaurant and paid for actors and singers to sit in acting like regular patrons, only for them all to suddenly break into song and sing a medley of the girlfriend's favorite love songs. All of which was followed by the guy getting down on one knee and proposing.

Raya had been animated when reciting the story to me, and how much she enjoyed it.

Once again, a part of me experienced a pang of guilt for going after her home and cafe. But I knew business was business. And if she wanted to, she could open a whole bunch of cafes and turn it into a chain of Cole's around the country.

She made herself a coffee and quickly checked to see if the other customers needed anything.

Standing on the other side of the bar, coffee cup in one hand and wiping the surface counters with another, it was only when I finished my plate and looked up at her that I realized she had been watching me.

What was it about people of a particular generation that always discerned it was perfectly fine to sit and stare?

"Thank you for that. It was delicious."

She took my plate away and returned with a smaller one in her hand, carrying a nice large slice of carrot cake. She also poured me a cup of coffee.

I needed to work out this evening, I could feel myself beginning to soften from all the delicious food.

"I know you said on the phone that you're fine, but how are you doing?"

Oh, here we go.

"I mean it. I'm fine. I wouldn't say I was distraught, nor would I say I'm happy now. But I'm getting by, which is more than I can say than the rest of my family."

"And what about Serena? Has she been helping you get through any of this?"

I felt my body begin to tense. Taking a large sip of coffee, I cleared the lump beginning to form in my throat.

"Things are complicated."

I didn't know what else to say.

"May I ask what happened?"

It was not surprising that she asked but I only opened up to a few people. And with the ones I did, I was always careful with what I said, as there were only a few people who cared. The rest wanted something to gossip about or manipulate me for their advantage.

I knew it was safe to talk to her because Mrs Cole looked into my eyes, not wanting, or expecting anything in return, genuinely caring and worrying about my well-being.

Everyone had been trying to get me to speak to them since the day my father died. Not one had succeeded.

"The last time I saw you, I was here with Serena. We were having a wonderful time. Then I got the call to say my dad had been rushed to hospital."

I watched as she nodded in understanding.

"She told me you had to leave due to a family emergency. As soon as you left, her face was full of worry."

I didn't think about how Serena was feeling. I knew I just needed to leave.

"The whole family stayed there that night. I remember every minute detail. They are as clear as if they were happening right now in front of me. Before my father died, he shared with me his last words and wishes. Part of me knew I should have run and called the family in, but I didn't want to risk missing what he had to say. I've played back every word he spoke a thousand times."

"Did he say something cryptic?"

"No. It's not that. I... I... I don't know. I feel like I'm seeking an answer to something even though there isn't one."

"When our loved ones pass, one of the biggest things that happens is we question everything. Wanting to find answers to things at any other given time, wouldn't have any relevance or importance. But grief hits people in mysterious ways."

I nodded in response, not sure how else to answer.

"Anyway, after he died, I just didn't know what to do. I knew I had to step up and be there for my family. Be their rock, shoulder to cry on, whatever they needed. There wasn't time for me to wallow in self-pity or give into my grief. I had too much to do."

Drinking more coffee, I did my best to stay focused on what I was trying to say. I couldn't let my emotions get the better of me. Not now.

"So, I shut myself out. I answered people's questions and concerns as simplistically as I could. Not wanting to get into things too deeply."

"I'm guessing that also included Serena?"

"Yes. It may have been the wrong thing to do. But it was all I could do. The only way of getting through each day. She did try. She tried getting in touch, offering me her support, but I couldn't. So, I shut her out, too. Then, one day, I desperately needed to see her. So, I did."

I explained what had happened, obviously omitting the part where we had sex.

"I hadn't planned to tell her I was falling in love with her. That wasn't my intention when I had gone around. It just came out. But as soon as I said the words, that was when everything went wrong. I thought I was doing the right thing, opening up and telling the woman who had been the only source of happiness the love I'd felt. Never in my life had I wished I could go back in time as much as I do to that moment.

Serena doesn't love me. And I wasn't planning to wait around to find out the reason. So, I left. The next day was my father's funeral and as I'm sure you can imagine, it wasn't an easy day. First, my brother Julian was a drunken mess, then my ex turned up."

"What was it that annoyed you more? Your brother's behavior or your ex's arrival?"

"Definitely the latter. The problem is that she and my mother believe it'd be best for me to be with her instead. I now know they had this crazy twisted notion that Serena's just a phase and that I would, for whatever reason, go back to Verity. Not once did they stop to think what I wanted. Anyway, I caused a massive scene, which obviously wasn't the time nor the place. Mother was devastated as it was and there I was making things worse."

I felt sick to my stomach. I should have had more control over myself. How had I allowed Verity to affect me so?

"After the funeral, I went back to my apartment. Anyway, later, I find Verity standing in my lounge, having let herself in. She goes off on a verbal rampage against Serena. She was spouting all about how Serena isn't the right type of woman for me, saying racist, vulgar, and degrading things. Then, to my utter shock, Serena appeared out of nowhere, and by the tears running down her face, it was clear she had heard the whole horrible thing. Obviously, I kicked Verity out. There was no way in hell I would want anybody that spoke about the woman I love anywhere near me. Nor would I let them hurt her any more than she already had. But there was no point. She didn't want to stay, she had clearly heard enough. So, she left. And once again, I was left, dealing with my father's death, having an upset mother, a crazy deluded ex, and the woman I wanted to be with, not wanting me."

I let out a deep breath.

"So that pretty much sums up everything. I haven't spoken to her since and that's probably for the best. I don't know what else to say. I've told her I love her, and she can't reciprocate. Why bother trying to chase someone and convince them to love you? That's not how it works."

Raising one eyebrow at me, I felt like I was back at school, about to get scolded by my teacher.

"You, dear boy. What you've gone through in the past few weeks would knock most people for years. You said you told her you love her, but do you think your actions have shown her? Words mean very little if there's nothing to back it up with."

"You're saying you don't think I love her?"

I didn't mean for my anger to flare, but her words made me angry.

"Of course, I know you love her. It's as clear as day. When you say her name, your entire face lights up. Many people think the perfect partner is your perfect fit, someone who slots easily into your life, your beliefs, and your world. That's what most people want. But a person who shows you everything that is holding you back, who brings things to your attention so you can improve your life, who picks you up when you're down, who helps you learn not just about your-self but also the world around you. Someone who's willing to put themselves at risk for your sake, knowing, believing, and trusting that you will catch them. That is true love. That is a true partnership."

Her eyes shone with unshed tears as I imagined her remembering her husband.

"But there are a few things you have mentioned that I don't

think you understand the extent, magnitude, and impact they have on your relationship with Serena."

"And what is that?"

I felt genuinely intrigued.

"Race."

I was left speechless.

"I know we live in a day and age where most normal and level-minded people don't discriminate. But the sad fact is that many still do. You two come from different worlds, not just because of your family being very wealthy and hers building their way up. You must understand that things are different for us. I grew up a Black woman from an impoverished working-class background, being told what I was likely to do with my life and who I was expected to date, marry, and have children with. My parents were stunned when I told them I had met someone who wasn't from our community. Isaac's family came from a small town in Texas. I'm sure you can imagine people's surprise in the fifties. After some time, my family accepted and adjusted. My father died when I was a teenager, and it was only my mother and me. Once she understood that he was the man that I loved, the rest of my family did, too."

"What about Isaac's family?"

"The day he told them he would marry me, they disowned him. They never spoke to him again. He'd moved to Georgia to be with me, as my mother was sick, and I was looking after her. Once she passed, we decided to move here. After many years of trying for children, we found out it wasn't in God's plans for us to be parents. So, when this space became available, we bought it. The cafe became our child. We loved, cherished, and devoted our lives to it. But when he died, it felt like a part of me died with him. The things that once joyed me about coming downstairs and opening now saddens me since he isn't here."

How was I supposed to respond to that?

I felt so confused, especially as part of my agenda of coming here was to tempt Raya into finally selling. But wouldn't I simply be manipulating a grieving widow?

She walked over to clear the empty plates left by the last other patrons and twisted the sign on the door to say she was closed.

Walking back, she now stayed on my side of the bar and sat on the stool next to me.

"There isn't a minute that goes by that I don't wish I could be with Isaac just one more time. He meant more to me than anything in this world but we had many challenges thrown our way. Over the years, certain people felt the need to remind us that he was a white man, and I am a Black woman. As if telling us would make any difference to one another. You must understand that I was made to feel inadequate for a lengthy period of time - that I didn't deserve to be with him, I wasn't good enough or white enough. And from what you have told me, Serena has experienced the same."

"But I have never and would never make her feel unworthy. She's more of a saint than I am!"

Raya laughed.

"I knew you wouldn't, but how would you feel if whenever you were around some of her family or acquaintances, they always made you feel less than you are? Making a point or statement that you'll never be right for her. All because of the color of your skin?"

"I'd lose it."

"That's the difference between you and her. You have grown up in a way where, if I dare say it, you've gotten what you wanted. Serena hasn't. She's always had to fight, always had to either explain or justify her actions. Now she meets you, the man who could be the one for her, and is met with hostility and menace from your ex and your mother. Imagine how that makes her feel?"

"But surely, she knows my mother's opinion would never become my own?"

"You must remember Serena is close to her family, especially her father. Growing up, with her mother having abandoned the family for another man when she was still a child, she's possibly struggled with understanding the dynamic of your relationship with your mother, as she never had one with hers."

I never thought that there'd be any connection. I knew her mother had left, but anytime anything relating to her came up, she'd shut it down and move on to lighter topics.

I knew how important her family was to her. She always spoke of her father and siblings. But having her mother leave her at an early age must have been a tough thing for her to deal with.

She always seemed so strong and sure of things. It almost seemed alien to see her in any other light.

It also made me feel like a fool with the way I pushed her away. No, I walked away, just like her mother.

My mind was beginning to flood with all the different thoughts of things I should have done and conversations we could have had.

"Serena is a remarkable young woman. She's achieved so much and takes genuine care and consideration of those around her. She was so worried after you left to see your father. I know when I see a woman in love. Even if she hasn't realized it yet, I know she wouldn't want to make things or life any harder for someone. Especially not you. And here she is faced with the risk that should she tell you her true feelings, it could affect your whole family."

I never thought of it in that way.

"You must think I'm such an ass."

"Of course not. You're a man who's just lost his father. So, is it so surprising that your head is all over the place? You've gone through a horrible couple of weeks, but maybe as time and grief settle, things may become clearer?"

"But what if I'm too late? What if anything I do or say won't have influence?"

"If you genuinely love her and want to give your relationship a real shot, you must take that chance. Reach out to her. Lay all your cards on the table and ask her to do the same. As all things that are meant to be will be."

My body began to vibrate. It was as if she gave me a new purpose or sense of direction.

Suddenly, I felt wide awake. As if the past few weeks, I had been in some coma-like trance, and now I had been shocked back alive. I knew I needed to see her.

Grabbing my wallet from my pocket, I go to pay.

"You put your money away. Just promise me you will at least give it your all. We only have one life, so it's imperative to make it the best we can."

This time, it was my turn to hug her. She, indeed, was a remarkable woman.

Chapter 28

Rhett

I waved goodbye as I made my way to the car.

"Where to, sir?" Russell asked when I got in.

"First, I need you to drop me back at my apartment. I need to have a shower and change. While I'm there, can you please pick up a bouquet? I want it to consist of lilies, stephanotis, peonies, roses, and carnations. And make sure they are the best."

"Yes, sir." Russell had a smile on his face, too. Obviously, my mood affected those around me more than I realized.

We were stuck in midtown lunchtime traffic, but for once, I didn't mind as it gave me a chance to think and plan what to say to Serena.

Scrolling through my phone, I realized there was a voicemail I'd never listened to. Goosebumps prickled my skin as I heard her husky voice.

My breath stopped.

Why didn't I notice this before?

Fuck. Fuck. Fuck!

She'd wanted to check on me and see how I was doing. She said there was something she wanted to tell me. It had been two days since she left the message. She must have presumed I'd listened to it and ignored her.

Frantically scrolling through my call list, I saw the call ended.

I must have rejected her call.

SHIT!

Was it already too late? No. I wouldn't allow it.

"Russell, change of plans. Please take me to Ms. Parker's office. And get there as fast as you can."

As I was scrolling through my emails, my mind was working out what I could do to fix it, as I knew what I wanted.

I knew I needed Serena. I loved her with every fiber of my being. I kept replaying my father's words in his letter, which only solidified things for me.

She was my future. I wanted to spend every day for the rest of my life showing just how much I loved her, her courage, determination, and passion. I wouldn't allow anyone or anything to come between us ever again.

The car stopped after we pulled up outside her office building. I realized I didn't just want to talk to her, I couldn't just dump this out.

I needed to show her how much she meant to me.

Prove that I was a man of my word and prayed to God and every other deity out there that she felt just as consumed as I did.

Grabbing my phone out of my jacket pocket again, I brought up my contact list and made the first of two calls I never imagined I would have to make.

~

As Russell pulled into the gate and drove down the drive to Mother's house, a slight pang of guilt settled over me as I realized I hadn't been back there since the wake.

Although I had been checking in and seeing how she was doing, and I knew my sisters had been to see her, it was just another reminder of how much things had changed.

I knew the conversation I was going to have wouldn't be easy, but one that was absolutely needed.

"Mother. How are you?" I asked as I kissed her cheek and sat on the couch opposite her.

"I'm as good as can be. What are you doing here? Surely there are lots of things in need of your attention at the office?"

Despite her clipped tone, I could see from the sad look in her eyes it was more grief-talking than enquiring about the state of my work affairs.

"Yes, work is busy. There is always something to do. But I've come to see you to talk about something. Something important."

"I see. Go on, then. I'm all ears."

"It's about Serena."

I unbuttoned my suit jacket, leaning back and making myself more comfortable. I watched her lips pursed slightly, tilting her head to the side as she wrung hands tightly in her lap.

"And what about Serena?"

This time, I could undoubtedly hear the venom in her voice, which made my anger boil.

"I have come here to tell you that she is the love of my life. She has made me happier than I have ever been. She makes me realize my self-worth and doesn't expect anything from me—there is no pressure to be or become something or someone when I am around her. I have understood the pressure and expectations that you and Father have put upon me all my life. And although I can understand them, to some extent, I still hate that I was never asked if this—taking over the company was something I wanted to do. Of course, I will make the company and my father and grandfather's legacy proud, but I will be doing it in my own way."

"What do you mean?"

She fretted. Her mouth pinched, and her eyes wide in alarm.

"I mean, I won't be carrying on the way things were done before. The world has changed, and we need to change with it. Since Serena came into my life, I have seen the passion and change she brings to those around her. That, among many other things, is what I wish to do. I want to create opportunities for those who are otherwise restricted. I want to diversify our portfolio instead of simply dismantling and rebuilding and then selling on to the highest bidder or adding more hotels, luxury condos and offices to our already remarkably lucrative portfolio and assets. I will keep what we already have, but moving forward, I will implement changes and create separate departments to start bridging the gaps in the market."

"And all of this simply because you love Serena?"

"Yes and no. She has opened my eyes, and I no longer can nor want to look away. Not only in the business side of things but also personally. That brings me to you."

"What about me?"

Her brow arched with both intrigue and clear annoyance that I was no longer holding anything back anymore.

"Since the moment you met her, you have been cold, judgmental, and, let's be honest, racist."

"How dare you? I am not racist. I have worked with charities and on boards to help people of all ethnicities and backgrounds."

"You know as well as I that means nothing when your son doesn't feel comfortable bringing his partner around you, for worry you or your friends will belittle her or insult her with microaggressions or prejudiced views. I will not allow you or anyone else to make her feel less than she is. That leads me to another issue. Verity. I will never be in that woman's presence again. If I ever hear her criticize or slander Serena, I will not be held responsible for my actions. I have never implied nor indicated that she and I have or ever would have any future together. She is a disgusting and manipulative snake. She preyed upon you as much as she has done me. She exploited your vulnerability with Father's diagnosis. I can only guess that she most likely fed you lies to perpetuate and possibly fan the flames of any issues you had with Serena. If you choose to continue to have any relationship with her, I will take that as your choice to effectively cut off any relationship I have with you. I will not sit back and have that kind of person in or around my life."

I watched as she stood, walked over to the window, and waited for her to speak.

"You know your father didn't want to marry me initially?"

"Excuse me?"

My tone showed shock, but she just nodded, continuously staring out the window.

"It had been a suggestion—in other words, an arrangement between our families. I'd always had a crush on him. Still, I don't think he ever really noticed me until I'd overheard him being told about the marriage. Then he and your grandfather argued as my father talked about me as if I were a piece of cattle. I'll never forget the look on your father's face when he stormed out and ran into me, seemingly having realized I must have heard everything. No one heard from him for over two weeks, then he came back and apologized, and we started dating. During that time, we realized how much we had in common and fell in love. We were one of the lucky ones. The letter your father left for me reminded me of that. Most others in our situation had sham marriages full of betrayal, infidelity, and animosity. Since the day you were born, I always felt that you belonged to your father—you were his to shape into the man you have become today. You never needed me. So, I thought this would be one thing I could do. I could help with. I thought I could help pick someone who knows the ins and outs of how things work. And with any luck, you would go on to have the kind of relationship I had with your father."

Her voice hitched, and I watched as she took a deep, steadying breath.

"I thought I knew what was best, but clearly, I was wrong."

Slowly, she made her way back over, sitting next to me.

"Your father would be so proud of you. I know there are many things you may have wished we had done differently, but you have to remember we brought you up in the way our parents had raised us. If you truly love Serena as much as you say, and if she feels the same way you do, as your mother, that is all I could ask for. I'd also like to apologize to her and get to know her. Maybe we can arrange a lunch? Or she could come over for some tea?"

I managed to suppress the chuckle that bubbled inside as I couldn't imagine Serena being too keen on having a lunch date any time soon with my mother.

"I'll speak to her and see what she says. I won't push her on it as I want her to feel comfortable and welcomed."

Rolling her shoulders back, she gave me a brief nod before asking if I would be staying for something to eat.

"Sorry, I have another important matter I need to get started on."

With that, I said my goodbyes, made my way back to the car, and as Russell started the drive back to my apartment, I scrolled through my contacts, making the next and most important call to hopefully begin putting the plan I had come up with into place.

Chapter 29

Serena

It was Thursday the 18th, and the office was closed the next day for Juneteenth, and everyone there was hesitant to approach me.

I'd tried to hide my feelings, but it was as if a black cloud had been following me, and no one wanted to risk coming too close.

Finishing off the last paperwork on a case, I called in Sarah.

"What's next on the agenda?" I asked as she took a seat in front of my desk.

"We are currently up to date on everything, simply waiting on the rulings for Drummonds, Hartley Ltd, and Mr Price. We are still waiting to hear back the counter offers from Blackthorne & Associates and the reps from the malpractice suit."

Slumping in my chair, I checked the time on my laptop.

"I'll send a memo and tell everyone they can head out early. We're clearly on top of everything."

Looking up, I noticed Sarah hesitate as she approached the door. Tentatively, she asked, "Is everything okay?"

Not wanting to talk about it, I paste on a smile.

"Yes, everything's fine. Go on. I promise everything's okay. Go and enjoy your weekend."

Clicking through my emails, I signed off on the last one before logging out, and my phone rang.

The sound was shrill and loud, making me realize how quiet the office was, as everyone else had gone home.

A warm smile spread when I saw my dad's picture light up the screen.

"Hey, Daddy."

"Hey baby girl, I was just calling to remind you about tomorrow."

Suppressing a sigh, I wished there was some excuse I could come up with to get me out of going to Dad's BBQ. Not because I didn't want to see my family but because I knew I wouldn't be able to keep it together the minute I did.

"Yeah, I'm leaving work now and heading straight home to make the macaroni salad. Are you sure there's nothing else you need me to bring?"

"No, sweetie, all the meats are already seasoning in the fridge, and Olivia will drop off some stuff in the morning. The twins have been working hard this week and have put together a production for us. It's called *Cinderella's Not the Best.*"

I couldn't help the laugh that slipped past my lips. God, when was the last time I laughed?

"I've got to say for once, I'm intrigued. Let me get going, and I'll see you tomorrow."

"Drive safe, and I'll see you then. Love you, baby girl."

"Love you, Dad."

Cleaning the kitchen, I forwent the wine and treated myself to hot chocolate and popcorn instead. I plopped down on the sofa and made myself comfortable. I'd got the TV on in the back-ground as I scrolled through Instagram.

As I was about to force myself to pay attention to the movie instead of continuously scrolling TikTok, my phone rang, and Ruby's name flashed. Knowing I needed to stop being such a shitty friend, I picked up.

"Hey, Rubs, how are you?"

"I'm good. You know me, busy, busy, busy."

Putting her on speaker, I notice the time. It was already 9:45 p.m.

"Anyway, I just wanted to check in and see how my girl is doing. You know, speak to her, and make sure she hasn't actu-ally been abducted, and some AI thing is simply responding to my text."

Despite my awkward laugh snort, guilt washed over me.

"I'm sorry. I've just been busy with work," I respond meekly.

"Babe, we both know that's bullshit, but I'll let it slide. Well, for now, at least. So, I wanted to let you know that I'm heading to that yoga retreat I was telling you about. You know the one where it's Kombucha at 5 a.m. followed by goat yoga?"

"Yeah, I remember. I thought you weren't going to that until next month?"

There was a long pause, but finally, she answered.

"I know, but I just need to rejuvenate. Get my Zen back."

I could hear from the tone in her voice she was keeping something back. And I guessed that Julian was the reason she chose to bump up this trip—not her goddamn Zen.

Ugh, this was just another reminder that while I'd been wallowing and moping about my own life, I'd been a shitty friend to her recently. She had enough of her own stuff going on, and I hadn't been there for her.

"You know I'm always there for you if you need to talk?"

"Yeah, I know, and I promise we'll have a girl's night when I'm back and properly catch up. Anyway, I've got to go."

"All right, enjoy, and let me know if any of those goats bite you in the ass!"

Bursting out laughing, she responded, "Will do! Love you."

"Love you too."

Deciding to call it a night, I cleaned up my mug and bowl, ran a bath, and chose to have an early night.

After hours of tossing and turning, I finally fell asleep as my mind drifted off to the image of ocean-blue eyes.

As I parked my car, I could already smell the delicious scents of smoked meat from the BBQ. Making my way through the house and into the garden, I saw my sister, her husband, the twins, and some uncles, cousins, and aunts scattered around the garden.

Auntie Rena screams were followed by a tornado of limbs as my nieces engulfed me in hugs. Looking down at them, I saw they were ready for their performance and dressed in princess dresses.

"I'm super excited to watch your show."

Just as Eden opened her mouth to say something, Amelia clamped her hands over it and said, "It's a surprise!"

Both darted a look over at my sister, who couldn't help but laugh.

Walking over, I said my hellos, and as my sister gave me a big squeeze, she said, "Don't ask."

Making my rounds of greetings, I saved Dad for last. Engulfing me in a bear hug, he whispered, "There's my girl."

My eyes shone with tears, but I wouldn't allow them to fall. I noticed my brother's absence and asked, "Where's Roman?"

"He had to grab something from the store."

I could feel my father's eyes deeply assessing me, and not wanting to get into it or make a fool of myself as I became a blubbering me, I made my way over to the rest of my family and busied myself by catching up with them.

After eating my weight in food and catching up with family, the twins got everyone's attention, and everyone simmered down, waiting for the show to start.

Looking around and noticing Roman still wasn't there, I leaned over to my sister and asked her if she knew where he was. I was just about to grab my cell and call him when Amelia cleared her throat and started reading from her pink fluffy binder.

"Once upon a time, there was a beautiful princess. She was prettier than all the others in the land because she had hair just like me."

Everyone laughed as Eden walked over, waving and shaking her curls, almost causing her plastic tiara to fall off her head.

"Her name was Sabrina, and she ruled over all the animals in her kingdom. Even the grumpy lion."

Suddenly, my cousin Anthony burst into a roar, making us all laugh.

"One day, she met a Prince, and he was the most handsome prince called Ryder. He was even more handsome than my dad," she whispered.

I looked over at my brother-in-law as he rolled his eyes but laughed.

"The prince fell in love with Sabrina and told the King he wanted to marry her and have babies, ponies, and unicorns! The King said yes, but the Queen wasn't happy. She wasn't a proper Queen. She was mean and evil. She didn't want the Prince to marry Sabrina because Sabrina was much prettier, nicer, and more fun than her. So, she put a spell on Sabrina and the Prince. Sabrina was locked away in a tower, and the Prince was hidden in a dungeon far, far away. He needed help from his friends Ruben the Rabbit and Edmond the Elephant to save the princess. They had to travel far and wide, but before they could go and rescue the Princess, the Prince needed to tell the Queen that her spell wouldn't work anymore."

Until then, the girl's elaborate and confusing story was amusing and utterly ridiculous. Seriously, who picked a rabbit and an elephant as sidekicks? But the more it went on, the more a cold chill ran through me. This story was hitting too close to home. The back of my eyes began to sting as my mind drifted back to Rhett and the regret of how everything ended. I wished things could have been different. My heart physically hurt. There was an emptiness there that had never been there before.

I forced myself to push those thoughts aside and focus on the show.

"After the Prince told off the Queen, he left the castle and set off to rescue the Princess. It took fourteen days and fourteen nights. The Prince was tired and scared that he'd never get to her, but Ruben and Edmond helped him along the way. Suddenly, they came upon a pond with the prettiest flowers around it, and in the middle were the biggest lilies he'd ever seen. And on top of the lily pads sat the prettiest fairy."

Suddenly, from behind Dad's tool shed, Ruby emerged wearing a glittery dress and huge fairy wings. What in the actual fuck was going on? My pulse was racing as a million thoughts rushed through my head. Looking around, I tried to understand what was happening and see whether anyone else was as confused as I was. Just then, Ruby sashayed forward, her eyes glittering with laughter.

Waving a plastic wand, she spun it three times as the girls

chanted, "Alakazam alakazish, now it's time to make your wish!"

Suddenly, a loud bang went off, and my head shot up as fireworks exploded above us, and beautiful pinks, yellows, and oranges dazzled and glowed up in the sky. I felt a tap on my arm and looked as Eden and Amelia held their hands for me to take.

Looking around, still confused and unable to wrap my head around what was happening, I noticed everyone's eyes were on me.

"Follow us," the girls loudly whispered.

As they pulled me down the path back towards the house, my dad stepped forward and handed me a beautiful red rose. That was followed by my three uncles, five of my cousins, and finally, Roman. My hands were shaking. No one was saying a single word, and my hands were full of roses when suddenly, out from the back door, My eyes landed on the crystal blue eyes that had been haunting my dreams.

Chapter 30

Rhett

As always, seeing Serena's beautiful face took my breath away. I watched as a tear slowly fell down her cheek.

My mind was still spinning that we had finally reached this moment after what felt like weeks of planning. But there wasn't a single thing I would change.

"What... what's going on?" she whispered.

My eyes briefly glanced at the two men who helped me put this together, then down at the two little girls I could see bursting with excitement. My initial nerves dissolved the second my eyes focused back on Serena's again.

"I needed a little help to show the woman who crashed into my life and gave me a reason to want more and live for more, that I am and always will be, utterly and madly in love with her."

Another tear fell down her cheek, and I gently brushed it away.

"From the first moment I laid my eyes upon yours, I've felt as if you have managed to pierce through my walls. Instantly seeing beyond the mask I have lived behind since I was a child, and you excavated the man hiding beneath. You made me realize the shackles I thought were restricting me could instead, be used as tools to build the foundation of something great. I know I was born into privilege. More fortunate than most I have been blessed enough never to experience financial worries, always had a roof over my head and have never gone without. But none of the houses, cars, millions or deals even come close to comparing to how rich, lucky, and fortunate I felt the day you let me in."

I took another step toward the woman who meant everything to me—the person who owned my heart and soul.

"Watching the passion, drive, and desire you have with your work has been an honor to witness."

I lent in closer toward her.

"Your determination to fight for those who cannot—your empathy for those in need, and your love for those who are lucky enough to experience it are only some of the things I love about you."

Her lip trembled, followed by more tears falling down her cheek.

"When I've had moments of struggle, arduous days, or fears that I'm not good enough or strong enough, all I have to do is close my eyes, and my heart instantly feels fuller as I think of you. You've shown me that love and care don't need to be shown in fancy gifts. They can be expressed in support, understanding, and even pushing that other person to strive for more. I thought my education had given me a good understanding of many things. But I can honestly say you have taught me more in the last few months than I could ever have imagined.

You opened my eyes to the ongoing issues facing those of varied ethnicities; you taught me to stop and listen to those who have experienced hardship and ridicule and have made me want to do everything in my power to stand up and make a change. You continuously fight, conquer, and survive all that is thrown your way. I know you are strong enough to manage it alone, but I want to stand by your side and do it with you."

I briefly glanced past her shoulder and saw her sister Olivia pass Ruby a tissue as the two of them were now also crying.

"You've shown me countless times that more is always possible. I know there have been those who have been both disgusting and cruel, and I am so sorry and will forever make it up to you that some of those are members of my own family. I want you to know I will never allow anyone to treat you like that ever again."

I took a deep, steadying breath, knowing I needed to get through this next part.

"After my father passed away, I realized what I wanted, no needed, more than anything in this world. And that's spending the rest of my life with you. I'm so sorry for shutting you out. I was scared of showing you how much I was struggling. Not that you would ever hold it against me. I just always wanted to be in control of my emotions. I was utterly overwhelmed by how much his loss and the responsibility of taking over the company had on me. And instead of turning and leaning on the one person who's been there, the one who would have the strength to care and support me—I hid away like a coward."

My thumbs continued wiping away her tears, and I wanted nothing more than to kiss away every ounce of hurt and pain I caused her.

"Every moment I have been away from you has been utter torture but I knew I couldn't just come to you and say I'm sorry. I needed to show you."

The smile that beamed across her face set off my own as I reached down to hold both her hands.

"There were changes that needed to be made to prove I

mean my apology. I want to show you how much I love you and take the first steps in hopefully demonstrating that I am worthy. Worthy to be in your life—in your mind and hopefully in your heart."

Again, she went to speak, but I stopped her as I cupped her face.

"As of yesterday, Chambers Industries is no longer interested in acquiring Cole's. I've set up a department specially tasked with collaborating with businesses and going into partnerships instead of acquiring them. You opened my eyes and reminded me that it's not just about my job and the company. This is just one example of how I want to learn how to utilize myself, my company, and my money for the better. It's about making a real difference. I will continue to educate myself, listen to those who have a real understanding, and follow through with action and change—not just empty promises and kind words."

I looked over her shoulder and nodded at Ruby, who made her way over and took the flowers out of Serena's hands.

"And there's one more thing."

I thought I would be shaking and pulsing with nerves by the time we got to this moment, but as I gazed into her stunning eyes, I had never felt as right as I did right then. I reached into my pocket, took out the Harry Winston pear-drop diamond ring, got down on one knee, and took her hand in mine.

"You are the most beautiful woman I have ever seen. You bring laughter, joy, and happiness everywhere you go. Your intelligence and determination are only outshone by the love you have for all that you do and all those who are lucky enough to be in your orbit. I now know and understand just how short and precious life can be, and I don't want to waste a single second of it without being by your side. I want to continue watching you fight for those who can't and embrace those in need. You ensnared my mind under the hood of a car and encapsulated my heart in the boardroom. As I'm sure you've guessed, you are the Princess in the story, but will you be the Queen of my life? Will you do me the honor of becoming my wife?"

Chapter 31

Serena

Tears were streaming down my face, and I didn't think I had taken a breath in what seemed like forever.

With shaking hands, I ran my thumb across his cheek, and for once, I was genuinely and utterly speechless.

As I gazed into his beautiful eyes and saw the unshed tears, I did the only thing both my head and my heart told me to.

I nodded.

Instantly lifting me into the safety of his arms, Rhett crashed his lips onto mine and it felt like taking my first gulp of air after being held underwater.

Cheers and applause brought me back into focus as he gently broke our kiss and slid the most beautiful ring on my finger.

"I love you, Serena, and I cannot wait to show you just how much every single day."

This time, I stopped him from continuing.

"I'm scared I'll wake up, and this will just be a dream. I love you so much, Rhett, and I can't wait to spend the rest of my life with you. I can't believe you did all this. How? When?"

I was still breathless when Eden and Amelia pulled us down as they continued screaming and jumping up and down.

"See, Rhett, we did it just like you said!"

Crouching down, he gave both girls a big hug, and just that image tugged on my ovaries. He whispered something in their ears, and they both turned and ran inside. Not long after, we heard screaming and hooting with excitement, and with the grin currently plastered on his face, I can only imagine what he'd gotten them.

From behind, Ruby and Olivia both screamed in my ears and crushed me in their arms.

"You both knew, didn't you?"

My cheeks hurt so much from smiling, and my eyes felt like faucets as I couldn't stop crying, yet these were tears of complete happiness.

"How on earth do you think he managed to pull all of this off?" Ruby screamed, and I was again reminded how lucky I was to have her as my best friend.

Roman came over, gave me a big hug, and offered his congratulations.

"There's another surprise for you out front once you've hugged everyone and caught your breath again."

Before I could ask him any more, I watched as he followed Ruby inside. I turned as Dad walked over and engulfed me in another bear hug.

"You knew too!"

"Of course I did. He called me about two weeks ago and explained everything. I'm not going to lie. Some of what I had to hear was tough to swallow, expecially when talking about his family. It's hard not just for you but also for me to wrap my head around someone being so different from their family, especially given how close we all are. But I know in my heart that that man loves you with his very being. You know, I never think anyone is going to be good enough for my girls, but I know he's as close as it gets. He came down five times to help the girls put this together. Now he knows that if he ever hurts you, I'm going to be mad because I won't be able to give you my hugs while I'm doing time for murder."

I couldn't help but laugh.

That morning, I never could've imagined the day would turn out like this. I felt so lost, so broken, genuinely believing there was no hope for us ever to get back together again.

There was never any question or doubt about whether I loved or wanted a future with him. I couldn't bear the thought of being the wedge in his family.

My mind drifted back to the words he said, and my heart felt like it was completely and utterly complete. I knew that any problems or battles that came our way, we'd face them together.

My eyes scanned the garden, looking for my fiancée. God, would I ever get used to that? I could see him being bombarded by hugs and kisses from my aunts, one of whom was overly handsy. Catching the slight fear in his eyes, I laughed as I made my way over to his rescue.

"I need you to explain to me how a woman as small and sweet as your aunt has the grip strength of a coconut crab. I'm pretty sure I'm going to have bruises all the way down from my arms to my ass."

Lovingly, I guided us to the loveseat in the back of the garden for some privacy.

"Can you imagine what it was like growing up and having your cheeks pinched by her every time she said hello?"

Tentatively, he brushed his lips along my jaw before finally capturing my mouth. He kissed me with such love I could feel it in every cell in my body.

We kissed until our lips were swollen, and then he

explained in detail how he came up with this plan and the difficulties he had persuading my nieces to keep it a secret.

Turned out that dolls and toys weren't enough. They bartered him into a trip to Disney Land, and that was only after he got them a whole wardrobe of princess dresses, riding lessons, and a damn pony each that he purchased and were living at stables a thirty-minute drive from there that they could go and visit any time they wanted.

He also spoke about how he'd met up with his mother and put everything on the table. She had to accept that I was the love of his life, and his future was with me, or she'd have no place in his life at all.

It turned out his father had also left a letter to his wife. Both that and the sudden death of her husband were making her realize what was truly important.

I wasn't going to get my hopes up and think that she was a changed woman, but apparently, she had asked if, at some point, I'd like to meet up with her as she wanted to apologize to me in person.

His sisters never had an issue with me, and it made me smile when he said how excited they were for him. I couldn't wait to get together to celebrate. He also produced a card from his back pocket that his nephew Kai had made, and for the first time, I knew everything was just as it was meant to be.

Hours later, I sat on his lap, running my fingers through his hair as we sat around the fire pit.

Whispering in my ear, he said, "Are you ready to make a move? I can't wait to get you into bed wearing only my ring."

As I gingerly ground my hips down on him, I could feel his hard cock beneath me.

Bringing my lips to his ears, I whispered, "Yes, future husband."

With a deep groan that vibrated through his chest, he squeezed my thigh before gently lifting me to stand.

After making our hasty goodbyes, I followed him out of the house, and parked out front was the car he bought at the auction. I couldn't help the squeals that left me. After everything that had happened, I'd asked Ruby to return it to him.

Although it was a dream, it was too heartbreaking not to enjoy it together. Even though I couldn't currently drive as I'd had a couple of drinks, I still couldn't believe he got me the car.

"Did you drive this here?"

As I climbed into the passenger seat, I almost crushed the cool box in the foothold.

"No, Roman did, as well as picking that up."

Rhett got into the driver's seat as I opened the box, and the sweet smell of peach cobbler filled the car. I grabbed the note that was tucked into the side.

> *Congratulations, my sweet dears. I wish you both a lifetime of true love and happiness.*
> *All my love, Raya.*
> *P.S. I wouldn't mind trying one of those pastries from Paris.*

I looked up in confusion as Rhett pulled the car away.

"What does she mean by pastries from Paris?"

Bringing my hand to his lips, he kissed first my ring and then every finger before answering.

"Well, I thought it's only fair we bring her back something as she made us this."

As excitement bubbled through me, I felt almost hesitant to ask.

"We... when... are we going to Paris?"

We stopped at the stop sign, and he pulled my face to his.

"I said I would show you how much I love you and I plan on doing that every day for the rest of our lives. So, what better way than to start right now in the city of love? Ruby packed a bag for you after you left this morning. The jet is waiting for us and you will be spending your first night as the future Mrs. Chambers beneath the stars as we cross the Atlantic."

Rhett

6 Years Later

Laying on the bed, I watched the sunset over the crystal-clear lagoon wrapping around the side of the water villa we were staying in.

I was waiting for my wife to finish getting ready for dinner. It was our last night there before heading off to the second part of our anniversary trip.

Today was our fifth wedding anniversary, and I couldn't think of a better way to celebrate than a candlelight dinner with the love of my life.

The past five years have been more than I ever hoped for. That was not to say everything had been easy.

Given that we both had demanding jobs, we did everything possible to carve out as much time for one another.

Family was just as important to her as it had always been and over the years, I'd grown closer to everyone.

I didn't think my wife and mother would ever have a close relationship, but seeing how happy she made me seemed to have thawed my mother exponentially.

Hearing the door to the bathroom open, I got up to get dressed when I saw her emerge, still donning her bathrobe.

Looking down at my watch and seeing the time, I was confused as to why she wasn't ready yet, especially given how long my wife took to get ready.

I was just about to ask her how much longer she'd need when she produced a box out of her pocket.

"What's this?" I asked as I kissed the top of her head.

The coconut and mango scent from her hair filled my nose.

"I wanted to give you your present before dinner."

Taking my hand, she walked back to the bed, sitting in the middle with her legs beneath her.

I stretched out beside her, propping myself up with one elbow and taking the box with the other. Lifting the lid, I saw an Oxblood Pin-dot Silk and Wool tie rolled up neatly in the center. Goosebumps settled over me, and I sat up straight as I immediately recognized it.

It was one that belonged to my father. It was his favorite. The loss of him never went away.

Every day, as I sat in what used to be his office, I was reminded of the remarkable man he was. Every day, I wished he was still with us, seeing that I found true love and knowing the happiness that would have brought him.

My throat felt tighter as all those emotions bubbled to the surface. My hand timidly ran over the soft, smooth material.

"Where did you get this from?"

My voice was barely above a whisper.

"I called Kara a couple of weeks ago. I knew I'd need it for your present."

Taking my other hand, she brought it to her lips, gently kissing each knuckle.

"I thought this would help with the main present. Go on, unravel it."

I was so confused, but curiosity got the better of me.

Gently, I unrolled it, and at the end, a tie pin pierced through it. Lifting it, I saw that it had been pinned to the inner lining of the box.

As I pulled on, it raised the lid to what I now realized was a hidden compartment. Looking over at Serena, I saw her hands clenched so tightly under her chin that her knuckles had turned white. Her eyes were shining with unshed tears. Carefully lifting the lid, I looked down, and it felt as though all the air had been sucked out of my lungs.

Nestled under the lining was a sonogram. My mouth instantly went dry, and my tongue felt like lead.

After what felt like eons of staring at the image in my trembling hands, I looked over at my gorgeous wife.

"We're having a baby?"

Tears gently rolled down her face, and her beautiful smile slowly stretched from ear to ear.

"Yes, we're having a baby."

Looking down at the picture again, I was in awe. And I knew I'd remember that moment for the rest of my life.

Spinning around, I scooped her up into my arms, and my lips crashed down onto her in a bruising kiss.

I could taste the salty tears on her lips, although I was unsure if they were mine or hers. I never thought I would be able to love this woman more than I already did, but I did.

Pushing her down on the bed, I continued kissing her. Pouring in every ounce of love I had for her. I swallowed the sounds of her moans which made my already hard cock pulse and seep with pre-cum.

Breaking the kiss, I look down at my wife. My salvation. My angel who is carrying our child.

Her curls fanned around the pillow, her lips were red and swollen, and her green eyes sparkled like the brightest emeralds. She looked like an ethereal mermaid. There were no words to describe how I was feeling.

Although she had her IUD taken out almost a year ago, we weren't actively trying or pressuring it. Both of us simply wanted nature to take its course.

Opening up the belt of her robe, I eased her arms out until she was bare beneath me.

She had never looked as beautiful as she did right then. Kissing my way down the column of her neck, I felt her pulse racing beneath my lips.

Not wanting to miss an inch of skin, I kissed, bit, and licked along her collarbone. Her breathing increased as her chest lifted up and down faster and faster with each touch.

Her brown nipples were erect, and I laved them with my tongue before gently nipping on them. She let out a deep moan, and my mind instantly wondered if they were more sensitive now.

I continued my journey down her body until I got to her belly. My hands gently rubbed over her, and I only now noticed the slight firm curve of it. How hadn't I noticed this? As my mind flitted back, I thought back and was only now piecing together her lack of drinking and being more tired than usual.

"How far gone are you?" I asked as I continued to kiss and lick down her hip to her inner thigh.

"Ten weeks," she said in a gasp as I ran my tongue along her slit, which was already dripping.

"Rhett, please, I need you."

"You have me."

I continued lapping up and down her lips before focusing on her clit.

Her legs clamped down around my head, and her body twisted and turned in pleasure. Her moans were growing increasingly stronger, and I couldn't wait a second longer to be inside her.

Lifting myself back up and over her, I ran my aching cock along her wet lips. Leaning down, I captured her mouth with mine as I slid into her soft, wet heat.

"You have made me the happiest man in the world, Serena Chambers. My life, my love, my queen."

Acknowledgments

I first wrote this book over 10 years ago. It had been an idea I'd had in my head for weeks and simply needed to put the words down.

I handwrote the whole thing and still have those papers, and never did I expect those scribbled down ramblings to be worked and reworked (*many times over*) and then finally taking the plunge and deciding to put this story that means so much to me, out to the world.

They say it takes a village to raise and child and the same goes for writing a book.

Firstly I want to thank my Mum and Dad for constantly telling me to go after my dreams and that if I set my mind to it and work hard, anything is possible.

I also want to thank my kids (despite the fact they will *never* see this) for putting up with rushed dinners, understanding when I play music loudly at my desk I am not to be disturbed and for always giving me a purpose to carry on, even when I wanted to give up.

A special thanks to Victoria Straw, my copy editor, who helped me fix and transform my words from British English to American English. A task I had been utterly reluctant to do, and you saved me hours of meltdown and frustration.

The ultimate shoutout to Samantha at SamanthaDesigns for putting together the most beautiful cover I could have asked for. You were able to transform my scattered and crazy ideas and suggestions and transform it into something truly spectacular. Not only are you unbelievably talented but you're an amazing woman and someone I now also count as a great friend.

I couldn't have gotten this book to where it is now without my PA and friend Natasha. J. PA. You've put up with all my incessant fears, worries, doubts and insecurities and you have done it without a single complaint. None of this would have been possible without you. I cannot wait for the book tour, and we are 100% adding on the food tour as well. I cannot wait to continue this journey with you and all up and coming releases.

Stacey at Stacey's Bookcorner Editing Services, your help and support will be something I never forget. Your eye for detail is superb and I am truly thankful for all you have done.

Rowena, I'm going to have to limit my thanks as otherwise it would be pages long. I don't want to know how many hours of voice notes and messages I have bombarded you with. Thank you for making me laugh when I was breaking down, for talking me off the ledge when I wanted to give up, for supporting me when I was hysterical and fearful no one would care. You were and are continuously there for me. I will never be able to thank you enough for everything you do and I'm so grateful for our friendship – soul sisters through and through.

I also want to thank my secondary school English teacher, Mr Smallman, your support and guidance is something I have always cherished. You never berated my unhelpful requests to have larger word counts on essays (because even back then I loved writing).

I want to tell my younger self, things will be ok. I promise.

And finally thank you readers. I honestly don't have the words to say just how thankful I am that you took a chance on me and this story. This is only the beginning, and I can't wait for you to come along the ride.

About the Author

Natasha Allen is a contemporary romance author born and raised in London, now based in East Sussex.

Inspired by the works of Sylvia Day and Kennedy Ryan, she loves to write about diverse and interracial relationships.

When she's not crafting steamy love stories, Natasha can be found lost in a good book.

With a focus on diversity, Natasha strives to create inclusive and relatable love stories that reflect the world around us.

Keep an eye out for her upcoming releases, as she continues to enchant readers with her heartfelt tales of love and desire.

instagram.com/natashaallenauthor

amazon.com/author/UK

tiktok.com/@natashaallenauthor